~THE POLYANDRIST~

MURDER~MYSTERY~ROMANCE

~MASON MALONE~

THE POLYANDRIST

Copyright © 2018

Mason Malone Publishing

ISBN 978-0991205851

masonmalone.com

Dedicated to the polyandrists of the world and the men who worship and adore them.

Foreword

A polyandrist is defined in the Oxford English Dictionary as a woman who has two or more husbands or male sexual partners at the same time.

I think that's oversimplifying the mindset of the polyandrist. She's a different creature than a woman who uses a man to get what she wants and then discards him afterward. She's a collector of men. It's a hobby, a sport and an occupation. She admires, organizes, labels and displays her conquests. Each has a specific place and purpose.

She rules over them. She directs them to protect her, compete for her and perform for her. She plays with men, and plays for keeps. She possesses the men who fall under her spell. They're hers to do with as she pleases until she decides otherwise.

If you ever have the pleasure of witnessing a polyandrist in action you walk away with a newfound appreciation for her guile, strength and conviction. A member of the weaker gender? Not hardly.

~1~

Lauren is a woman accustomed to getting what she wants. At twenty-five she's in the prime of her life, and far too ambitious and heart-stopping gorgeous for any one man alone. Don't take my word for it. Ask her, she'll tell you as much herself. She should come with a label cautioning men of the danger of prolonged exposure to her. Trouble is, they'd all ignore it. She's that irresistible. As addictive as a narcotic, and twice as lethal.

Standing in front of a full-length mirror, she applies the final touches to the pussycat costume she'll be wearing this evening. It consists of a skintight leopard print bodysuit with a furry tail sewn on to it and a headband holding matching ears in place. She completes her ensemble with glue-on long fingernails, stiletto pumps and whiskers drawn on to her cheeks with eyeliner. A final 360 turn to view herself from all sides, and she's good to go.

She'll be attending tonight's Halloween party solo. Her husband would go if she asked him to, but she didn't. It's not that she's embarrassed by him. Quite the opposite. He's a tall, handsome, well-built man with wavy dark brown hair, a beard to match, and deep-set brown eyes. It's just that with him at her side, she wouldn't be free to explore and exploit certain opportunities. And one never knows when such an opportunity might present itself.

Lauren's husband is Nolan Drake. With a successful business, money in the bank and an expensive Tuscan style suburban house, he's almost perfect. He's an architect, with his own architectural design firm. At the moment, he's holding the phone to his ear with one hand while the other pecks at a computer keyboard. The image on the screen before him is the floor plan of a client's space within a high-rise office building. The person on the phone is Dana Porter, a colleague from work. She's relaying the latest changes the client is requesting.

"They want a private bathroom with a shower in the offices of the CEO and the president?" Nolan says, confirming what Dana has told him. "We can do it. I'll have to take a couple of hundred square feet of space from somewhere else. It will probably cut down on the office space for the middle management and clerical staff."

"Personally," Dana says, "I think adding washrooms to the executive offices sends the wrong message to the rest of the employees. I mean they're the ones putting in long hours and doing most of the work. And they probably make a fraction of what the CEO does. But instead of rewarding the workers, the muckety-mucks are going to rub their faces in it by having upscale bathrooms for themselves while their underlings have to share a toilet down the hall."

"I hear what you're saying. They can take it up with their union representative. We answer to the CEO because she's the one who signs our check, without which I'd be out of business and you'd be out of a job."

"So, keep my opinion to myself, is that what you're saying?"

"You're free to express your opinion, but not to the CEO, and don't post it on social media for the whole world to see."

"Roger that, boss."

"Is that the only change they wanted?"

"As of this minute it is."

"I appreciate you letting me know, but this could have waited until Monday. Why are you hanging around the office this late on a Friday, anyway? You do remember you're on salary, don't you? There's no extra pay for working late."

"Yeah, I know, but all there is waiting for me at home is a microwave dinner and a Meg Ryan movie. So, I'm in no rush to leave."

Nolan starts to ask about the guy she's been seeing, but can't remember his name. And besides, he's probably a part of her past by now. Dana goes through men like infants go through diapers.

"You should get a dog. I hear they can be real affectionate and don't ask for much in return. You feed them, give them a place to sleep and when you come home, they meet you at the door, nuzzle your crotch and lick your face."

"That sounds like my last boyfriend. Actually, it sounds like half the men I've dated since high school. You're lucky you met Lauren. Do you have any advice for those of us who are still single? What's the secret to finding Mr. or Mrs. Right?"

"If there is a secret, I didn't stumble on to it during the thirty-three years I was single. I just got lucky. And the only words of advice I have for you are don't give up, he's out there somewhere."

"Yeah, right. He's out there hiding from me. Well, enjoy your evening with Mrs. Right. Do you have anything special planned?"

"I don't, but I never know what Lauren has in mind. Have a great weekend, and give some more thought to getting a dog. I'll see you, Monday."

Lauren is standing in the doorway as he ends the call.

"Mrrreow," she purrs. "How do you like it?"

"Come here, so I can have a closer look."

He takes her hand and pulls her toward him, careful of the fingernails which appear to be sharpened.

"Don't pull my tail. You'll rip a hole in my bodysuit."

She raises her arms above her head and turns in a circle so he can see her from every angle.

"All in all, I like it, even the whiskers. And I've never cared much for facial hair on women."

He runs his hands up her thighs, past her waist, continuing until reaching the zipper at the collar of her bodysuit. Then, he starts to slide it down.

"No, no," she says, pushing his hands away. "I don't have time for what you have in mind. I'm running late as it is."

"Running late for what?! Where are you going?"

"To the office Halloween party. Don't you remember? I told you about it a month ago."

"No, I don't remember you telling me about a party. I figured the sexy outfit was for me."

"Sorry, I rented it for this party."

"Are spouses invited, or is it an employee only get-together?"

"Some of the women will probably bring their husband, but I knew you wouldn't be interested."

"And you knew that because…?"

"It's not your kind of thing, Nolan. You know that. You make fun of adults dressing up on Halloween. Besides, you don't know any of the people I work with. You'd want to leave the second we arrived."

"That's not true. I can be a fun sort of guy when I want to be."

"I seriously doubt that, but I don't have time to discuss it, now." She bends over to kiss him on the cheek. He twists his face to kiss her lips, but she pulls back. "I don't want to smear my lipstick. It's difficult to apply because of the whiskers." She pats his cheek and turns to leave.

"Maybe when you get home I can help you out of your costume."

"It will probably be pretty late. Don't wait up for me," she says over her shoulder as she's walking out. Then, she seems to have a moment of indecision over leaving him like this. "I don't have to return the costume until Monday. That gives us two days with it. We can have our own private Halloween party. That is, if you can come up with a costume for yourself."

"I'll start working on that. Have fun at the party."

He hears the garage door open and her car—the brand new Lexus SUV he bought her on the one-month anniversary of their marriage—back out of the driveway. Then the garage door closes and all is quiet in the house. He goes to the kitchen for a glass and the bottle of Smirnoff vodka in the freezer. Before he met Lauren, this was how he spent many a Friday evening—alone at home, just himself and a bottle of vodka.

They had known each other only briefly, and were on a weekend getaway in Jamaica when it happened. One minute they were frolicking in the water flowing over Dunn's River Falls and the next they were saying 'I do' at their own sunset wedding on the beach. That was nine months ago, and although neither has expressed second thoughts about it since, that doesn't mean they don't exist. It was influenced by the tropical setting and completely spur of the moment. Statistically, impulsive decisions like that seldom turn out well.

Nolan's phone sounds an incoming call as he's pouring himself a second glass of vodka. He recognizes the number. It's Lauren's brother, Greg.

"Hi Greg."

"Hey bro, how's it going?" Greg says, in his usual upbeat manner. "Is Lauren home? I've got a question for her."

"Sorry, Greg. She's out for the evening at a company Halloween party."

"Why didn't you go with her? You're not working are you?"

5

He starts to say he didn't go because he wasn't invited, but that would sound like him grousing, so instead he says, "It's not my kind of thing."

"Yeah, I know what you mean. I was never into dressing up like that. Not past the age of twelve, at any rate. Well, tell her to give me a call tomorrow, if you will."

"I'll tell her if I see her before then," Nolan replies, and starts to hang up.

"Hey, Nolan. Is everything alright between Lauren and you? I don't mean to pry, but I know she can be difficult, sometimes."

"Things between us are normal. There's no need to be concerned."

"Okay, if you say so. Listen man, if you ever need to talk, about Lauren or anything else, I'm here for you. You're my brother-in-law. We're family, right? And besides that, I was the one who introduced you two, so I'd feel bad if there were problems and I didn't try to help."

"Thanks, Greg. That's good of you to offer, but really, everything between Lauren and me is just fine."

~2~

It is technically correct for Greg to say he introduced Nolan to Lauren, but it isn't as if he's the one responsible for them hooking up. That was simply nature taking its course. Nolan was at a sports bar with a buddy of his, Jeremy. Jeremy had broken it off with his fiancé and was in need of consolation. They were in the middle of a game of eight-ball when Greg lays a quarter on the pool table.

"Okay if I play the winner?" he asks.

"Fine with me," Jeremy says. "Maybe you'll do better than me. I've lost three in a row."

Nolan noticed Greg earlier, joking around with some other guys in the place, like he's a regular here. He's a friendly guy with an easy manner, nearly six foot, clean-shaven with close-cropped black hair, who dresses and looks like a successful type. Maybe he's a lawyer or realtor. Hell, maybe he's a pool shark. He sips from a bottle of Heineken while he waits patiently for the game to end.

As predicted, Jeremy loses. Greg feeds quarters into the coin slot to release the balls, and racks them for the next game. Nolan is chalking his cue in preparation to break when Jeremy nudges him and says, "Check it out." Nolan follows his gaze to see what has his attention. That's when he gets his first glimpse of her.

Lauren is a few feet inside the front door, walking slowly as she scans the room looking for someone. She's wearing a loose-fitting silk tunic dress. The place is dark except for the neon beer signs and big TV screens. Each time she passes in front of the light, her near-perfect body is silhouetted beneath the fabric. Nolan can't stop staring at her.

Suddenly her head pivots in his direction, and her eyes lock on him. They seem to glow in the dark, like the eyes of a feral beast at night. She smiles, and then starts in his direction. He drops his cue stick and bends to pick it up. When he looks up again, Lauren has her arms spread to embrace Greg. Close up she's even more striking. Tall, maybe five foot ten, with long strawberry blonde hair and piercing gray eyes.

Nolan is thinking, what a lucky guy, until Lauren says, "Well, big brother, are you going to introduce me to your friends or should I do it myself?" She was looking directly at Nolan and he felt sparks fly. Or at least that's how he remembers it. Next she says, "Is this a guys-only game, or can a girl play?"

Nolan and Jeremy trip over each other getting her a cue stick. When she bends over the table to line up her first shot the entire place falls quiet, as if someone hit the mute button. Every man there is mesmerized by the gorgeous babe playing pool.

"I can't decide which ball to shoot at, Nolan. Which one would you choose?" she asks.

He steps closer until their shoulders touch, and says, "Maybe the 9-ball. It's a straight shot into the corner pocket."

"I don't know if I can do that. Show me how to line it up."

"Alright. Put your left hand here," he says, guiding it to a spot four inches behind the cue ball. He reaches around her to position her right hand near the butt of the cue stick. She leans against him as he does.

8

"I don't know how to stop the cue ball from going in."

"Flatten your left hand slightly, so the tip of the stick strikes the cue ball below the equator. That's right, just like that. Now, make the shot."

She jabs the stick forward, striking the cue ball too low and causing it to hop before rolling into the 9-ball, which comes to a stop at the lip of the pocket.

"Oh, darn," Lauren says. Nolan bumps the table with his hip, and the 9-ball falls in. "Look, I made it! Did you see that, Greg? That's so exciting!" She throws her arms around Nolan's neck, and kisses him. It isn't a passionate lingering kiss, just a friendly smooch, but from that point on, he's completely under her spell.

The game takes forty minutes to complete. No one challenges for the table. No one wants Lauren to step away from it. Under the spotlight of the tiffany shade lamp hanging above, Lauren is the center of attention, and seems to enjoy every second of it. The men ogle her and whisper to one another. She responds to their lecherous leers with a flirtatious smile. Any one of them would kill for a minute alone with her, but for whatever reason she chooses to spend her time with Nolan.

While they play they exchange small talk about their occupations, their homes, what foods they enjoy, their interests and marital status. While he racks the balls for a second game of eight-ball, she applies a layer of chalk to the tip of her cue stick. Nolan looks up from the table as she parts her lips, blows the excess powder away and winks.

"I'm not very good at this. Would you show me how?" she says, when it comes time to begin the game.

"You can place the cue ball anywhere behind these dots. The objective is to knock it into the triangle of balls as hard as you can, without sending balls off the table. Here, I'll help you set up the shot." Again, he guides her hands into their proper positions, then says, "Okay, break 'em."

9

The cue ball glances off the racked balls, separating only three of them from the pile. A half dozen men applaud, and she rewards them with a smile and a curtsy. The second game lasts longer than the first, and when it's over they notice both Greg and Jeremy are gone.

"Is he coming back for you?" Nolan asks.

"I don't think so. He probably assumed you would take me home. Do you mind?"

"Not at all. I'll be happy to. Do you want to play another game?"

"Not really. I'm ready to go, if you are."

"That's fine with me, but there are a lot of guys in here who are going to be disappointed to see you leave."

"At the moment, there's only one man I'm concerned about disappointing."

Prior to meeting Lauren, Nolan's architectural design company had an inflow of work, from a stable list of clients which included some of Houston's most prominent builders. He put in forty hours a week, and spent his spare time with friends and clients having drinks or playing golf. His long-term business plan was for slow steady growth over the next few decades, and when the time comes, sell the company and retire.

Since marrying Lauren, Nolan has been expanding his business and putting in more hours. He works at home before and after his day at the office, as well as on Saturdays and Sundays. And because he no longer has any spare time, his friends have taken a back seat to his career. Lauren doesn't mind him devoting so much time to work and neglecting her the way he does. In fact, she encourages it.

In response to his apologies for spending more time working than with her, she tells him, "I don't want to be with some poor schmuck who's struggling to get by. I'm proud of you for being ambitious and wanting a better life for us. It makes me love you that much more."

Whenever the heavy workload begins to take a toll on him, and he feels his energy level waning, Lauren finds a way to motivate him. She'll get all dolled up and have him take her someplace fancy, where all the men turn their heads, envious of Nolan as he walks by with her on his arm. Or she'll greet him wearing sexy lingerie when he comes home late from the office. It's a not-so-subtle reminder of what he gets in return for his hard work.

"I've done without for most of my life. I'm not interested in living that way any longer," Lauren confesses, two days after they meet. "That's the thing about you, I find most attractive. You're a go-getter. You have a nice home, a good income and money in the bank. You're going to make something of yourself, and I want to be there when you do."

The statement was so Lauren, as he would later learn. She stroked his ego, and at the same time invited herself along on his climb up the ladder.

"Really! That's what you find most attractive about me, my house, bank account and earning potential? And here I thought it was my Dodge truck with four-wheel drive."

"Well, it's a nice truck, but it falls a little further down the list. Your good looks are what got my attention, but without your financial status, we wouldn't have made it past that first night. I have high standards, as you can see."

"Some people would refer to that as high-maintenance."

"It goes with the territory. Nice things sometimes require additional upkeep. And I think you're the kind of guy who likes nice things."

The conversation was eye-opening for Nolan. Lauren is a breed of woman he's unfamiliar with. She knows what she wants, isn't shy about pursuing it, and is confident her gorgeous looks and savvy smarts will get her everything and everyone she's after.

~3~

The Halloween party is taking place at the home of Gordon Weston and his wife, Erica Dupree. Gordon manages the investment firm where Lauren works. She enters the address into her GPS as she leaves her house and it directs her to a big sprawling estate in the River Oaks section of Houston. According to office gossip, the home belonged to Erica before she met Gordon. Her father is supposedly some kind of old-money oil tycoon. After a look at the estate, Lauren feels it must be true. It's too expensive a property for someone with Gordon's income.

A valet greets her as she pulls up to the entry of the mansion. "Great costume," he says, with a lascivious wink and a smile.

The front door opens before she can ring the bell. A young Vietnamese woman in a servant's uniform escorts her through a foyer into a huge room decorated with tombstones, jack o' lanterns, skulls and crossbones. Ghosts, bats, skeletons and witches on brooms hang from the ceiling. There's an open bar and a buffet table of food with servers standing by. Most of her coworkers have already arrived. They're appropriately costumed and spread around the room, standing or sitting with a drink in one hand and a plate of hors d' oeuvres in the other.

"Lauren, we're so glad you could make it," Gordon Weston says. He is decked out in a devil costume with horns on his head and a barbed tail pinned to his ass. It's a world of difference from the conservative tailored suits he wears to the office. "This is my wife, Erica."

"It's so good to meet you, Erica. You have a beautiful home, and I love your costume."

Lauren guesses Erica to be thirty-five, give or take, a few years younger than Gordon, but a decade older than herself. She is dressed as Cleopatra, Queen of the Nile, and giving Lauren a run for her money in the sexy costume competition.

"Thank you," she tells Lauren. "Your husband didn't come with you?"

"No, he's not really a partygoer. He'd rather stay home and watch TV."

"Well, that's a shame. I would love to have met him."

Roughly translated that means, she'd rather he was there keeping an eye on Lauren, so she and the other wives at the party wouldn't have to.

"I'm sure you'll enjoy yourself, nonetheless," Gordon tells Lauren.

"Yes, I'm sure she will," Erica agrees. "Get something from the bar and the buffet table, and then join your friends. We're going to do karaoke later, after everyone has a few more drinks. It should be a lot of fun."

Lauren has the bartender make her a vodka martini, extra dry with three olives. She strolls around the room chatting with coworkers while sipping her martini. All eyes are on her, and she's well aware of it. She performs for her audience, taking the olives from her glass and sliding them off the toothpick, one at a time with her lips, and then rolling them on her tongue before biting into them. The bartender brings her another martini with two toothpicks holding three olives each as soon as she finishes the first. He's hoping for an encore. She doesn't disappoint him.

An hour later, when everyone who is coming has arrived, they take a vote for the best costume. Gordon moves around the room holding a hand over each partygoer while the others applaud. The end result is a tie between Lauren and Erica. The prize is dinner for two at Houston's finest steakhouse. As party host, Erica doesn't feel right about taking it.

"You take it," she tells Lauren. "Your husband will give up a night of TV for a nice steak dinner won't he?"

"I think I can persuade him. And, thank you. That's very generous of you. I hear their food is excellent."

"I can assure you it is. I've eaten there many times."

Even though everyone is well lubricated by the time the karaoke music begins, no one is eager to go first. Never one to shun the spotlight, Lauren steps onto the makeshift stage and selects a song by Shania Twain, 'That Don't Impress Me Much'. The best-selling video of Shania performing the song features her in a smoking-hot leopard print outfit. Lauren looks the part and she sings in a sultry, albeit somewhat off-key voice.

Her performance inspires a few others to take a turn. With help from a couple of guys from his office, Gordon sings a Van Halen song, 'Running with the Devil'. It draws plenty of laughs, and applause. To close the karaoke session, Erica selects a Celine Dion number, 'My Heart Will Go On'. No one there realizes Erica has had years of voice training. Her performance is spectacular. Everyone watches in awe, and afterward there is no question of who's won this competition.

"You have an incredible voice," Lauren tells Erica. "Have you ever sang professionally?"

"Not really. I've performed at various venues for charity events. You did a very convincing imitation of Shania Twain. Do you have acting experience?"

"I played the role of Maria in our high school's rendition of 'West Side Story'. That's the extent of my acting experience."

14

Several others are nearby listening to the conversation and waiting for an opportunity to tell Erica how much they've enjoyed the party and her performance. Lauren's phone buzzes. She takes it from her purse to glance at the screen.

"You can take it in the kitchen where it's quieter, if you like. It's through that door there," Erica suggests, and points the way.

A member of the catering staff is cleaning cooking utensils at the sink as she enters. It is only marginally quieter than the big room. Lauren moves to the other side of the kitchen, puts the phone to her ear and says, "What do you want, Greg?"

"Hey, babe. Are you still at the party?"

"Yes, I am. I'm in the kitchen where it's not as loud. Why are you calling?"

"I talked to Nolan, earlier. He didn't sound happy about you going without him. You've been with him for almost a year. I'd hate to see it all go to waste because you wanted a night out."

"Look, Greg. If it all goes to waste it will be because of you, not me. You don't need to call Nolan, and you don't need to check up on me. I've got my end handled. Nolan worships the ground I walk on."

"Every man has his limits. You can only push him so far."

"Every man? Does that include you? Is this call about me and Nolan, or is it more about you and me?"

"Lauren, don't get upset. I'm just reminding you of the time you have invested, and asking you to be careful. That's all."

"Fine, Greg. Message received. Now if there's nothing more, I'm going to return to the party." She disconnects and lets out a sigh of exasperation.

"Was that your husband wondering where you are?" Gordon Weston asks. She has no idea how long he's been standing behind her or what he might have overheard.

"My older brother," Lauren replies, as she turns to face Gordon. "He's always been overly protective of me."

"Yes, I got that impression from what I heard of your end of the conversation." Gordon is standing close. He has a glass of bourbon in one hand and a martini with three olives in the other.

Lauren gestures to it and asks, "For me?"

"Who else?"

The woman who had been washing pots and pans when Lauren came into the kitchen has since left. It's just the two of them, standing closer than their spouses would think appropriate. If it worries either of them, they don't let it show.

Lauren came to this party anticipating Gordon would try something with her. There's been a sexual tension between them at the office for a while now. He's a little old for her, but not bad-looking for a guy his age. He seems to stay in shape. His sandy brown hair is graying at the temples, which gives him a distinguished look. He's nowhere near as handsome as Nolan, but at the same time, Lauren sees potential there. She lets her eyes wander around the room.

"This is a huge kitchen. Do you entertain often?"

"Erica belongs to several charitable organizations. She hosts one function or another at least once a month. They're usually pretty boring compared to this one. Would you like a tour of the rest of the house?"

"Are you sure Erica would approve of you showing me around?"

"She probably wouldn't, but she'll be busy with the other party guests for a while longer. Follow me. We'll go this way."

He takes her by the hand to lead her from the kitchen and down a hallway past several closed doors.

"This is what we call the servants' wing. We have one maid and a man who is Erica's assistant living here. She stays in that room." Gordon tilts his head toward one of the closed doors. "He's in the one across from that."

16

He pulls Lauren into a room farther down the hallway. It's a good-sized bedroom with its own bath, a queen-size bed, an armoire and dresser. She gives herself a tour of the room, running a hand over the dresser, glancing into the bathroom and finally sitting her pussycat-clad ass down on the bed.

"It's very comfortable. These are nice accommodations for the household staff."

Gordon shuts and locks the door. "Careful with your tail. I wouldn't want you to break it," he says, as he crosses the room to join her on the bed.

"Worry about your own tail, you devil. Mine is just fine. Why did you lock the door?"

"Why do you think? I don't want anyone walking in on us. I've been dreaming about this for a long time." He moves in to kiss her, but she holds him off with a hand to his chest.

"You can dream about it all you want, but that won't make it happen. I'm not interested in having any more than a working relationship with you. And even if I was, I'm not going to screw you right here under your wife's nose in her own home. That's a little too risky, don't you think?"

"Don't worry about Erica. We have an understanding."

"Really?" Lauren says skeptically. "The two of you openly discuss your extramarital affairs?"

"Of course we don't. That's why it's called an understanding. There's no need to talk about it. Besides, I don't have extramarital affairs, I have fun. That's all this is. We're two people looking to have a little fun. Come on, Lauren, we're wasting time."

"I think not, Gordon. We have different ideas about what is fun. Thanks for the home tour. I'm going to rejoin the others. I'm not confident Erica didn't see you follow me into the kitchen. She could be standing outside this room with her ear to the door, right now."

She gets up from the bed. He grabs her left wrist to stop her. She brings her right hand around to slap him, but he grabs that wrist as well. Holding her arms to her sides, he pushes her back against the armoire, pinning her there with his body. "Gordon, what are you doing?"

"I've wanted you since the first time I laid eyes on you. You want it, too, don't you?"

He kisses her roughly as she squirms to break free.

"Let go of me, Gordon. You're hurting me."

Her distress only seems to excite him all the more.

"Stop fighting me and give it up."

"No, I'm not doing this. Quit it, now!"

He tries to wrestle her back onto the bed. She stops struggling. Her expression is one of resignation.

"Alright," she sighs.

He relaxes his grip on her arms and eases back. As soon as he does, she lays her hands on his shoulders, and sinks her knee into his balls three times in quick succession.

"You jerk," she says, and pushes him away. He's still bent over in pain when she returns to the big room. The party is winding down. Several are saying good night to Erica and leaving. Lauren decides the time is right for her to exit, as well.

"It was a terrific party. I had a wonderful time. That was my husband on the phone. Apparently he's feeling lonely, so I'll leave now."

"It was a pleasure meeting you, Lauren. Hopefully, your husband will come with you next time and you won't have to rush home."

"I can't speak for him, but maybe. I don't see Gordon anywhere."

"I'm not sure where he's wandered off to. He should be back in a minute, however."

"Well, tell him thanks for inviting me and I'll see him at the office."

~4~

From the street, Curtis Leyden surveys the house of his newest client before turning into the circular drive. His mind is instinctively running various calculations—its size, value, vulnerability to a home invasion and visible deterrents. Security consulting is what he does and has done for the past ten years, ever since taking early retirement from the FBI. His clients are corporations with big budgets for curtailing security threats. He started to explain this to the woman who called him at 9 a.m. and asked for a noon meeting. Then she gave her name, which was vaguely familiar, and her address in River Oaks, a section of the city where some of its wealthiest citizens reside.

"If you'll come to my house, we can discuss the matter over lunch. How does a crab salad sound?" Erica Dupree asks.

"Fine with me. What is it we'll be discussing?"

"I'd rather not say over the phone, Mr. Leyden. It's a rather delicate matter. You come highly recommended. Drew Rondel assured me you're very capable and always discreet."

The doorbell is answered by a slightly-built young man wearing black slacks and a white dress shirt. He escorts Curtis to an outside garden overlooking the swimming pool and seats him at a table set for two. A waterfall which seems to emerge from a man-made tropical forest flows into the pool where

Erica is floating face up on an air mattress, wearing only a bikini and sunglasses. Curtis cautions himself not to stare like a pubescent boy, but his brain isn't transmitting the message to the rest of his body.

The young man, goes to inform Erica of her guest's arrival. Erica paddles the air mattress to the shallow end, gracefully dismounts and ascends the steps out of the pool. She's of medium height with a slender, yet curvaceous figure, and shoulder-length red hair. Her attendant diverts his gaze deferentially and hands her a towel to pat dry her legs—the only part of her that touched the water—and then holds her robe as she slips it on.

"Thanks for coming, Mr. Leyden," she says, as she seats herself across the table from him. "You're right on time. I appreciate your punctuality."

"I appreciate the opportunity to be of service."

"Hernando, could I have an iced tea, please?" Erica says. "Would you like one, Mr. Leyden?"

"Yes, I would, thanks."

Erica takes her time getting around to the reason she asked Curtis here today. It doesn't bother him. He's pushing sixty with mostly gray hair and a sizeable midriff bulge. It isn't often he has the pleasure of sitting across the table from a beautiful young woman like Erica. Hernando delivers a serving cart with two trays to their table. One tray has two glasses of ice, a pitcher of tea and a bowl of lemon slices. The other holds the crab salads. Once Hernando has placed everything on the table, Erica dismisses him.

"I know you're curious as to why I've asked you here. Thanks for your patience," Erica begins. "I suspect my husband is cheating on me."

"Ms. Dupree, before you go any further, I'm a security consultant. My customers hire me to advise them of threats to their assets and employees. If you're looking for someone to surveil your husband's activities, I can probably refer you to someone, but it's not what I do."

"As I mentioned in our earlier conversation, you came highly recommended by Drew Rondel. He's worked for my father for several years and his recommendation carries a lot of weight. Perhaps if I explained what is involved, you might reconsider."

"Go ahead. I'm listening."

"I'm an heir to the Dupree business empire, as in Dupree Oil and Gas."

"Yes ma'am, I'm aware of that. I viewed information about you ma and your family after we spoke this morning. I did so to be better prepared for this meeting, and for no other purpose. I know your grandfather did quite well in the oil business a few decades ago."

"Good, that will save us some time. My husband, Gordon Weston, and I were married five years ago. At the time, my personal assets were valued in excess of two hundred million dollars. Gordon's assets were valued at less than fifty thousand dollars. For obvious reasons, I had him sign a prenuptial agreement. In the event of a divorce, he gets twenty million."

"That's a pretty generous settlement, if you don't mind me saying so."

"Yes, it is, I agree. In hindsight, I used poor judgment, both when I agreed to the prenup and when I married Gordon. I wish I could say it was because I was young and foolish, but the truth is I was old enough to know better. There is a clause in the agreement I haven't told you about. And it's something I think you'll find interesting. If Gordon commits adultery he loses his right to any part of my estate, and walks away with nothing but the shirt on his back."

It takes Curtis no more than a nanosecond to understand the monetary reward for saving Erica from paying out twenty million to Gordon could be a substantial chunk of change. Erica can hear the gears inside his head gnashing together.

"As you can see, this is a little more complex than you originally thought. Would you like to reconsider, now?"

"I'll admit you've piqued my interest. Why don't you start by telling me what makes you think Gordon has been cheating on you?"

"I can do better than that." She calls to Hernando, "Please bring me the large manila envelope from my desk." A minute later, it's lying on the table between Erica and Curtis. "That contains detailed information about Gordon—where he works, the country club he belongs to, some of the places he frequents. There's also the name of a woman he works with. I have a bad feeling about her, call it a woman's intuition. Anything else you need to know, you can reach me on my personal phone."

He scans the contents of the envelope. "I can see you're a very organized person. This stuff will be helpful." The last item he sees is a check made out to him. "We never discussed my fee."

"I made an assumption on what you would ask for as a retainer. I doubled the figure, hoping it would be incentive enough for you to accept the job. Did I assume correctly?"

"Yes ma'am, twenty thousand is more than adequate. I'll take the job and start immediately."

"Good, I'm glad to hear it. Don't rush off, Mr. Leyden. Stay and enjoy your crab salad. I hope you won't think me rude if I return to my air mattress. I need another few minutes of sun on my backside to even out my tan. Hernando will show you out when you're finished."

Curtis leisurely enjoys his lunch as she ambles away. He considers diverting his eyes, but feels Erica is the sort of woman who is more offended by those who don't look, than by those who do. This is further evidenced when she stops at the edge of the pool, lets the robe drop to the deck and turns to wave goodbye to Curtis.

She is without question a very desirable woman, and filthy rich to boot. What would possess a man like Gordon to throw it away for a tryst with a coworker? It leads him to believe there's more to this than he's being told. Maybe, Erica has a lover and wants Gordon out of the picture, but doesn't want to pay him the twenty million. That would make more sense than Gordon screwing around on her, knowing what's at stake for him. If that's the case, what does Erica want from him? Evidence to support the supposition Gordon has committed adultery, even if it's fabricated? Tread lightly, he tells himself. This could get crazy before all is said and done.

~5~

Lauren receives a call from Greg as she arrives home after work on the Monday following the Halloween party.

"We need to talk," he says. "Is Nolan home?"

"He has some kind of meeting at the office. He won't be home for a couple of hours or more."

"Alright, I'll be there in twenty minutes."

In the meantime, she changes out of her work clothes. Then, she takes two glasses from a cupboard, fills them with ice, gin and tonic water, and tosses a lime wedge into each. She hands one to Greg when he arrives and he drains half of it in one gulp.

"So, what is it we need to talk about?"

"Was Nolan pissed when you got home, Friday night?"

"I don't know. It was two a.m. Saturday when I got home, and he was asleep. When he woke at seven, I screwed his ears off and he was happy as a lark after that."

"I don't want to hear about that."

"You seem concerned with Nolan's happiness, so I'm simply reassuring you there's nothing to worry about."

"I'm not concerned with his happiness. I'm worried you're going to jeopardize your plan. Leaving him at home while you party is going to get old for him, sooner or later."

"First of all, I wasn't out partying. I was at a social function at a very upscale home in River Oaks, and rubbing elbows with some rich and influential people. One can never have too many irons in the fire. And second, I've jeopardized nothing. Nolan couldn't be happier. Besides, this arrangement was your idea."

"My idea?! Where do you get that? You planned this whole thing from the start. I've gone along with it, but only because I had no other choice."

"That's not true, Greg. You convinced me I have a gift with men and encouraged me to use it. There's something about me that makes them want to spend their money on me, is the way you put it. You implied I was wasting my talent on losers. It was you who chose Nolan and dared me to seduce him. You orchestrated the whole thing."

"Your selective memory never fails to amaze me. Here's what really happened. You picked Nolan out of a dozen or so others for what was supposed to be a one-night stand. Next thing I know you're marrying him."

"It was a fluid situation from the beginning. I had to improvise as it progressed. Look, regardless of how things reached this point, this is where we are, now. I'm doing what's necessary on my end, and you need to trust my judgment. I'll get us another drink. Sit down and make yourself comfortable."

He is slouching in a recliner with his eyes shut and his forehead furrowed when she comes back with the drinks. She sets the drinks on the coffee table and steps behind him to massage his temples and neck.

"Does this help?"

"Some, but that's not the part of my body that needs attention. How long is this charade with Nolan going to continue? You keep telling me you're going to divorce him and take half his money. Do you have any idea when it will happen?"

"As I've already explained, it's a fluid situation. The longer I'm married to Nolan, the more wealth he accumulates

25

and the more money I walk away with. And in the meantime, he's a terrific lover."

"Damn you, Lauren. Why do you taunt me this way? It's bad enough my wife sleeps with other men. I don't need the constant reminders."

"Greg, I'm not a one-man sort of woman. I never have been, and I've never hidden this from you. You knew this when you met me. Did you think that after we married I'd have a change of heart? Did you picture us with a dog and three kids? You don't want that life any more than I do."

"I don't know what I thought would happen when I married you, but I never imagined this." He picks up his glass and sips from it as he sulks.

"Nolan won't be home for another hour. Between now and then, I could give those body parts you mentioned the attention they need. That is, unless you'd rather sit here and pout, instead."

He follows her into the bedroom, where she has him sit on the bed while she undresses him. Then, she slowly and seductively strips out of her own clothing. He lies on his back and she mounts him. It's over in less than a minute. Lauren has that effect on men. It's a curse.

"That was great," he says. "I needed that in the worst way."

It's his way of letting her know he's done. She rolls off to lie beside him. He pulls her close. After a moment, they both doze off. Lauren wakes an hour later. She glances at the clock, and then rouses Greg.

"Get up and get dressed. Nolan will be here any minute." He's slow to respond, so she jabs him in the ribs. "Hurry, he can't find us like this."

She grabs her clothes and goes into the master bath to dress, check her hair and fix her makeup. Greg is not on the bed when she comes out, and his clothes are no longer on the floor. She is straightening the bed cover when she hears the front door opening. It can only be one person.

"Lauren," Nolan calls to her.

"Hi hon," she calls back, then goes to meet him. On the way, she scans the house for Greg. "You startled me. I didn't hear the garage door."

"Greg's car is parked in the driveway on my side. Where is he?"

"I don't know. He was here a minute ago. I went to the bathroom. I was just coming out when you called my name."

"Hey, bro," Greg says, as he enters the room. "I thought that was your voice I heard. How was work?"

"It was a long day, but other than that I can't complain. Is everything alright with you?"

"Yeah, everything's super. I just stopped by to return Lauren's purse." Nolan looks perplexed by that. Greg explains, "My girlfriend borrowed it for this thing we went to."

"Your girlfriend?" Nolan questions. "I thought you were...,"

Lauren clears her throat to catch Nolan's attention, and then gives a barely perceptible shake of her head to warn him off what he's about to say.

"You thought I was what?" Greg prompts. He looks at Lauren, and then back at Nolan, but neither reply. "You thought I was gay? Is that what you were going to say? Where'd you get that idea?"

"Uh...," is all Nolan can say.

"Greg, it's nothing to be ashamed of," Lauren says.

"But...," Greg starts.

"Really, Greg. It's alright, you don't need to say anything more. We're family. No one is passing judgment." Her eyes plead with him to let the discussion of his sexual orientation end there. He reluctantly abides.

"I should leave. I'm sure Nolan would like some quiet time alone with his wife, after a long day at the office. Wouldn't you, bro?"

"Don't rush off for my sake. Stay for dinner if you like."

"I'll take a rain check on that. I've got other plans." He gives Lauren a brotherly peck on the cheek before going.

"I didn't know he was still in the closet," Nolan says, after Greg is gone.

"He's always had trouble coming to terms with his homosexuality. It's a constant struggle for him."

"What was that thing about borrowing your purse?"

"No one borrowed a purse from me. That was just something he said because he was embarrassed over the real reason he stopped by. He's in a jam with a creditor and asked if we could loan him some money. I told him I'd talk to you."

"How much does he need?'

"Five thousand dollars. He says he'll pay you back, but I wouldn't count on it. I wouldn't ask this of you, but he's my brother and I hate to say no."

"Five thousand? Is this creditor a drug dealer?"

"Probably. He struggles with depression due to his homosexuality, and when it gets to be too much for him to cope with he turns to drugs. He doesn't have anyone else he can count on. I hate to think what might happen to him if he doesn't pay off the dealer."

The thought of causing Lauren pain or disappointment precludes all others for Nolan. He doesn't hesitate for even a second.

"Okay, I'll write him a check for five thousand."

"Make it out to cash. If Greg is involved in anything illegal, I don't want there to be a record of you giving him money."

"Good thinking. It's best if there's no paper trail connecting me to him."

"Thank you for doing this, Nolan. Your support means a lot to me. I love you so very much." He pulls her into his arms for a kiss.

"Anything for you, sweetheart," he says. "And, I love you just as much."

"That reminds me. With all the hours you're spending at work, you've fallen behind on your conjugal duties. I think we should go to the bedroom so you can catch up."

~6~

The Investment Diversity Advisory Group, usually referred to as IDAG, is the company Gordon Weston manages, and the place where Lauren Drake works. They specialize in investments which generate big returns over a short period, but have a high risk factor associated with them—a fact they sometimes neglect to mention to their clients. The startup capital for the business was provided by Erica shortly after she and Gordon married. IDAG has operated in the red since its inception, but that's of little concern to Erica. Gordon has a swanky office and an important-sounding title, which helps with appearances. She has a tax write-off.

Midmorning Wednesday Gordon is in his office with the door closed. He is viewing images of his employees on his desktop computer screen. Cameras mounted throughout the office complex allow him to monitor, zoom in on and record their activities. At the moment, his attention is focused on Lauren. She is introducing herself to a prospective client, which is her primary function at IDAG. A guy makes an appointment to speak with someone about handling his money and hers is the first face he sees upon entering the office. She greets him in the reception area wearing a slinky low-cut dress and a come-hither look. Before long, the guy is bragging about how much money he has to invest. That's when Lauren escorts him into the inner office area to be fleeced. Gordon turns up the audio.

"Where did you hear about IDAG, Mr. Leyden?" Lauren asks.

"I saw something online," Curtis lies, because he can't very well say he heard about IDAG from Erica Dupree and he's there to find out who is playing hide the sausage with Gordon.

"Then, you probably already know we specialize in high-return investments. These aren't available to everyone. Our new clients have to invest a minimum of five hundred thousand dollars, and that money cannot be withdrawn for one year."

Part of Lauren's job is to read the client's reaction when she tells them about the half-million-dollar minimum. Curtis doesn't flinch, which she takes as a good sign. But Curtis isn't concerned with the amount, because he knows his dealings with IDAG will never go that far.

"Could I have a look around?" Lauren is confused by the request. "If I'm going to invest that kind of money I'd like to get a feel for the company that's overseeing it."

"Of course," Lauren says, without hesitating. "I'll introduce you to Palmer Medford. He's our chief investment strategist."

He follows her from the reception area through the door into the inner offices. Along the way he makes mental notes on the layout. He sees the cameras, several other employees on the phone or at their computers, the stark office furnishings and Lauren's ass swinging to and fro as she walks in front of him. They enter Palmer Medford's office, she introduces Curtis and leaves the two of them to get acquainted.

"Lauren is a real looker," Curtis says to Palmer, after she's gone. He's fishing for information, like an office rumor about Lauren and Gordon.

"She is that, alright," Palmer agrees. Curtis waits for him to elaborate, but instead he launches into a sales pitch.

From his office at the far end of the hallway Gordon calls, "Lauren, could I have a word with you in my office?"

His tone is appropriately professional. He holds the door for her, then closes it once she's inside. They haven't uttered more than a perfunctory good morning to one another since Gordon put the moves on her the night of the Halloween party. She stands before him with her arms crossed over her chest.

"What?" she says in a tone which makes it clear to Gordon his actions at the party haven't been forgotten or forgiven.

"Look, I had a little too much to drink at the Halloween party. I might have misread your body language and said some things I shouldn't have."

"You more than said some things you shouldn't have! You pinned my arms and tried to assault me!"

"Shush, not so loud. The whole office will hear. I'll admit I tried to kiss you, but it didn't go any further than that."

"It didn't go any further because I stopped you. What would your wife say if I told her?"

She considered doing just that the day after the incident, but decided against it. All it would serve to do is get Gordon in hot water. And if she doesn't tell Erica, it's something to hold over Gordon. Maybe it will be worth something to him to keep it secret.

"It's your word against mine. I'd tell her it was the other way around. You came on to me. Who's she going to believe, her husband of five years or a woman in a pussycat costume who she's only met once?"

"She's a woman. She'll believe another woman before she will a man, husband or not. It's what women do. Do you want to test that theory?"

"No, I don't. Lauren, I'm trying to apologize. That's why I asked you in here, to tell you I'm sorry for the way I acted

32

and ask you to forgive me. I promise it will never happen, again."

If she tells him he's forgiven, she loses her leverage over him. There's no incentive to give in so easily.

"It will never happen again because I won't let it, but I don't know if I'm ready to forgive, forget and act like it never took place."

Gordon can see the wheels turning as Lauren calculates the possibilities. His lips turn up to form a smug smile.

"You know, you and I are a lot alike," he tells her.

"How so?"

"You're sizing up the situation and trying to figure what you can get out of it. You're not offended by me coming on to you. That probably happens all the time. Your mind is totally focused on the bottom line. I can respect that. You're a woman after my own heart."

She is somewhat unnerved by his observations because they are surprisingly accurate. He takes a wad of one-hundred-dollar bills from his pocket, peels off three and hands them to Lauren.

"What is this?"

"An apology. The only kind people like us understand."

She considers it for only a second before folding the bills and stuffing them into her bra. Then, she turns to leave.

"Lauren," Gordon says. She pauses at the door, but doesn't turn around. "I'm not such a bad guy once you get to know me, and I can be very generous to my close friends. We could have a lot of fun together, you and me. Think about it."

Now he's got her attention. She turns around to face him.

"You phrased that as if making me an offer. What does very generous equate to in dollars and cents? And, what do you expect in return?"

It's the beginning phase of the negotiations, they both realize. Each has something the other wants. Now it's just a matter of coming to terms.

"You like to travel, don't you, Lauren? I'll be making several business trips in the near future, going to places like Paris, Rome, Rio de Janeiro, to name a few. I'll be taking an assistant along with me. Does that sound like something you might be interested in doing?"

"Possibly," she replies.

"All expenses would be paid by the company. There would be an additional allowance for shopping and sightseeing."

"When will these trips take place?"

"There's nothing scheduled. It's still in the planning stage. If I knew you'd be coming with me, it might be enough to make me solidify my plans."

"Well, if I knew when and where we were going, and how long we'd be gone, it would help me to decide. I'm going to leave your office now, because if we're in here any longer with the door shut, people are going to start spreading rumors about us."

Curtis has been halfheartedly listening to Palmer point out the dismal returns received from conventional investments when Lauren exits Gordon's office. Her expression is unreadable, but her face isn't flush and her clothing isn't disheveled. If the two of them are involved in an office romance, they're keeping it discreet.

"So, what do you say, Mr. Leyden. Would you like to open an account with us? The sooner you do, the sooner your money starts working for you."

"The information you've provided has been helpful, but I have another few investment places I'm considering. I expect to make a decision by the end of the month. I'll let you know what I decide."

~7~

Curtis Leyden finds Erica Dupree in her garden overseeing the pruning of her rose bushes when he arrives at her home. It's an overcast day and the temperature is considerably cooler than on his previous visit two weeks earlier. She is wearing bib overalls, a flannel shirt, sneakers and gloves. It's a far cry from how she looked when he saw her last, but it can't erase the memory of her in a bikini, floating in her pool.

"Thanks for coming to see me," she says.

"No need to thank me, Ms. Dupree. I'm at your service when and where you request."

"Let's talk in here." She ushers him into a greenhouse, out of earshot of her gardeners. "I'm anxious to see what you have so far. That's why I asked you here, today."

"I'm afraid I don't have much. I've been to his office. His interaction with the women who work there appears strictly professional on the surface. I observed him at the country club where he played a round of golf and in a cocktail lounge at a popular Mexican restaurant. He chats up the waitresses in the lounge and the beverage cart girls on the golf course. I haven't witnessed anything you can use against him to claim adultery. If he's cheating on you, he's covering his tracks."

"What about the woman in his office, Lauren Drake? Have you seen Gordon with her outside of the office?"

"No, I haven't. Her husband owns an architectural firm. His name is Nolan Drake. They're a nice-looking couple who have been married for less than a year. She is certainly pretty enough to tempt most men, but as you know, that's not enough in itself. There is one other thing I came across while looking into Lauren's background. She was married to a Greg Malloy prior to meeting Nolan. I didn't find any record of their divorce, but I didn't pursue it very far because it isn't pertinent to your case."

Erica considers that last bit of information for a minute before saying, "I'd like you to continue watching Gordon. I believe it's just a matter of time before he slips up."

"To be honest with you, I'm not so sure of his guilt, but if he is cheating on you, I'll find out."

"That's what I want to hear, Mr. Leyden." She takes a check from a pocket of her overalls and hands it to him. "I'm sure the retainer I gave you is mostly spent by now. Here's another twenty thousand dollars, so you can continue to give this your full attention."

"That's generous of you, and you can rest assured I'll do that."

~~~

The next day, Erica drops by the IDAG offices shortly before noon on the pretext of taking Gordon to lunch. He'll have a reason ready and waiting as to why he can't—an important meeting with a new client, a teleconference scheduled for twelve thirty, or maybe a doctor's appointment—but it doesn't matter to Erica. She has an ulterior motive for coming here. After greeting and conversing with a few of his coworkers, she enters his office without knocking. He's on the phone.

"Just a minute," he says into the phone and covers the mouthpiece.

"I was in the area and thought you might like to have lunch with me."

"I'd love to, but I can't. I'll be tied up on the phone for the next hour at least. Sorry, dear. We'll do it another time, okay?"

"Of course, sweetheart. Another time."

Next, Erica finds Lauren. Her timing is perfect. Lauren is getting ready to take her lunch break.

"Hi Lauren. It's so good to see you again. Were you about to take lunch? I stopped by to invite Gordon to lunch, but he's too busy. Would you join me? I hate to dine alone."

"Well, I…," Lauren starts, but can't think of a reason not to. And besides, getting to know Erica better might be beneficial later. "Uh, sure. I'd love to."

"Splendid," Erica says. "I know of a great little bistro right around the corner. We can walk there."

On the way, they chat amiably about fashion, music and celebrities in the news. When they enter the bistro, Erica asks for a corner booth where it's somewhat quieter. Once they're seated the conversation turns to topics of a more personal nature.

"I understand you and your husband are newlyweds," Erica says.

"Not exactly. We're coming up on our first anniversary, soon. How did you know that?"

"Gordon mentioned it. We talk about his job and the people he works with over cocktails, some evenings."

Lauren is skeptical the statement is true. She seldom shares details of her life away from the office with her coworkers, but it is possible she said something to someone, and it got back to Gordon. However, at the moment she is more curious over the reason for Erica's interest, rather than where she obtained the information.

"How long have you and Gordon been married, if you don't mind me asking?"

"Five years. We met at a gala benefitting the Children's Hospital, began seeing each other afterward, and a few months later eloped. I'm guessing it was much the same for you and Nolan. Am I right about that?"

That's not something anyone at the office would know. Of this, Lauren is certain.

"Ms. Dupree," she says.

"Please, Lauren. Call me Erica."

"Alright, Erica. You're either very intuitive, or you've been checking up on me. Which is it?"

"To be honest, it's a little of both, combined with my own personal observations of you. But don't be offended. My intentions are harmless. I have a project I need assistance with, and I think you might be the ideal person to provide it."

"Is this a project for one of the charity organizations you're involved with?"

"No, but before I tell you more about it, let's order an appetizer and a carafe of wine. How does that sound?" She signals the waiter to come to their booth. They agree on an order of king crab appetizers and Chablis.

"I only get an hour for lunch," Lauren says to Erica.

"That's no problem," the waiter assures her. "I'll be right back with your wine and appetizers."

While he's getting the order Erica says, "The first year of our marriage was the best. We were still in the process of getting to know one another and discovering new things along the way. Some of the things I learned about Gordon, I wish I hadn't. I suppose we all have secrets we would rather not reveal."

Lauren is listening closely, wondering why Erica is confiding this, and curious over what is coming. Erica pauses as the waiter returns with their order.

"Go on," Lauren coaxes, once he's gone.

"Gordon and I were raised in entirely different circumstances. My family was wealthy and Gordon's family lived more modestly. Don't get me wrong. Not being rich isn't a strike against a person, and it didn't make me love him any less. In fact, if my attorneys hadn't demanded he sign a prenuptial agreement, we would have gone ahead with the wedding and he would be entitled to half of my estate in the event of a divorce."

Lauren is listening distractedly to Erica while nibbling on an appetizer. And then, something occurs to her.

"Erica, are we just making idle conversation, or does this have something to do with the project you mentioned?"

"The latter. Now that we've had this chance to talk and I feel I know you a little better, I'd like to confess something to you. I'm embarrassed to admit it, but I suspected you of having an affair with Gordon. At the Halloween party, I noticed how Gordon couldn't take his eyes off you. I see now it was an overreaction on my part, and I apologize."

"Just to be perfectly clear, there isn't and never has been anything going on between Gordon and me."

"Frankly, I wish there was."

"Excuse me."

"If Gordon was having an adulterous affair with you or anyone else, it would greatly decrease the amount he receives if we divorce. Now that I've revealed that, you can better understand how you can assist me."

"You're asking me to spy on Gordon? Is that it?"

"Not exactly."

"Then, what exactly do you have in mind?"

"I'm hoping to obtain indisputable evidence of Gordon committing adultery. It's not enough to suggest he is capable of it. Third person testimony or rumors is insufficient in court. He has to be caught in the act, and the person who can best do that is the one he's sleeping with. That's where you come in."

"Let me get this straight. You're asking me to sleep with your husband. And then what? Take pictures of us in bed, so you have proof he's cheating on you? I'm sorry, that's just creepy bizarre."

"I'll admit it sounds sleazy when you put it that way. But, I'm not asking you to do it as a favor for me. You'd be paid well for your service. I'd venture to say it would be a sum of money larger than you have ever before held in your hands." Lauren appears dumbstruck by the idea. Erica places a hand on her forearm. "Just give it some thought. I don't need an answer today."

"How much are we talking about? What's it worth to you if I do this? If I'm going to seriously consider it, that's an important factor."

Erica doesn't hesitate. She wants the number to have maximum impact. She wants Lauren to be speechless. "One million dollars," she says.

It has the desired effect. It's a full minute before Lauren can get the words out. "Is this some kind of cruel joke?"

"No, Lauren. I've never been more serious in my life."

~ 8 ~

Of course Lauren will sleep with Gordon and pretend to be his lover for a million bucks. It's a no-brainer. She has slept with men for far less. That's not the part of Erica's plan that gives her pause. At present Nolan doesn't know her true relation to Greg, and Greg doesn't know her true feelings for Nolan. It's enough of a juggling act already without adding another man to the mix. Sneaking around with Gordon while not letting on to either of her husbands is going to be difficult, to say the least.

If Nolan gets wind of it, he'll be gone in a heartbeat, and she's not ready for that to happen. Greg, on the other hand, would be a little more understanding. She doesn't have to tell him everything, just enough to have him play along. He could serve as an accomplice of sorts. If there ever comes a time when she needs to explain her whereabouts to Nolan, Greg would provide her with an alibi. Any number of scenarios involving Greg's drug problem or debts could be fabricated, and Greg would willingly go along with the ruse.

"Tell me again. How is it Ms. Dupree picked you?" Greg asks.

"He's my boss. The Halloween party was at their house. She saw how he looked at me. Based on that, she thought he'd fall for me if I gave him a little encouragement."

"You already explained that. I get that part, but how did she know you'd go along with it?"

"I think she's good at reading people. And besides that, she's the type who believes everyone can be bought. It's just a matter of offering them enough money to get what she wants."

"That's another thing. Ten thousand doesn't sound like much if she's as rich as you say she is. Can't you squeeze more out of her?"

"I might be able to later, but I didn't want to push too hard initially. It wouldn't be difficult for her to find someone else. I mean let's face it, you'd screw her husband for ten thousand dollars, wouldn't you?"

"Ha, ha. Real funny, Lauren. But, I see what you're saying. For less than a thousand she can get a woman from an escort service to do the same thing."

That's not true, but Lauren isn't going to discourage Greg from believing it. Erica can't hire a hooker to bed her husband. It would look like nothing more than him paying for sex, and although technically that is adultery, it might not appear so to a male judge in a court of law. The affair with Gordon will have to be staged to look as if it has been going on for a while, and is serious enough to threaten his marriage to Erica.

"I'll have to improvise as I go. I may need you to cover for me with Nolan if I'm delayed getting home because I'm with Gordon. If that happens and Nolan calls you, make up something believable. Tell him I mentioned going to a yoga class or whatever."

"Don't worry, I understand. I won't tell him you're sleeping with your boss and might be gone a while."

~~~

42

Nolan calls to tell Lauren he'll be an hour late getting home. She uses the time to pick up Italian takeout and red wine. The table is set with the food on plates, the wine uncorked to breathe and a candle burning in the center of it as Nolan walks in. Lauren isn't the domestic type. She never decorates or cleans the house, and she rarely cooks. Nolan stops in his tracks upon seeing the meal prepared and waiting.

"Wow, you cooked this?"

"No, I picked it up at Angelo's."

"Wow, you picked it up, all by yourself? There are only two places set. Is this what it looks like, a romantic dinner for two?"

"That's exactly what this is. And, wait until you see what's for dessert."

They embrace and kiss, remaining in that position for a long time, enjoying the scent and feel of one another, and wanting it to continue.

"I'm thinking we should skip ahead, and go right to dessert," Nolan whispers in her ear.

"No way. Not after I've gone to all this trouble. You're going to eat your dinner and drink the wine at a slow leisurely pace, savoring every bite. Afterward you'll relish your dessert in the same manner. I'm going to make you wait for it, and then I'm going to make it worth the wait. Capisce?"

"Yes, ma'am."

True to her word, Lauren makes Nolan feel like he's the most important man on the face of the planet. He doesn't know why she chose to do this tonight, but assumes it has to do with the long hours he's been putting in, and the effect it's having on their bank account.

~~~

The next day Nolan goes to his office feeling like he's on top of the world. Lauren goes to her office knowing she has her ducks in a row and is fully prepared to do what needs to be done with Gordon. He buzzes her at ten thirty and asks her to come to his office.

"I've got a business trip scheduled for next week. I'll be spending four days on Grand Cayman Island, leaving this coming Monday morning. Would you like to come along as my assistant?"

"What would I be assisting you with?"

"Come on, Lauren. Don't play coy with me. You know how this works. It's a business trip for tax purposes only. The real reason we're going is to get away and have some fun."

"I'll reword the question. What do you expect of me?"

"I expect you to enjoy yourself. I'm offering you a paid vacation. Don't look a gift horse in the mouth. Would you rather stay here and work?"

"Let me be more specific. Do you expect me to sleep with you? Is that what you mean by assistance?"

"Alright, so you want me to spell it out for you, is that it? I've booked one room with one bed for the two of us, hoping I can convince you to share it with me."

"You're taking a lot for granted. What if we get there and I decide I'm not ready to go that far with you? Are you going to try and force me to have sex with you, like you did at your house the night of the party?"

"No, that won't happen, again. I said it once and I'll say it again. I'm sincerely sorry for my behavior, then. From here on, whenever I'm in your presence, I'll be a perfect gentleman."

Erica informed Lauren of Gordon's planned trip ahead of time, so Lauren could rehearse her response when he asked her to come with him. Gordon broached the subject one evening as he and Erica were having dinner. He told her the trip was to Mexico City to meet with potential clients. She knew it was a lie, but played along, praising him for going to such lengths to build the business.

"An investigator who works for me will be following you. Chances are you'll never see him," Erica explains to Lauren. "He'll be there to document your affair with Gordon. Don't overdo it with the PDA. It can't look like a performance. But, don't be so discreet it's impossible for my investigator to do his job."

"I understand. Will he sneak a camera into our room, to get pictures of us in bed?"

"I can't be sure, but it's possible. It would give me the proof of adultery I'm looking for. Are you okay with that?"

"Yes, I've got one million reasons for doing this. What about you? Are you okay with seeing pictures of your husband with another woman?"

She doesn't tell Lauren she has twenty million reasons for wanting to see Gordon with another woman.

"I'm more than okay with it. I'm deeply grateful to you for your help."

The day after Gordon asks Lauren to accompany him to Grand Cayman Island, she confirms with him her decision to go. That same evening she tells Nolan. His reaction is subdued. She expected it would be. However, she is surprised by the pang of guilt she feels for deceiving him.

"How many from the office are going with you?"

"Four or five people, I think. Two other women and two or three men."

"It will be strange to have the house to myself for four days. I've become accustomed to having you close."

"I know what you mean. I like our evenings together, but being apart occasionally is good for us in the long run. As the saying goes, absence makes the heart grow fonder."

"I'm not sure I can grow any fonder of you than I already am, Lauren."

"I feel the same about you, Nolan."

~9~

Nolan offers to drive Lauren to the airport for what he believes to be a business trip to Mexico City.

"That's okay. I'll take my car. I'd prefer to have it there when I return, in case my flight is delayed for some reason. That way, you're not tied up waiting at the airport or by the phone until I get in."

"I don't mind waiting, if it comes to that. Besides, wouldn't it be nice to receive a hug and a welcome home as soon as you step off the plane?"

"If the welcome home is from my husband, then yes, it would be nice, but it really isn't necessary. However, I would like a hug before I go."

They hug and as she kisses him goodbye her eyes involuntarily well up with tears. The surge of emotion is an odd sensation, and one she's unfamiliar with. It might be mistaken for love, if she didn't know better. She often uses the phrase, 'I love you', with Nolan, Greg and others, but they're empty words, nothing more. Actual love has always eluded her.

After parking and then hopping a shuttle to the terminal, Lauren checks her bag before proceeding to the gate. A glance at a flight information screen tells her the flight is running on time. Gordon isn't at the gate when she arrives.

Boarding isn't scheduled to begin for another forty minutes, so she takes a seat to wait.

Across the concourse at another gate, Curtis Leyden is sitting with coffee in one hand and his phone in the other. He's texting a message to Erica to let her know Lauren has arrived. He's unaware of the scheme Erica cooked up involving Lauren. All he knows is that Gordon is going on a trip and Erica has suspicions regarding it.

It was no easy task finding out what flight Gordon was booked on. The airlines aren't as free with passenger information as they were twenty years ago. He called in a favor with a friend at the Bureau and was able to connect a charge on Gordon's corporate MasterCard to United Airlines. The amount of the charge narrowed it down to three possibilities. He reserved a seat for himself on each. This flight to Grand Cayman is the first of those, and luckily for him, the right one. Now he can cancel the other two.

Lauren spots Gordon approaching the gate. He's wearing a charcoal gray Brooks Brothers suit, a paisley silk tie and black wingtip shoes, looking like he's flying off to an important business meeting. She waves to catch his attention. His face creases into a broad grin upon seeing her.

"Good morning, Lauren. Today's weather forecast for Grand Cayman is sunny with a high temperature of eighty-five degrees and calm seas," he says cheerfully.

All the while he's speaking his eyes are roving over Lauren, checking out her hair, makeup, clothing and every inch of her marvelous body. She's wearing a black jumpsuit which covers everything below the neck and above the ankles. It's casual, comfortable, ideal for a three-hour flight, and best of all, it isn't revealing or suggestive. She doesn't want Gordon getting worked up and making an ass of himself on the plane.

While Lauren and Gordon are chatting, Curtis uses his phone to inconspicuously snap pictures of the two with the gate number and destination showing in the background.

47

They're seated in first class and are among the first to board. Curtis is one of the last. It takes ten minutes to work his way down the aisle to the back of the economy section. He stows his carry-on and takes his seat. He won't see the couple at all during the flight, but it doesn't matter. Nothing worth photographing will happen while they're in the air.

~~~

By late afternoon, Lauren and Gordon have checked into their oceanfront hotel, changed into swimsuits and are sipping pina coladas while lounging on the beach. They have a late dinner at their hotel, listen to a band playing reggae beside the pool, then walk the beach afterward and are back in their room at midnight. It's show time, Lauren realizes. She can't be sure Erica's investigator has been able to get a camera in the room, but she has to do her part and assume he'll do his.

"Lauren, I've made no secret of my desire for you. Being with you on the beach today, sitting across from you at dinner and now here, just the two of us alone in the room. All day I've had one thing on my mind, and I think you know what it is."

"I've enjoyed the day too, Gordon. You were right. You're not such a bad guy, now that I've had a chance to spend time with you."

He eases nearer. When she doesn't step back it emboldens him to wrap his arms around her waist. He kisses her tenderly. She responds by pressing herself closer. The kissing intensifies and is followed by groping. Articles of clothing begin falling to the floor, and after a few minutes of that, they're in bed. It's not at all what Lauren expected from Gordon. He's fifteen years older than her and not as fit as Nolan or Greg. She assumed he would lack stamina and disappoint her as a lover. Instead, he's surprisingly virile.

48

The next day they go sailing in a rented dinghy. Gordon learned to sail as a young man growing up in Florida. Lauren has never been on a sailboat. She's impressed by how well Gordon handles it and amazed at how energized she is by the experience. They return to the room after dinner that evening, and soon are in bed going at it again. Gordon's performance is even better the second night.

On the third day they splash around in the ocean near the hotel. They are both all smiles and thoroughly enjoying themselves. There is a lot of PDA in plain sight of everyone around, even a little groping when they think no one is watching. They go back to their room for a nooner at midday, and are back in the ocean an hour after that. By this time, Lauren feels certain Erica's investigator has enough evidence to prove Gordon guilty of adultery. And if not, there's another day and two nights in which she plans to give him plenty of other photo opportunities.

Friday morning they need to rise early, in order to pack their things and get to the airport on time for the flight home. Before sunrise Gordon rolls on top of Lauren to make love one last time before they leave Grand Cayman Island.

In the throes of ecstasy he cries out, "God, I love you, Lauren."

That's when she realizes she's gone too far. He's under her spell, which means he'll be spending every minute wanting to be with her and she can't discourage him until his divorce from Erica is final. She'll have to string him along for at least another three months. Her biggest fear is that Gordon might do something stupid in the meantime, like tell Nolan.

On the plane ride back to Houston, Gordon holds her hand. It reminds her of the way Nolan acted when they came back from Jamaica as newlyweds. He has the same faraway look in his eyes, and the same stupid grin on his face. From the baggage claim area in Houston he walks with her to the shuttle stop. He bends toward her to kiss her, but she pulls back.

"That's a little too risky, now that we're back where someone we know might see us."

"You're right, I'm sorry. I've never met anyone like you, Lauren. These last four days have been the best of my life. I hate to see it end."

"I had a wonderful time in Grand Cayman, but we're back in the real world, now. My husband can't find out about where we went or what we did there. Do you understand?"

"Of course, I do. My wife can't find out either. I understand that. But, that doesn't mean we can't see each other. We just have to be discreet."

"We have to be more than discreet. Let's take it one day at a time. We'll see one another at work, but we can't let on that anything has changed between us. No touching, lascivious looks or conversation in low voices should pass between us. Nothing at all that can be misconstrued by our coworkers."

"Can I call you? We can use a code. For instance, if I call at a time when you can't talk because your husband is nearby, you say wrong number."

"Absolutely no calls. Our spouses can view our call logs. You have to be patient, Gordon. Again, one day at a time. Alright?"

"Do I have a choice?"

"No, you don't. Here comes my shuttle. Go home and kiss your wife like you've missed her terribly. I'll see you Monday."

~10~

Curtis Leyden has to wait until after Gordon and Lauren check out of the hotel in Grand Cayman before he can go into their room to retrieve his cameras and audio recording gear. As a result he misses his return flight home, Friday. It turns out to be something of a blessing in disguise. After all, there is nothing more to do where Lauren and Gordon are concerned. The video captured of them and the recordings of their intimate conversations will provide Erica with the indisputable evidence she needs to hang Gordon out to dry, six ways to Sunday.

With that in mind, Curtis decides a celebration is in order. And what better place and time, than here and now. Back in Houston, it's cold and rainy. There's no rush to get back. He can spend the day sipping rum drinks on the beach and watching young girls in bikinis walk past. Tomorrow, he'll rise early to get to the airport in plenty of time to catch a flight out.

The plan goes awry Friday evening when he meets forty-nine-year-old Nancy Saris, who is a few hours into her own celebration. Her divorce from that cheating skunk of a husband was finalized two days earlier. The first item to be checked off of her post-marriage to-do list is to screw the first man she meets in Grand Cayman, and send her ex a selfie of it, as it is happening. Hell hath no fury, and all that.

51

It's Sunday night before Curtis finally manages to drag his ass home to his faithful and loving wife of twenty-five years. On the flight home, he rehearsed the lie he's about to hand her, but her expression says, don't even think about it. After twenty-five years, she knows him better than he knows himself. She can read guilt in his body language as well as a gypsy reads palms. She doesn't admonish him for the sins she's certain he's committed, nor does she ask him to confess them. He takes his place in the dog house where he'll remain for a few days, or weeks, or months, until she decides he's served his time and can come out. He has yet to fully recover from the weekend when his phone sounds at eight a.m. Monday.

"Good morning, Ms. Dupree," he answers.

"I hope I'm not calling too early, Mr. Leyden. I'm dying to hear how it went this last week. Gordon just left for his office. When can you come over to show me what you have?"

"I can be there in two hours, if that's alright."

"The sooner, the better, as far as I'm concerned. I'll see you, then."

He showers, shaves, and then eats two pieces of toast, while his wife reads the morning newspaper and ignores him. Erica greets him at the front door when he arrives. She's wearing a workout top and shorts which are soaked in sweat, with a towel draped over her shoulders.

"Come in, Mr. Leyden," she says, and steps aside. "Please excuse my appearance. I've just finished my cardio on the treadmill. Do you exercise?"

"Not as often as I should. It's on my list of things I'm going to do after I retire."

"I see you brought some things with you. I hope this means your trip was a successful one."

"Yes, ma'am. I think you'll be very pleased with what I have."

"Splendid, let's talk in the study. It's this way."

Once they're in the study with the door shut, Curtis says, "I have video with sound taken inside the hotel room they shared. It's unedited and very graphic. It might be too disturbing for you to watch."

"You're right, it might be, but show me anyway. I've got to see for myself the treachery Gordon is capable of."

Curtis sets his laptop on a desk and has Erica sit down before slipping the first disk in. The video frame appears on the screen. "Go ahead and play it," she coaxes. He clicks the arrow.

It begins with the couple entering the dark room and turning on a lamp. The audio is poor, but Gordon can be heard telling Lauren of his desire for her. They embrace, kiss and move to the bed. Lauren pulls the sheets away, Gordon lies on his back, she fondles him while he gropes her breasts, and then, she mounts him. Erica appears transfixed as she watches. After twenty minutes, she has Curtis turn it off.

"This is better than I hoped for. You've done an incredible job. Now I know why Drew Rondel recommended you."

"There's more than four hours of video taken of them in the room, as well as pictures of them in Grand Cayman and boarding the plane in Houston. I'll edit it down to an hour or less of usable video, and I'll have stills made of the more incriminating parts."

"Please, put a rush on those. I'll pay extra for that, of course. I want to get my attorney working on the divorce proceedings as soon as possible."

"Yes, ma'am." Curtis doesn't begin packing up his gear and preparing to leave. Instead, he stares pensively at his feet for a moment.

"Is there something else, Mr. Leyden?"

"I'm not sure," he begins. "It's just that as I was reviewing the video footage afterward, I couldn't help but notice how cooperative Lauren Drake seems to be. She pulls the sheets

53

back, turns on a lamp nearby and appears to fake an orgasm at one point. Or at least, it looks that way to me."

"What are you saying?"

"I'm saying that someone who is trained and knows what to look for, might come to the same conclusion as me. They might think Lauren is acting, and the affair between Gordon and her is phony."

Erica didn't expect Curtis to put it together so quickly, and she doesn't know whether to show anger or incredulity in response.

"I'm afraid I don't agree. From what I saw, Lauren looks every bit as smitten with him as he is with her."

"Ms. Dupree. I work for you. I have no obligation to anyone else involved, and I won't betray you. That being said, I feel duty-bound to point out something I feel might be problematic down the line somewhere. For instance, if you had a conversation with Lauren Drake prior to this trip, and this came to light during the divorce proceedings. The conversation may have been unrelated, but Gordon's attorney could use it to cast doubt on the adultery claim."

"You make a good point. I appreciate you bringing it to my attention, and I appreciate your loyalty, as well. I sense you have a suggestion for how I should proceed with this matter."

"Yes, ma'am, I do. Your claim of adultery is based solely on the evidence I provided you, and you paid me to gather it. That discredits the information to some extent. Your suspicions have no weight in a court of law. To solidify your case against Gordon, you need someone to corroborate your claim of adultery. Someone unconnected to you who has witnessed or is otherwise aware of his indiscretions."

"I see what you mean. If someone who I've had no connection with came forward to support my claim it would help a great deal. A woman he's had an affair with before Lauren, maybe. I suspect there have been others, but I don't know who they are. Do you have any ideas for how to go about finding one of those women?"

"I do have some thoughts on it. Give me a day or so to mull it over while I edit the videos."

"Of course, Mr. Leyden. While you're here, I'd like you to look at the servants' wing. The video you showed me gave me an idea. There's a separate entrance to that area, used by my household staff among others. It might come in handy one day if there were hidden cameras monitoring who comes and goes."

"I'll be glad to give you my recommendations for camera placement. If you like, I can have an installation crew come out tomorrow."

"Excellent. I don't want anyone else to know the cameras are there. I'll find a reason to have Hernando and Phuong out of the house on an errand while the installation is being done."

~11~

Nolan leaves his office early on Friday afternoon in order to pick up flowers, wine and takeout food. He has the wine uncorked, the flowers in a vase and the food in takeout containers on the table as Lauren arrives. He greets her at the front door and wraps his arms around her.

"Welcome home."

Her response is a dispassionate, "Thanks," and she gives him a quick peck on the lips.

Nolan hides his disappointment. "How was the business trip?"

"Too long and very boring. I'm completely exhausted."

"There's a bottle of wine opened, and I picked up Mandarin food."

"I'd like to change clothes and clean up, first. We had to get up early to catch our flight. I feel like I've been going nonstop since Monday."

"Sure, go ahead," Nolan says, but what he's thinking is, *we* had to get up early. He cautions himself against reading too much into it as he watches her head toward the bedroom. The whole group of people from her office, that's most likely what she means by *we*. His phone sounds. He sees it's Lauren's brother calling.

"Hello, Greg."

"Nolan, did Lauren get home, yet?"

"Yes, she got here a few minutes ago. I think she's in the shower, though."

"Have her call me when she gets out, okay?"

"She's feeling pretty beat. Can it wait until tomorrow?" He hears Greg let out a sigh of frustration.

"I need to ask her about something. It won't take long. Could you tell her for me, please?"

"Is everything alright, Greg? Is there anything I can do?" Greg lets out another sigh.

"Everything is good. Just tell her to call me."

Greg disconnects abruptly and leaves Nolan wondering why he didn't call Lauren's phone if it's something Greg doesn't want to discuss with him. In the master bath Lauren has the shower going while texting a message to Gordon. He texted her once on the way home and twice since, but she hasn't returned them. The message to him is brief and simple. *STOP TEXTING*. Greg has called twice since she arrived back in Houston. She hasn't responded to his calls either, because she doesn't want to deal with Greg or Gordon, right now. She's home with Nolan, and needs to focus on him. Otherwise, if she's not careful, she's going to slip and call him Gordon.

She steps into the shower, adjusts the temperature warmer and lets the water cascade down onto her back. The tension begins to dissipate and the pounding in her temples eases. For the first time since agreeing to help Erica, Lauren questions the decision. There are three men in her life. Each believes they love her. Each wants her for himself. Each has something to offer. Greg is the one she has known the longest and the one she can confide in. He understands her desires and passions better than anyone else. Nolan is handsome, tall and strong. He personifies stability and security. He's the one she would cling to in a storm. Gordon is her newest acquisition. His effect on her has been unexpected, and she is rethinking her initial impression of him.

"Lauren," Nolan calls from the other side of the bathroom door. She hears the knob turn, and then, "Are you okay? You've been in here for so long, I was beginning to worry."

"I'm fine. The water feels so nice, I didn't want to get out."

Through the frosted glass of the shower enclosure she can see him coming toward her. The shower door opens and he stands there in the buff looking at her unabashedly. She cringes slightly, hoping he doesn't notice her reluctance to invite him in.

"Can I join you? I could help you clean those hard-to-reach spots."

"I can hardly believe I'm saying this, but I'm too exhausted for that. Right now, I need sleep more than anything else."

He stands there a minute longer, hoping against hope she'll change her mind and pull him to her.

Instead she says, "You're letting all the heat out. Close the door. I'll be finished in a minute. Then, we can have dinner and I'll tell you about my trip."

He leaves her in the shower as she requests and redresses in sweatpants and a T-shirt. The rebuff from Lauren stings more than he cares to admit. He knows he shouldn't let it get to him, but what's going on with her sure seems like more than exhaustion. While he waits for her to finish showering, he pours himself a tall glass of vodka with no ice. He drinks it down and is pouring another when Lauren comes in the room wearing her robe, with a towel wrapped around her head. She notices the vodka bottle in his hand and his glazed over eyes.

"Nolan, you'd better slow down or you're going to end up passing out before you've finished eating."

"So what if I pass out? Am I going to miss out on something?" The words are slurred, and he appears eager for an argument.

"Forget I said anything," Lauren responds, hoping that's the end of it.

"I mean it's not like we'll be up all night screwing, is it?"

"What is wrong with you, tonight? This is some way to treat your wife after she's been gone for almost a week. And all because I don't want to jump into bed with you, the second I walk in the door."

"What's wrong with me? Is that what you're asking? I'm supposed to be kind and considerate, while you act as if I'm not even here?"

"I explained that to you. I told you I'm completely exhausted from all the business meetings and the plane ride home. I wish you would try to be a little more understanding."

Nolan's phone sounds. He checks the display.

"It's Greg. He called earlier while you were in the shower."

"Don't answer it. I don't want to talk to him, now," Lauren says, but Nolan takes it, anyway.

"Greg, I told you before, Lauren is tired, she'll call you tomorrow." He starts to disconnect.

"Nolan! Don't hang up on me. I need to talk to Lauren, now," Greg demands, emphatically. So Nolan hands his phone to her.

"What do you want?" Lauren asks, irritably.

"I want to know if you're okay. You won't answer your phone, and Nolan sounded mad when I talked to him."

"When I don't answer my phone, I'm either unavailable or I don't want to speak to the person calling. In your case, it was the latter."

"He didn't hit you did he?"

"Who?"

"Nolan. I've been worried he's mad about the trip. I can come over, if you need me to. I can be there in ten minutes."

"Greg, everything is fine with me. That is, everything would be fine, if certain people would stop bothering me. Don't call me again, tonight and lose Nolan's number. Good night." She hits end and hands the phone back to Nolan. "Please don't answer it if he calls back."

"What's he so upset about?"

"That's just Greg being Greg. He thinks you're mad at me because I've been out of town."

"Why would he think that? Is there something you're not telling me?"

"No, there's not. Again, it's just Greg being his typical overprotective self, nothing more. Look, let's sit down and eat. That might be part of why I feel weak and tired. I haven't eaten since early this morning."

"Would you like a glass of wine with dinner?"

"No, I don't. I want to have a quiet dinner with no more interruptions, and then I'll probably go to bed early. Is that okay with you?"

"Of course." They sit down and begin scooping the Mandarin food out of the boxes onto their plates. "I'm sorry for the way I spoke to you," he tells her. "I missed you a ton while you were away."

"Forget about it. I missed you, too. I do love you, Nolan. You know that, don't you?"

"Yes," he lies, because it's what she wants to hear, but the truth is he's beginning to have doubts.

~12~

Saturday morning, Lauren wakes feeling rested. Friday evening was horrible. The men in her life were coming at her from all directions, vying for a position at the front of the line, and wanting to be recognized as the main person in her life. She let herself become overwhelmed by it, and now it's time to regroup and get a handle on it. Saturday afternoon, she has a long conversation with Greg to set him straight. He's a part of her life for as long, and for no longer than, she wants him to be.

"You have only two options," she explains. "Accept me as I am, or walk away. You are not going to screw up my plans for Nolan or Gordon."

She designates Sunday as Nolan's time with her. For an entire day, he can have as much of her as he wants, as often as he likes. By nightfall he's groveling and fawning over her like an obedient servant.

"I've never been more in love with you than I am at this moment," he tells her after they couple for the fourth time in as many hours.

"I know, Nolan. I feel the same," she replies.

Two down and one to go.

In the course of the weekend, Gordon sent Lauren eight text messages. She responded to the first two with STOP and GO AWAY. After that she turned her phone off and stuck it deep inside her purse. Come Monday, she'll deal with his obsessive behavior. She'll sit him down to explain in terms his hopelessly-infatuated mind can understand. And if that doesn't work, she'll stab him to death with the gold-plated ink pen on his desk.

She arrives at the offices of IDAG at nine. Fifteen minutes later, Gordon calls her into his office. All eyes are on her as she walks past her coworkers on the way. It isn't lost on them that Gordon and Lauren took a vacation at the same time, last week. Lauren ignores their inquisitive stares. Screw them, anyway. As soon as she gets the money from Erica, she'll be out of this place.

Gordon is waiting for her behind the door as she enters. He pushes it shut and lunges toward her with his arms spread. She puts both hands up with the palms facing him.

"Stop," she says, through gritted teeth. "I'm going to speak slowly, so you can grasp what I am about to say. What happened in Grand Cayman, stays in Grand Cayman. We had a wonderful time, and we have some great memories, but that is now a part of the past."

"It doesn't have to end, Lauren."

"Shut up, and listen very carefully. You are not to ever call my phone, again. Do not text me, attempt to talk to me or leave a voicemail message. Now, tell me you're hearing this, and promise you'll abide by my wishes."

"Jeez, Lauren, I hear you. Why are you being so cold to me?"

"I'm not being cold, I'm being angry. I'm angry because I told you not to call me, and within the hour you've either forgotten or ignored my instructions."

"Look, I'm sorry. Alright? I didn't expect this reaction from you."

"That's because you don't know me, Gordon. You can't get to know me in four days. I'm too complex a person."

62

"And I appreciate that about you. You're beautiful, complex, fun to be with and sexy as hell." He tries to wrap his arms around her, but she pushes him away.

"You have the attention span of a gnat, and a memory just as short. Everyone in the office already suspects something is going on between us. I'm going back to my desk, now, and you need to try to get your mind on business and off of me."

"Wait, what about lunch? There's a motel in Westchase with hourly rates. What do you say?"

"That isn't happening, Gordon. Not today or any other. Besides, I'll be out of the office for a dental appointment during the lunch hour."

From his office she goes to the ladies room, where she locks the door so she isn't disturbed while making a call to Erica.

To Erica's voicemail she says, "This is Lauren Drake. We need to speak in person, today. Meet me by the Sam Houston monument in Hermann Park at one."

It is three days before Thanksgiving. The temperature is sixty-two when Lauren arrives at Hermann Park wearing a jacket and sunglasses. She takes a seat on a park bench by the reflection pool. Erica arrives five minutes later, wearing a turtleneck cardigan, jeans, suede booties and a headscarf. She sits down next to Lauren.

"This is sort of cloak and dagger, don't you think?" Erica says. "You sounded upset in the message you left on my voicemail.

"Your husband is obsessed with me. He's going to say or do something stupid, and I'm worried it will get back to my husband."

"My investigator came by this morning to show me some of the video taken of you and Gordon in your hotel room in Grand Cayman. I must say, I'm not surprised he's enamored with you. That was quite a performance."

"That's what you wanted, isn't it?"

"Yes, it is. It's everything I wanted and more."

Erica smiles at the memory of the video, still fresh in her mind. It comes across as smug to Lauren.

"Good, I'm glad you're pleased. Now that I've done what I agreed to do, when can I expect to be paid? I want to get this over with."

Erica calmly examines her manicured nails as she says, "The agreement is for you to help me obtain a favorable divorce settlement with Gordon. It will be a few months before that can happen. There's a certain period of separation required by law before a divorce can be granted and the settlement is finalized."

"The agreement was for me to provide you with evidence of Gordon's infidelity, in exchange for one million dollars," Lauren says, with a little grit in her tone. "I've done my part and I'd like to be paid for my services, now."

The smug smile returns to Erica's face as she replies, "Lauren, did you really think it would be as easy as that? You get one million dollars to screw Gordon once? I think I made it clear from the first, this can't look like a fling or an isolated event. It has to appear as if it's one incident among several, demonstrating a pattern of behavior."

"What about installments? You can pay me half now and half after the divorce is final. The hardest part of the job is already done."

"If I pay you five hundred thousand dollars, you might decide that's enough, and not follow this through to its conclusion."

"And if you don't pay me something now, Gordon might get wind of the game you're playing before the settlement. Then, you'll wish you'd paid the one million to me, rather than twenty million to Gordon."

Erica tries, but fails to hide her surprise at the mention of the twenty million. Lauren must have somehow finagled that information from Gordon, probably while they were in bed.

"Careful Lauren, it wouldn't be wise to threaten me. I have a lot of very influential friends in the right places. It could come back to bite you."

"Who's threatening whom? You came to me and offered me the money. You're the one with everything to lose if things don't go as planned. I'm merely reminding you of this. Don't be foolish. You can rid yourself of Gordon, and save nineteen million, or renege on the deal, and lose the whole twenty. Think about it Erica, but don't take too long. Patience is not my strong suit."

Erica rises from the bench and walks away without another word, and without looking back. Lauren hopes she hasn't overplayed her hand. She watches Erica until she is out of sight. Then, she takes the miniature recording device from her purse and turns it off.

From the other side of the Sam Houston monument Curtis Leyden uses a telephoto lens to photograph the meeting between the women. He gets a shot of Lauren slipping the recorder back into her purse, and a few more as she's leaving the park.

~13~

At two o'clock Wednesday afternoon, the day before Thanksgiving Nolan is working in his office. Six members of his eight-person staff have already left for the long holiday weekend. They've gone to be with family for tomorrow's feast. Nolan won't be spending Thanksgiving with his family for the first time ever, because Lauren isn't ready to meet them yet, even though they've been married for almost a year. The reason given for her trepidation, is the fear of dredging up the painful memories of past holiday seasons spent with her own parents. She and Greg were still in their teens when their parents died in a horrific traffic accident. Dana knocks on the open door to his office.

"Unless you need me here for something, I'm taking off," she says.

"I don't know why you've stayed until now. The phone hasn't rung all day, and there's nothing on the slate that won't wait until next week. Have a great holiday. Are you spending tomorrow with family?"

"I'm going to my mom and stepdad's place. My brother and his family will be there, along with two stepsisters."

"That sounds like it should be fun."

"Would you and Lauren like to come?"

"Seriously?"

"Yes. Mom loves to cook for big groups of people—don't ask me why—so there will be plenty of food. We'll watch whatever football game is on TV, eat until we puke, and all talk at once. That's the way it is every year. So, what do you say, do you want to come over?"

"That's sweet of you to offer, and I'd say yes if it was just me, but I don't think Lauren will want to. She has some issues with holidays. It has to do with losing her parents when she was a teenager. Thanks, anyway."

"I understand. Call me if you change your mind, and if you don't, I'll see you next week."

Things haven't gotten back to normal between Nolan and Lauren since she returned from the trip. She's distant and preoccupied most of the time. Whether it's because of something that happened, or the upcoming holidays, he can't say. She won't be home until late this evening because she's going over to her brother's apartment to help him cope with the holiday blues. Because of her absence, Nolan isn't eager to go home. There's another rap on the door. Thinking it must be Dana returning, he says, "What did you forget?"

He raises his head to see a woman standing in the doorway. He's never seen her before. He would remember if he had. She's wearing knee-high boots, a short plaid skirt and a tight-fitting sweater. It's a look suitable for a naughty school girl, and not for the thirty-something woman standing before him, but he has to admit, she's making it work.

"I'm hoping to speak with Nolan Drake. Are you him?"

He is rattled by her sudden appearance and slow to respond. His eyes focus on her boots for a second before slowly venturing north. They're only halfway through their journey when she speaks again.

"There was no one in the reception area. I hope you don't mind me letting myself in. Am I intruding?"

"No, you're not. I'm sorry, I thought you were someone else. Yes, I'm Nolan Drake. What can I do for you?"

"I'm Erica Dupree." She steps toward him and extends her hand. He squeezes it briefly, and then releases it. She casts an appraising glance around the room before settling it on him. A playful smile forms on her lips and she says, "You're not what I expected."

"You're not the first to tell me that, though I'm not sure what it means."

"What it means is, I didn't expect you to be tall, handsome and charming. Instead, I imagined you to be less...," she searches for the right word, and chooses, "desirable."

"Thank you, I guess. As much as I like hearing that from an attractive woman like yourself, I sense it's not the reason you're here. Did someone refer you to me?"

"Not exactly. You might say it is fate that brings us together. You see, we share the same dilemma, and I thought if we put our heads together we might come up with a solution."

Erica seems reluctant to reveal the reason for her visit. Nolan glances at his watch, and then says, "I was about to close up and go home. Is this dilemma you mentioned something that can wait until next week?"

"I'm afraid not. You'll want to hear what I have to say, now. Do you mind if we sit? I have some things I'd like to show you." She indicates the thick manila folder tucked under her arm.

"Let's go in here," he says, and leads the way into a small conference room. They sit on opposite sides of the table and Erica sets the envelope down between them.

"There is no easy way to tell you this, so I'm just going to come out and say it. Your wife, Lauren is having an affair with my husband, Gordon. I'm not sure how long it's been going on."

Nolan is looking her in the eyes, waiting for a blink or twitch to signal a lie. She stares back impassively, giving away nothing.

"Gordon manages IDAG, where Lauren is employed," Erica continues. "I met her a few weeks ago, at a Halloween party given in our home. She's a beautiful girl. I can see why Gordon has become infatuated with her. However, I don't know what she sees in him. I know it's not his looks, after meeting you. Gordon can't hold a candle to you in that department. That's what I meant when I said, you aren't what I expected."

"Speaking of unexpected," Nolan says to her. A part of him refuses to believe what he's hearing. "What's in the envelope?" he asks, but he already knows it's something which supports her allegation. Why else would she have brought it?

"I suspected my husband was cheating on me and hired an investigator to surveil him. It was my hope he'd find my suspicions were wrong, but that wasn't the case. The envelope contains pictures of Gordon and Lauren together. I'll warn you the images are very graphic, but until you see them with your own eyes, you won't believe what I'm telling you."

Nolan opens the envelope and slides a stack of pictures onto the table. The first one shows Gordon and Lauren standing in a dimly lit room, embracing and kissing. In the next one, they're standing in the same spot with most of their clothing removed. Each subsequent picture which follows shows increasingly more graphic images of the couple engaged in conventional and not-so-conventional sex in a variety of positions.

"The pictures are frames of video recorded by my investigator while Gordon and Lauren were in a hotel in Grand Cayman, last week."

"The so-called business trip to Mexico."

"Yes. Gordon told me the same lie. That stack is just a sampling. There are plenty of other pictures and audio as well."

"I don't need to see any more." He pushes the stack of pictures away and sits with his gaze fixed on the tabletop. It's difficult to get the images out of his mind. Erica reaches across the table to place her hand gently atop his.

"I know this must be difficult for you. You feel betrayed. The person who has vowed to be your partner in the best and worst of times has deceived you, and you feel like someone pulled the rug out from under you."

"I appreciate you bringing it to my attention. I can't say I'm happy about it, but it's better that I find out now, rather than later."

"That's exactly right. The longer you're married to her, the more intertwined your lives become, and the more difficulty you'll have with the division of property when you divorce."

Nolan hasn't processed the information long enough to consider a divorce. For most men it would be their first thought after viewing graphic pictures such as those. But, most men don't have a wife as beautiful as Lauren. It's enough to make him think twice.

"I don't mean to be rude, but I don't think you've come here out of concern for me. Did you come here to ask me to tell Lauren to leave your husband alone?"

"No. I don't think that would help either you or me. Are you familiar with Dupree Oil and Gas?"

"I've heard the name."

"I'm a Dupree by birth. I won't bore you with the history of the family business. I'll just tell you that I'm a very wealthy woman. I've recently come to realize it's the reason Gordon married me. Fortunately there is a prenuptial agreement in place to protect the bulk of my estate, but it still entitles Gordon to a substantial sum of money if we divorce. There's a clause in the agreement which precludes him from receiving it in the event he is unfaithful to me."

"Now, I understand why you hired the investigator. It looks like he's gathered all the evidence you'll need to prove Gordon's infidelity."

"It would appear so on the surface, but Lauren is making it difficult." She pulls the picture of her and Lauren on the Hermann Park bench from the bottom of the stack. "That one was taken a couple of days ago. Lauren called me and asked to meet. Then, she demanded money. She somehow found out about the prenuptial agreement. She's threatening to testify that I put her up to the affair with Gordon in order to get a more favorable settlement in our divorce."

"That doesn't sound like Lauren. Not the one I know, at any rate."

"How well do you really know her? I think she's using Gordon to get to my money. I think it's the kind of person she is. If I'm right about that, she's probably using you in the same way."

The thought has crossed his mind before, but it vanishes the instant he looks at her.

"I suppose it's possible she takes advantage of me sometimes. No offense intended, but that's my problem, not yours. You haven't answered my question. Did you come here to ruin my marriage and get even with Lauren, or is there another reason?"

"Your directness doesn't offend me. I find it refreshing. I brought you the evidence of Lauren's infidelity because it will be helpful when you divorce her, which I'm certain you will, in due time. I'm hoping you'll return the favor by testifying to Lauren's duplicity during the divorce proceedings against Gordon."

~14~

In a two-star motel a block off Houston's North Loop Lauren lies underneath Gordon in the queen-size bed trying not to think about how many people have used this same bed in this same manner before them. It's making it difficult to concentrate. Typically, her performance in bed is of academy-award-winning quality. She can fake an orgasm on cue as well as Hollywood's greatest femme fatale. Gordon has tried every move he's learned in the twenty-four years since losing his virginity, and none seem to be having the desired effect on Lauren.

"What is it sweetheart? You're a thousand miles away. Are you having second thoughts about being here with me?"

"It's not you, it's this motel. It makes me feel cheap and dirty. I'm not accustomed to slumming it."

"Come on, Lauren. It's not so bad. The sheets are clean, and the mattress is firm enough for our purposes. What more do we need? It's not like we're spending the night here. Try not to think about it."

"I can't help but think about it. Take care of yourself and don't worry about me. And hurry up. I want to get out of this bed. It feels like something is crawling on me."

After he completes his end of the task, she goes to rinse off in the shower. He's still in the bed when she comes out with a towel wrapped around her.

"Come here," he says, pulling the bed sheets back for her to slide in.

"I really don't want to, Gordon. This was a bad idea."

"We'll find a nicer hotel, next time."

"There's not going to be a next time. This whole thing is a bad idea. It's insane for me to risk a sure thing with Nolan for whatever this is with you. I won't do it."

"Lauren, I don't like sneaking off to a cheap motel any more than you do. I wanted to be with you—needed to be with you. This was the best way I could think of."

"No, Gordon. It was the fastest, easiest and cheapest way. This is how a man treats a hooker. He takes her to a motel, screws her and tosses the cash on the bed on his way out."

"That's not fair. It wasn't like that at all."

"Wasn't it?" She undoes the towel, lets it drop to the floor, straightens her spine and poses like a model. "Take a good look, Gordon, because this is the last time you'll see it."

The bed is in the center of the room. On the back wall is an open vanity area. Lauren turns her back to Gordon and bends over the vanity sink to wash her face. He's mesmerized by the sight. It is without a doubt the finest female body he has ever seen unclothed. The thought of never touching it again, has him on the verge of tears. In the vanity mirror she sees his expression and for a brief moment almost feels sorry for him. Men are such simple creatures. Getting what she wants out of them is child's play. She turns to face him, once again.

"I'm not going to be taken for granted. Not by you or anyone else."

"I'm not, and I wouldn't."

"If you want this," she says, sweeping a hand to indicate her body, "you have to give me what I want in return."

"What is it you want?"

Lauren turns back to face the mirror, picks up her lipstick and begins applying it. She lets Gordon feast his eyes on what he is about to lose if he balks at her demands.

"I want you to divorce Erica. I'm not going to be the other woman, for you or any other man."

"I can't do that. You don't know what's involved."

"You're wrong, I know exactly what's involved, all twenty million of it."

"How do you know about that?"

"You told me. It was in Grand Cayman after you had several pina coladas and smoked a little weed. You said if Erica caught you screwing around on her, it would cost you twenty million dollars. That's what it says in the prenuptial agreement you signed when you married her."

"So, now you know why I can't divorce her. Not yet, anyway. If she gets suspicious, she might have someone take a closer look at me."

"What is it you don't want her to know? I mean, besides the fact you're screwing around on her."

"It's not important, just stuff a husband doesn't want his wife to know. Every marriage has some of that. You don't tell your husband everything, do you? Of course, you don't. What I'm trying to say is, it will be better for me, better for us, that is, if Erica decides she wants out."

"The problem with that is, we don't know if or when that will happen, and I'm not a patient person." She reaches for her clothes on the chair beside the bed and begins dressing.

"Don't go, yet."

"Sorry, I should never have come here. You aren't going to leave Erica, which means you aren't going to be able to afford to treat me like I deserve to be treated. This," she says, gesturing to the dingy room, "is the most I can expect from you, and this won't cut it." She grabs her purse and starts for the door.

"Lauren, what if I leave her. Will that change your mind?"

"There's still the issue of whether or not you can afford me."

"I've been taking money from the business and stashing it in a bank in the Caymans, building a nest egg, just in case. It's not a lot, but if you'll give me a little time, I'll get more."

"I'll give it some thought," she says, then walks out.

From the motel she drives to Greg's place. On the way she organizes her thoughts in an attempt to prioritize her objectives. That was much simpler a year ago. She wasn't faced with the same number of opportunities as she is now. She had Greg, and he had dreams, none of which were ever likely to come true. Then, she meets Nolan who has a house, a business and a solid future. He has a million dollars in assets, and is accumulating more every day. As his wife, half of that is hers.

Now, she has Gordon. The second she entered their home the night of the Halloween party, her vision was blurred by dollar signs floating in front of her eyes. This is the motherlode, she remembers thinking. It represents fifty times what Nolan will ever have. All she has to do is finagle a chunk of it out of Gordon, Erica or both. Erica offered her a million dollars, but then the bitch wanted to dangle it in front of her and threaten to take it away. She's going to regret doing that when Gordon divorces her, and Lauren helps him get the twenty million he's due. That comes to ten million for her, when she marries Gordon.

~15~

Lauren leaves Greg's apartment at ten p.m. to drive home, where she expects to engage in an argument with Nolan. When she arrived at Greg's earlier that evening, he said Nolan had called asking for her.

"He was mad. I could tell from his voice. I told him you went to the store to get me something for my cold. Then, I asked him if he wanted you to call him, and he hung up on me."

That was three hours ago. Hopefully his anger has subsided some, since. She can't be sure of what he knows or suspects, but on the way home she rehearses her reaction to every imaginable contingency. She adopts a cheerful persona that belies the dread she feels over the impending confrontation. He's leaning against the island counter in the kitchen with his arms crossed and a glass of vodka beside him when she enters.

"Where have you been, out with your boyfriend, Gordon?" The verbal slap catches her off guard, but she stays cool.

"Gordon? My boss, Gordon Weston. Is that who you're talking about? You think I'm running around on you with him? How much have you had to drink, Nolan? You're talking nonsense."

"As far as how much I've had to drink. Not enough to drown the image of you screwing Gordon out of my mind. I know you were in Grand Cayman with him when you told me you were in Mexico."

He knows more than she anticipated. Denying it at this point would just be digging the hole deeper.

"Who told you?" she calmly asks.

"So you admit it. We've gone from I'm talking nonsense one second, to who told me in the next."

"I'll admit I haven't been completely honest with you. And yes, I lied about going to Mexico, but I can explain all of it."

"Really, you can explain away you and Gordon holed up in a hotel on Grand Cayman Island, screwing like monkeys?"

Lauren realizes this probably means he's seen pictures taken by Erica's investigator. Which means one of them contacted Nolan.

"Where did you get your information?"

"I believe my source prefers to remain anonymous for now."

"I have a right to know who's accusing me, and of what. I can't defend myself otherwise."

"This isn't a court of law. Nor is it a legal matter, yet. I'm skeptical you can explain your actions to my satisfaction, but if you think otherwise, you'd better get started."

"I *can* explain. The thing with Gordon in Grand Cayman was staged. It was all an act. I can't tell you much more than that because it would void the agreement with the person who paid me to do it. I'm asking you to trust me for a little longer. When the project I'm on is done, I'll tell you everything."

His stern veneer is starting to crack. She can see he wants to believe her.

"You were paid to sleep with Gordon? Who paid you, and why?"

"I didn't have sex with Gordon. I made it look like we were. I can't tell you who asked me to do it or why. Please, trust me. Is that too much to ask of you. I am your wife after all."

"I don't know what to think here, Lauren."

"Then don't. Put it out of your mind. We can talk more tomorrow, and the day after that. You don't have to decide anything tonight. Look, I'm going to shower and spritz myself with perfume. Wait for me in bed. I'll only be a minute, okay. Don't fall asleep before I get there."

She puts her hands around his neck and pulls their faces together for a kiss, before going to shower. He watches her backside until it disappears through the doorway into the master bedroom, then downs the rest of the vodka in his glass and follows her. He feels shame over how easily she manipulates him, but helpless to resist her at the same time.

The steam has fogged over the glass surrounding the shower when he goes to the vanity to brush his teeth. In the mirror he watches her nebulous image as she cleans herself. She knows he's watching her. He can tell from her body language. She's performing for him, portraying herself as the person he wants to see. If he wants a seductress, she becomes one. If he wants a submissive consort, with a little more effort, she can be that, as well. She's a chameleon, capable of changing personas as quickly and easily as changing clothes.

Earlier in the day, Erica asked Nolan how well he really knows Lauren. He was evasive with her then, the same way he is with himself now. The shower door opens just wide enough for Lauren to stick her hand out and waggle a finger at Nolan, drawing him to her like steel to a magnet. He shucks his clothes and obeys her command. The specter of the man he was before meeting Lauren remains at the vanity, shaking his head at Nolan as he vanishes into the haze, and the shower door closes.

"Do you remember the first time we were in this shower together?" Lauren asks. "It was the morning after we met. We made love in your bed all night. Neither one of us slept a wink. In the morning we took turns scrubbing each other clean."

"I remember. It seems like a long time ago."

"Not to me, Nolan. It seems like yesterday, to me. We have something very special, you and me. You possess a part of me, no other man will ever see, much less own. Please, don't give up on me."

"I won't. I couldn't if I wanted to."

That night, Lauren sleeps soundly, but Nolan is unable to. For a while, he lies on his side gazing at her still form and the sweet look of innocence on her face. Then, he lies on his back staring up at the ceiling. His close proximity to her makes it impossible to think about anything other than her. She's awakened before daybreak by the sound of him pulling clothing from drawers.

"What are you doing?"

He sits down on the bed beside her. "I'm going to my parents' house for Thanksgiving. I'm packing enough to stay until Sunday."

"When did you decide this?"

"Sometime during the night, while you were sleeping."

"Are you going for your parents' sake, or is it because I lied to you about going to Grand Cayman?"

"A little of both. I can't think clearly when I'm here with you. I want us to be together as husband and wife, but maybe for all the wrong reasons. I need some time away from you to think things through."

"What time do you think you'll be home on Sunday?"

He wonders about her reason for asking and feels a pang of jealousy as he considers the possibilities. "I'm not sure," he answers.

~16~

The time spent with his parents brings Nolan no closer to resolving his conflicting thoughts about Lauren. He returns to Houston on Sunday every bit as confused as when he left on Thursday morning. He checks in at a motel, instead of going home to face her. The mere sight of her causes him to make bad decisions. She calls him on his cell phone at ten o'clock on Monday morning.

"Where are you?" she asks.

"I'm sitting at my desk in my office."

"You didn't come home yesterday. I thought that's what you said you would do. I've been worried. Are you alright?"

"Physically I'm fine. My head is sort of screwed up, though. I'm having difficulty understanding where this is going, or if you and I even have a future together."

"I asked you to trust me. You said you wouldn't give up on me. Has something changed while you were with your parents?"

"Nothing has changed. I was confused then, and I still am. It's better if I don't come home, yet."

"Don't you think we should talk, and work through this together? Wouldn't that be best?"

Before he can answer, a voice sounds over the intercom to let him know the client scheduled for ten has arrived.

"Send him in," Nolan instructs. Then, to Lauren he says, "I have to go. A client is here to see me."

For the rest of the morning, Nolan feels bad about ending the conversation so abruptly and causing Lauren to worry unnecessarily. He should have called her Sunday to say he was going to stay in a motel for a few days. In his mind, he's putting distance between them to think about things, but she sees it as him punishing her. He takes his phone from his pocket to call her, but reconsiders. Why not tell her in person? Let her look into his eyes and see for herself he's sincere.

"I'll be back after lunch," he calls on his way out the door.

He's never been to the IDAG offices, but he knows the building they're in. It's only ten minutes away. There's no one at the reception desk when he arrives, but it's the noon hour. Most of the people there will be at lunch. Lauren might be as well. He passes through to the inner offices looking for her or anyone else to ask if she's there. Two people are having lunch in their cubicles, but they're talking on the phone as they eat, so he continues farther.

In the rear of the complex of cubicles he hears the voices of Lauren and another person talking in low tones. The sound is coming from behind the closed door of an office. The name on the door is Gordon Weston. He raps on the door and the voices go quiet.

"Lauren," he calls. "It's me, Nolan."

"Nolan?!" she calls back, sounding alarmed. "Just a minute."

It's the worst possible thing she could have uttered at that moment. There is only one way to interpret its meaning. He interrupted them at a bad time. Overcome by a surge of anger, his hand is reaching for the knob before he can stop himself. Lauren is trying to fasten the buttons of her blouse and Gordon has his hand on his zipper when the door flies open.

"Nolan, don't make a scene," Lauren pleads.

81

"I'm not," he replies, in an eerily calm voice. He takes her by the arm and pulls her out of the room. "Wait here," he instructs. Then, he walks back into Gordon's office, shuts the door and locks it.

Gordon is smiling as if Nolan and he are good friends. It's an odd expression on the face of a man who's about to have his ass handed to him, and the only explanation for it Nolan can come up with is, Gordon thinks he's going to talk his way out of it. He's dead wrong about that.

"I think you've formed the wrong impression as to what just happened," Gordon says, maintaining his smiling facade.

"Is that right?" Nolan replies, and then jabs Gordon in the nose.

It stuns him momentarily. He raises his hands to protect his face, a second too late to block the right hook that lands on his jaw, and knocks him on his back. Nolan grabs his tie, pulls his head off the floor a few inches and smashes Gordon in the face with his fist repeatedly, until he lies motionless. For good measure, he kicks Gordon in the ribs three times before unlocking the door and leaving.

A half dozen office workers have heard the ruckus and are standing around gaping at him as he comes out of Gordon's office. Lauren is not among them. His anger is replaced by shame over scaring Lauren. She's never seen him like this. She probably thought he'd be coming after her next. He told her to wait here, which she interpreted as I'll be back in a minute to clean your clock.

His self-loathing is interrupted by two building security guys entering. They look around for the disturbance they've been notified of. In unison, the office workers point at Nolan. He offers no resistance as they escort him out of the IDAG offices and into the elevator. Neither he nor they speak on the ride down to the ground floor. He's hoping they'll tell him to leave the building and not come back. No such luck. They hold him in a room until the police arrive to take him to jail.

~ ~ ~

This is the first time Nolan has seen the inside of a jail cell. He's seen movies and read books where Americans are imprisoned in a foreign country. He always thought the filthy and dangerous conditions in those third-world jails were overdramatized for shock value. Now, he's not so sure. The overcrowded and inhumane conditions inside the Houston jail where he is taken couldn't be duplicated on a movie set without the heavy use of special effects.

After a few hours of detainment and no contact with the world outside by phone, email, carrier pigeon or intermediary, Nolan prepares himself for a long stay. Midway through the next day he hears someone call out, "Nolan Drake." He threads his way through the sea of inmates toward the voice.

"I'm Nolan Drake," he tells a man with a clipboard who's standing on the other side of the bars. The cell door is opened by a second man who steps aside and motions for Nolan to come out.

"I'm taking you to be processed," the first man says.

Nolan follows him to a room with a clerk behind a window, similar to one used by a teller in a bank. He signs a few papers, the clerk gives him a plastic bag containing his personal belongings and just like that, he's a free man, once again. He walks out of that room into a lobby area, where a well-dressed and rather stern-looking woman is waiting for him.

"Mr. Drake," she greets him. "I'm Karin Hearn, an associate at the law firm of Drury, Sutton, Leman and Stovall. We represent Erica Dupree. She put up the bond for your release."

"Why did she do that?"

"You'll have to ask her. Can I give you a ride somewhere?"

"I'd really appreciate it if you could take me to where I left my car. It's in a parking garage, next to the Broder Building."

As she drives him to his car, he asks, "Do you know anything about my case?"

"Quite a bit, actually. You're the focus of a lot of gossip in our office."

"Really? What are these gossipers saying about me?"

"They're saying that you punched out Gordon Weston because of his inappropriate behavior with your wife. And, that it was the last straw for Erica Dupree. At her request, we served him with the divorce papers in his hospital room this morning. We're handling the closing of the investment firm, as well."

Nolan is bowled over by the news. He shouldn't have lost his temper that way, but he never considered it would lead to this. Gordon loses his wife and business, and all the IDAG employees, including Lauren, lose their jobs.

"If it's any consolation, the divorce and closure of the business have been in the works for over a month. You may have helped things along, but you weren't the cause."

"You say he's in the hospital. I didn't realize I'd hurt him that badly."

"I think he's been released by now. They kept him overnight for observation. If you ask me, I'd say he had it coming. I mean, he was screwing your wife. What did he expect you to do?"

"I hope the jury feels the same way about it."

"I don't think you have to worry about that. Gordon Weston hasn't officially filed assault charges against you. He still can, but it's unlikely the District Attorney's Office will pursue it. It would be different had you shot or stabbed him, but you didn't."

"It's that one there," Nolan says, indicating the parking garage where his car is. "You can let me off here."

She pulls to the curb. Before he gets out she hands him a business card. It looks expensive—glossy card stock with two colors of ink and embossed lettering. Nolan figures her hourly rates aren't cheap, either.

"What's this for?" he asks.

"You never know when you might need a divorce attorney."

~17~

Gordon calls Lauren from his hospital bed to ask for a ride. She's the only person he can think of who might be willing to come get him. The attorney who served him earlier, explained that in addition to divorcing him, Erica is barring his access to their bank and credit card accounts, as well as cancelling his membership at the country club and gym. So, besides being homeless, he's strapped for cash.

Lauren isn't excited about the idea of chauffeuring him around, but the closure of IDAG has left her with a lot of free time on her hands. She pulls to the curb in front of the hospital where Gordon is waiting in a wheelchair. It's not that he's hurt that badly, it's a hospital policy. No one walks out of there unassisted, lest they trip and fall, and have to be readmitted.

"He really did a number on you," she says, as he gets into the car.

"He sucker punched me while I was looking the other way. He better not try that again. I'll be ready for him, next time."

"Where am I taking you?"

"I was hoping I could stay with you. Erica cancelled my credit cards and I've got less than one hundred dollars in cash on me."

"Stay with me? You mean, at the house I share with Nolan? He must have shaken something loose upstairs. You're talking crazy."

"Nolan's in jail. He doesn't have to find out."

"The answer is still no. I don't know what's going to happen with Nolan and me, but the last thing I need is you sleeping in his bed when he comes home. Or rather, if he comes home. I'll loan you two hundred dollars to get a room somewhere, and I'll take you to get your car. You have to figure it out on your own from there. I've got my own problems to deal with."

Gordon's car is still in the parking garage next to the Broder Building, the same place where Nolan's is. Gordon gets out of Lauren's car at the curb and is walking into the garage at the same moment Nolan is driving out. Nolan brakes and they lock eyes on one another. Gordon has a black eye with a bandage underneath it, a fat lip and a neck brace. Nolan allows himself a satisfying smile, then he sees Lauren. She gets out of her car and comes toward Nolan.

"Nolan, please wait a minute." Then, she says, "Gordon, keep walking and don't stop until you're in your car." He obeys, and once out of sight, Lauren tells Nolan, "Don't hurt him again. He isn't worth it. I don't want you to go back to jail. What happened is all my fault. We need to talk. Follow me back to our house."

"I don't think we have anything to talk about. It's plain to see you've been cheating on me and lying to me about it. I'm at the point where I don't believe anything you say."

"I can't blame you for feeling that way, but at least give me one more chance to explain. After that, if you want me out of your life, I'll accept your decision without an argument."

Reluctantly, he goes to his house to have the talk. They sit on opposite sides of the dining table.

"I'll fix you a drink before we begin," she suggests.

"No, thank you. Let's do this stone cold sober. You start."

"Our feelings for one another have been intense since the very first. We married before we knew much about each other. Some of the things you're learning about me are making you question that decision."

"That's true. We might have acted too hastily. You apparently feel the same. Otherwise you wouldn't feel the need for another man."

"That's where you're wrong. I don't regret marrying you. I'm happy with you, but it has no bearing on my relationship with other men. I don't feel the need for another man, but if I meet a man I find useful in some way, I might form a working relationship with him."

"Define working relationship."

"It's self-explanatory. You have a working relationship with the people in your office, men and women alike. It's the same for me. Whether it's my coworkers or a client, we interact for business purposes."

"So, when I walked in on you and Gordon interacting, that was strictly business, nothing more. Is that what you're saying?"

"That's exactly what I'm saying."

"I don't know why I listened when you asked me here to talk." He gets up to leave.

"Nolan, sit down. You're here, and for better or worse you're learning a few things about me. Don't leave, yet." He sits back down. "When we met, you brought me here to your house, told me about your business, took me to expensive restaurants and bought me gifts. Why?"

"Because I'm a nice guy, and I wanted you to know that."

"That's not true. You did it to impress me. You wanted to show me that you were worthy of my attention. You lured me to you by appealing to my materialistic nature. And you've continued to give me whatever I ask for. I'm a taker. It's who I am. I was when you met me and I still am."

"I'll admit it. I used whatever seemed to work in an effort to win you over. Was that wrong of me?"

"Most of the time, right and wrong are relative terms. You did what was necessary to get what you wanted. We both entered into this marriage with our eyes wide open. We both knew everything you owned became community property after that. It was the price you paid to be my husband."

"It sounds more like a corporate merger than a marriage when you put it like that."

"It is a business deal, plain and simple. We entered into a mutually beneficial partnership. I've benefitted from it physically, spiritually and financially. What about you?"

"I've benefitted in those same ways, and up until a week ago, I've been happy."

"You're referring to the thing with Gordon in Grand Cayman?"

"Apparently, it didn't end there."

"I know it's difficult to accept me being with another man that way, but there were other men before I met you. It was the same for you. What I'm doing with Gordon is strictly business."

"Really. Does he know this?"

"I'm honestly not sure how much he knows. Erica Dupree came to me and asked me to stage an affair with Gordon, in order to get a more favorable divorce settlement. She offered me a million dollars."

"That's hard to believe."

"It's true. The thing with Gordon is part of a business agreement between Erica and me." Nolan's expression says he's still skeptical. "You're a skilled architect. You earn a good living designing buildings. If you'll pardon me for saying so, I'm a beautiful and very desirable woman. Maybe it's not a skill, but it is how I get the things I want."

"You weren't honest with me when you said there was no actual sex between Gordon and you, were you?"

Up until that point Lauren felt she was getting through to Nolan. She drops her gaze to avoid his reproachful glare.

"Yes, I lied to you about that, but only because I was afraid you'd leave me if I told you the truth. Some things can't be faked. The sex with Gordon was real. I did it for one million dollars, not to please Gordon, and not to hurt you. I'm sorry I lied to you, Nolan."

It's too much for him to take. In a voice as cold as ice he says, "I want you to leave my house."

"It's our house," Lauren replies, in an equally dispassionate manner. "And, I can't leave. I can't afford to because I lost my job this morning."

"Fine. Then, I'll leave. I'll come back for my things tomorrow or the next day."

"Will you call ahead to let me know you're coming?"

"You're unbelievable," he says, and walks out.

~18~

The next morning Nolan is in his office absentmindedly shuffling paperwork around on his desk, picking up a page from a stack, scanning it and then restacking it in a different spot. Dana raps on the open office door. He acknowledges her with a glance. She enters, followed by James and Trisha. They form a line, standing side by side in front of his desk.

"This is an intervention," Dana, the self-appointed spokesperson of the group says. "I've looked into an anger management program, that I'd like you to consider. They meet Tuesdays and Thursdays, from six until nine in the evening."

James and Trisha are nodding their heads in a show of solidarity as Dana speaks. They've obviously been coached.

"Do me a favor," Nolan replies. "Shut the door on your way out."

"Nolan, we're trying to help," Dana says.

"Yeah, we're here for you, man," James adds.

"The problem is, James, I'd like you to be there for me, man. On the other side of that closed door. Could you do that, please."

"I give up," James says, and turns to leave, muttering under his breath as he does, "The dude is hopeless."

"I told you it wouldn't work," Trisha says, before retreating as well.

Dana isn't ready to give up so easily. She takes a seat to let Nolan know she'll be there as long as it takes. "So, talk to me. What's going on with you?"

"Dana, I appreciate what you're doing, and I know you're trying to be a friend, but sometimes the best thing a friend can do is mind their own business."

"How long have we known each other, Nolan? If memory serves me right, we met five years ago when we both worked at the Plan Factory."

"I've tried to erase that place from my memory, but yes, that's where it all started. The main reason we've remained friends for so long is because of our mutual respect for each other's privacy outside of the workplace."

"I agree, but sometimes what happens outside of the office spills over into the workplace and affects how you do your job. In your case, it affects how you run your business. And since I work for your business, if it suffers, I suffer with it. Two days ago, you left for lunch and didn't come back until this morning. Then, it comes to light you've been in jail, because you assaulted your wife's boss. Come on Nolan, it's me, Dana. Talk to me."

"If I give you a few details to satisfy your curiosity will you go away?" Dana nods eagerly. "I walked in on my wife's boss hitting on her, so I hit him, and he called the police. End of story. Shut the door on your way out."

"No you don't. You're not getting off that easy."

"That's the whole story in a nutshell. There's nothing more to tell you."

Nolan's cell phone chirps, he gestures for Dana to go. She mouths the words, 'This isn't over,' as she leaves. He mouths back, 'Shut the door.'

"Hello," he answers.

"Good morning, Nolan. This is Erica Dupree."

"Ms. Dupree, I'm glad you called."

"Call me Erica, Nolan."

"I heard you've filed for divorce, Erica. I don't know whether to offer condolences or congratulations."

"Neither for now, the process of ridding myself of the man will go on for a few months. Wait until it's done to congratulate me."

"I wanted to call and thank you for getting me out of jail, but I realized I don't have your number."

"You do now, and you can call me at this number whenever you like. As far as getting you out of jail, I felt an obligation to you. No, obligation is not the right word. I felt a camaraderie toward you, because of our spouses' deception and involvement with one another."

"I don't know how to repay you for your kindness, but I'll reimburse you for your expense, of course."

"I'm not concerned about that, Nolan, and you shouldn't be either. If at some point I need your testimony in my divorce proceedings, then that would be repayment enough. How are things between you and Lauren, if you don't mind me asking?"

"We're still on speaking terms, for now. I'm not sure what good it will do. I guess, time will tell. She said something I wanted to ask you about. Did you offer her money to sleep with Gordon?" The line is quiet on her end. For a minute Nolan fears she hung up. "Erica?"

"I'm still here. I owe you an explanation, but I don't want to do this over the phone. Would you join me for dinner, tonight?"

"Uh…, tonight?"

"Do you have other plans?"

"Uh…, no, not really."

"Splendid! I'll text you with the address after we hang up. Does eight o'clock work for you?"

"That's fine."

"Then, I'll see you at eight, Nolan. Dress casual. Bye now."

~~~

The address in the text message is Erica's house in River Oaks. Nolan is inspecting the leaded glass transom above the door when it opens and Erica appears. He's wearing Khaki slacks and a pullover cashmere sweater. A bottle of wine is tucked under one arm. She gives him an approving once-over. He returns it. Erica is dressed in black slacks and a black top with a plunging neckline which stops just above her navel.

"Come in, Nolan. It's so good to see you, again."

"You too, Erica. I didn't know what we were having, so I went with a Chardonnay," he says, holding the bottle for her to see.

"I love Chardonnay. I'll have Phuong chill it for us. Let's sit by the fireplace to chat before dinner. What would you like to drink—scotch, bourbon, brandy?"

"Scotch will be fine."

They sit at opposite ends of a sofa and turn to face one another. There's a fireplace with a gas log burning at a low setting. It doesn't generate much heat, but it gives the room a romantic ambience. Erica's Vietnamese maid, Phuong appears from somewhere bringing their drinks.

"You have a beautiful home," Nolan says, after Phuong is gone. Erica shrugs her shoulders, as if to say, it will do in a pinch.

"What about me? I spent an hour at the spa today, and another two hours at the salon having my hair and nails done. I'm hoping you'll tell me it was time well spent."

"I'm sorry, I should have said something when you first opened the door. I'm a little rusty at this sort of thing."

"I won't hold it against you. You're out of practice, that's all. It won't take long to get back into it. It's like riding a bike, as the saying goes."

"Let me start over and try again. Erica, you look absolutely gorgeous."

"Much better. You're obviously a quick study. I think we're going to have a lovely evening. However, there's something we should get out the way, first. As I told you earlier, I owe you an explanation regarding the agreement I made with Lauren. She approached me saying she knew about my arrangement with Gordon, referring to our prenuptial agreement. She asked what it would be worth to have proof of Gordon's infidelity. I thought she was joking, so I blurted out, a million dollars. That's how it started, and it just evolved from there."

"So, she wasn't lying to me when she said you offered her a million dollars to sleep with Gordon."

"It's a half-truth at best. She said she would provide me with proof of his infidelity. I didn't know until later she intended to sleep with him to get that proof. I'm sorry that I had a small part in breaking up your marriage, but knowing what I know now about Lauren, I think you're better off without her. I hope you feel the same."

"I don't know that you broke up our marriage. I haven't decided whether or not to end it, and Lauren says it's not what she wants."

"Lauren is self-serving above all else. She'll keep you around as long as you have something she wants. She thinks she can get to my money through Gordon, so she'll string him along while she formulates a plan on just how to do it."

Nolan has come to the same conclusion about Lauren. She told him as much, in so many words. It saddens him to think about losing her, but the woman he thought he knew was apparently nothing more than a fantasy, all along. He brings the glass of scotch to his lips, peering at Erica over the

95

rim as he does and acknowledges to himself how good it feels to be with her.

"Let's not talk about Lauren, anymore. I appreciate the explanation of how the agreement came about, but I'm ready for a change of topics. Tell me about Erica Dupree."

"You want to know more about me, do you? Would you like to hear my life story, or do you want the abridged version?"

"Take as long as you like. I'm in no rush to go anywhere. I want to know everything about you."

The light from the fireplace glistens off the moisture in her eyes, as she replies, "That's the sweetest thing any man has ever said to me." Then, she moves closer until their arms wrap around one another and their lips meet.

~19~

Since there are no children involved, and both parties want out, divorcing Gordon would normally be a simple procedure. There would be the mandatory waiting period after the initial filing, then the paperwork would be rubber stamped through the system, signed by a judge and that would be that. But because of Erica's sizable fortune, any time she's faced with a legal matter, there's a team of lawyers standing by. They descend on her like buzzards and drag out the proceedings for as long as possible.

Her large team of lawyers meet with Gordon's much smaller team every day in an effort to negotiate a settlement favorable to their client. Sometimes the meeting takes place at a restaurant, and the cost of the meal with tip is itemized under miscellaneous expenses on the client's bill. Other times the lawyers meet over cocktails. These too, fall into the miscellaneous expenses category. Erica understands how things work. She doesn't let herself get frustrated by it. The divorce will happen when it does, and fretting over it won't speed up the process.

Meanwhile, her relationship with Nolan is moving ahead swiftly. Because Lauren occupies his house, Erica offers him a guest room in her home. He keeps his clothes there, but shares Erica's bed every night. They've settled into a comfortable routine of having dinner together, and then cocktails each evening. Afterward, they couple and cuddle in bed until falling asleep snuggled against one another. It's an ideal life, except for one annoying fly in the ointment, by the name of Lauren. She still attempts to control and manipulate Nolan two months after he moved out.

"What is it now, Lauren?" he asks, when she calls him at the office one afternoon.

"The power is out in the guest room. Can you come over and fix it?"

"Have you checked the electrical panel?"

"What does it look like?"

"It's a rectangular-shaped gray metal panel on the wall in the utility room. Open the panel and see if one of the breakers is tripped."

"I don't know anything about that stuff. That's your area of expertise. Can you come by and take care of it, for me. Please, Nolan. If it's as easy as you say, it won't take two minutes for you to fix it."

Nolan calls Erica to let her know he'll be later than expected getting to her place.

"She using you, again. This is the second time this week. I hate to see you let her treat you this way," Erica says.

"I know she's using me."

"Then, why do you let her. Stand up to her. Tell her to call an electrician."

"It's easier to go over there and flip a breaker, than it is to argue with her about it. I'm just taking the path of least resistance."

Twenty minutes before Nolan is due there, Lauren tells Gordon to make himself scarce for a few hours.

"Where am I supposed to go? And, why do I have to leave, anyway? I can be in the bedroom with the door closed. I'll stay quiet and he'll never know I'm here."

"No, I want you out of the house when Nolan arrives. He doesn't know you're staying here, and I don't want him to find out. I'll call you when it's safe for you to return."

As soon as he's out the door, Lauren goes around the house straightening the bed, putting away anything of Gordon's, changing clothes and freshening her makeup. When the doorbell sounds, she answers it wearing running shorts and a sports bra. She waggles a finger at Nolan for him to follow, and then turns away. In the guest room there's a treadmill and other exercise gear.

"I was only a minute into my workout when it stopped working." She pushes a button on the treadmill control panel, but nothing happens. "See. The machine is brand new. You don't think I broke it, do you?"

"I don't know, Lauren. I'll check the electrical panel first."

She follows him to the utility room where the panel is located on the wall beside the washer. He feels her close behind him looking over his shoulder as he inspects the breaker switches. The one for the room with the treadmill is in the off position. It's been turned off manually, not tripped by an electrical surge. Nolan returns it to the on position.

"That should do it. Let's go check the treadmill, to be sure."

He turns around. Lauren presses closer.

"Why don't you stay for a while? There's no need to rush off, is there?"

"We've had this conversation, before. Things didn't work out for us."

He makes a half-hearted attempt to gently shove her away, but she pushes his hands down and remains where she is.

"Are you sure? You haven't divorced me. That must mean you still have some lingering doubts about it."

"I'll always have doubts, and you'll never change."

"I never will and never have. I'm the same woman you fell in love with. I think you still love me, you're just too stubborn to admit it."

"What I felt for you was lust, not love."

"You think too much, Nolan. Stop trying to apply a set of rules to it. Just follow your heart. Let's go to the bedroom."

"No, I don't want to do that."

"Yes you do. You just don't want to be controlled by me. Fine, then you take charge. Drag me into the bedroom, rip my clothes off and do whatever you want to me."

"No," he says, but his voice is unconvincing.

"Yes, Nolan. You know you want me. You know how good I feel to you. Do it, Nolan. Right now, before I change my mind." She pulls her sports bra off, takes his hands and places them over her breasts, then repeats, "Do it, Nolan. Right now, before I change my mind."

He sweeps her up, and cradles her in his arms all the way to the bedroom. There he drops her onto the mattress and quickly undresses while she removes her shoes and running shorts. He pounces on her like a leopard on its prey and they begin copulating furiously. Afterward, they lie on their backs with shoulders touching, sweaty and out of breath.

"I have to go," he says, after a minute.

"Alright. Thanks for fixing the breaker. And, thanks for recharging my batteries while you were here."

She remains on the bed while he dresses, letting him have a long look at her nude form stretched atop the covers before he leaves, knowing the memory will linger in his thoughts for weeks to come. She doesn't ask him to stay longer. He gave her what she wanted and she's done with him, for now.

~~~

100

"Were you able to fix her problem?" Erica asks, when he arrives at her place, thirty minutes later. She's curious as to whether he slept with her. She feels certain that's what Lauren really wanted.

"Uh..., yes. It turned out to be something small. I was able to fix it."

"I thought you'd be here earlier."

"I got stuck in traffic. There was an accident on the interstate."

"That's a shame. Would you like a cocktail before dinner?"

"Sure, that sounds good. I'm going to clean up first, though. I'll only be a few minutes." He starts toward the guest room.

"Aren't you forgetting something?" Erica says. She spreads her arms, inviting him to her.

"Sorry," he says, before hugging and kissing her. The smell of Lauren's perfume is still on his clothing. She probably suspects he's been in Lauren's bed, but she has too much class to ask the question. Or maybe, she doesn't want her suspicions confirmed.

He showers and changes clothes to rid himself of Lauren's scent, then goes to join Erica. He finds her on the patio beside the pool, sitting on a rattan loveseat. Behind her, the red and blue underwater lights in the swimming pool cast a purplish glow to the steam rising from the water. It's warm for early February, but still there's a chill in the air this evening. She's changed out of the dress she was in a few minutes earlier and is wearing a satin kimono robe.

"Aren't you cold?" Nolan asks.

"A little, but now I have you to keep me warm."

He sits at one end of the loveseat and lets her nestle against him with her back to his chest and his arms around her.

"That's much better," she coos.

Phuong appears with two snifters of warm brandy.

"Thank you, Phuong. You've had a long work day. Take the rest of the evening off," Erica tells her.

"Was that so we could have privacy?" Nolan asks, after Phuong is gone.

"It's so I can have you all to myself. I don't want to share you with another woman, not even Phuong."

It's clear to Nolan, Erica is referring to sharing him with Lauren, not Phuong.

"I didn't go to Lauren's today because I wanted to see her. You know that don't you?"

"You went there because she asked you to, and when Lauren calls, you go to her like an obedient dog."

"That's not fair, Erica. She's still my wife, even though we're separated. I'm obligated to her."

"You're still in love with her, Nolan."

"I still have feelings for her. I wouldn't call it love. You still have feelings for Gordon, don't you?"

"None whatsoever."

"I don't believe you. There's bound to be some pleasant memories of your experiences with him. It's only natural. You and I are still getting to know one another. I can see our love overshadowing our past loves someday, and who knows, maybe that day is not far away. "

"I like the sound of that, Nolan. Someday soon, we'll forget our past loves. Then, the one we share will be all that matters. And on that note, I think we should celebrate."

"What did you have in mind?"

"Let's go skinny-dipping."

"Seriously?"

"Yes, seriously. Every now and then, we need to do something spontaneous, so we don't fall into the same old monotonous routine, night after night. Don't you agree?"

She stands up and undoes the obi tied around her waist. The kimono drops to the ground. She's wearing nothing underneath it.

"I do agree. We certainly don't want to get bored with one another."

"I won't let that happen, Nolan. Now hurry and undress, then I'll race you to the pool."

~20~

There are moments when Lauren feels badly about taking advantage of Nolan, but those moments pass quickly. Besides, it's his own fault. He's always willing, eager even to drop everything to come to her aid whenever, and for whatever reason she can cook up. In the two months since they separated, he hasn't denied her access to his bank or credit card accounts. He doesn't hound her to move out or question her about who she sleeps with. He makes it too easy to get whatever she wants out of him. His passive attitude toward her mistreatment of him was beginning to concern her, until she learned he's seeing Erica.

"Phuong says he's staying there. He keeps his clothes in the guest room, but he sleeps with Erica every night," Gordon reveals to Lauren.

"Who's Phuong?"

"She's one of Erica's household staff."

"Why did she tell you?"

"She didn't. She told her boyfriend and I paid him ten bucks for the information. I thought it might come in handy, later."

It's the first time since meeting Nolan she's had a rival for his attention, and it rankles her. It's a contingency she hadn't taken into account.

"The information is reliable?"

"Completely. He has no reason to lie to me. You look pissed. I didn't think you'd be so bothered by it."

"I'm not bothered," she lies. "I'm just a little surprised, that's all."

Gordon has been sponging off Lauren since Erica threw him out. She's put up with him in order to get a payoff from Erica, though she still hasn't worked out all the details of when or how it will happen. In the interim, she uses Nolan's money to pay the bills for Gordon, herself and Greg. It's a little tight as it is. If Nolan was to cut her off, it would all collapse like a house of cards. She calls Nolan to feel him out.

"A little bird told me you've moved in with Erica Dupree."

"Would that be the bird that flew the coop you're referring to?"

"How'd you know I was talking about Gordon?"

"Just a hunch. I know you're still seeing him."

That surprises her, but she brushes it off. "You didn't answer me. Have you hooked up with Erica?"

"I'm going with, that's none of your business."

She changes tactics. "The front porch light is burned out. Would you mind coming by to change the bulb?"

"Yes, I would. Have ol' Gordo take care of that, next time he's there."

This is far worse than she thought. "Why are you being cold to me, Nolan? This is so unlike you."

"I'm not being cold, Lauren. I'm just getting tired of being used by you."

Next, she calls Erica to arrange a meeting.

"Hello, Lauren. To what do I owe the pleasure?"

"I thought we should get together, so I can give you an update on Gordon. He has a card or two he hasn't played," Lauren lies.

"I'm content to let my lawyers handle that. Are you sure you're not calling to inquire about my interest in Nolan?"

"I confess I am curious as to how it came about."

"Let's discuss it over lunch. We can meet at The End Zone, the sports bar on Richmond, if that suits you."

"I didn't picture you as the sports bar type, Erica."

"I'm not, but then neither are any of my friends, which is why I chose it. Is one o'clock good for you?"

"Yes, that's fine. I'll see you there."

~~~

The lunch crowd at The End Zone is a mix of blue-collar types, suits and frat boys, with a ten to one ratio of men to women. Erica arrives wearing baggy sweatpants and shirt, sneakers, a ball cap and sunglasses. A basketball game which played the night before is showing on a half dozen screens mounted throughout the place. She passes by the men at tables and on barstools without drawing a second glance from a one of them, as she heads toward a table in the farthest corner of the room.

Lauren comes in a moment later. She's wearing jeans so tight they look to be painted on and a scoop neck crop top. She stops just inside the front door and scans the room. Every man in the place stops what he's doing to visually undress her. Erica raises a hand inviting Lauren to come join her.

"As usual, you look fetching, Lauren," Erica comments.

"Thank you. And I like the incognito-look you've got going, Erica."

Lauren inspects the three unoccupied chairs at the table, selects the cleanest of the bunch, and then wipes it off with a napkin before seating herself. After a quick glance at a menu, they each decide to skip the food and order a glass of the house white wine.

"Nolan is the most genuine man I've ever met. I think of him as my best friend. I know you're not pleased to hear that, but if it's any consolation to you, our getting together has nothing to do with you or Gordon."

"That's not true, and you know it. The trouble between Nolan and me began with you telling him I slept with Gordon."

"Nolan finding out about you and Gordon, might have provided the catalyst, but the reason he left is because he finally realized what kind of person you are, which he would have discovered sooner or later, anyway."

"Is that so? How do you think he'll feel when he learns of your elaborate scheme to toss Gordon aside and renege on the prenuptial agreement?"

"That isn't an accurate account of what happened, but let's stop bickering over what's already done and talk about the future. My divorce from Gordon will be finalized, soon. Afterward, you'll receive the money you're due, but Gordon will get nothing. What will you do, then?"

"I'll go straight to the bank and pray the check clears, that's what I'll do. But, I know that's not what you're asking. You're wondering if I'll leave town, or at least leave Nolan alone. Isn't that right?"

"You're a smart woman, Lauren. I've never doubted that. And yes, that is what I'd like to know. Nolan is very dear to me. I won't stand by and watch you profit from manipulating him."

"Is that some kind of a threat? You can't stop Nolan from seeing me if that's what he wants."

"I'm not threatening you, I'm negotiating with you. I believe your only interest in Nolan is what you can get out of him. I'm sure you've done a few calculations. How much do you think you'll walk away with? One hundred thousand, two if you're lucky? What if I were to pay you more than that to walk out of Nolan's life and not return?"

Lauren has spent many an hour trying to devise a plan to get a chunk of Erica's money, and now Erica is offering to save her the trouble.

"I'm listening."

"I've been considering settling with Gordon. I haven't mentioned this to anyone. I'm thinking of giving him five million in order to expedite the divorce."

"What does that have to do with you, me and Nolan?"

"Don't play dumb, Lauren. It doesn't become you. I'm giving you a heads-up, so you can position yourself to take advantage of Gordon's good fortune. I think you know what I mean. You can marry him before he gets the money and be entitled to half of it when you divorce him a month later."

"That sounds complicated. Why not pay me the five million to divorce Nolan? Wouldn't that be simpler?"

"Please don't take this the wrong way, but I don't trust you to hold up your end of the bargain."

"Yes, I have some trust issues of my own. Besides, Nolan is very dear to me, as well. I'm not ready to end things with him."

"I advise you to give my proposal due consideration, without delay. Timing is of the utmost importance. For instance, if Nolan decides to divorce you, that would change everything. Needless to say, the offer of five million to Gordon would be off the table."

"The notion of divorcing me hasn't crossed Nolan's mind. You know this, or else you wouldn't be here trying to pay me off."

"I wouldn't be overly confident of that if I were you. Call me when you've reached a decision, Lauren." Erica pushes the untouched glass of wine aside and stands, preparing to leave.

"Say hello to Nolan for me. Tell him I hope to see him soon."

Erica doesn't respond. She drops a twenty on the table and walks out. As soon as she's out the door, Greg moves from the barstool, where he's been sitting since Erica arrived, to join Lauren at her table.

"What'd she say? Are you going to get the ten thousand, or not?"

"Not yet. The plan has changed some. She wants me to divorce Nolan and marry Gordon."

"Why?"

"Two for the price of one. She gets rid of Gordon, and at the same time frees Nolan to have him all to herself."

"How much is she offering?"

"Another ten thousand on top of what she owes me."

"That's it? Twenty grand total? The broad is driving a two-hundred-grand Lamborghini, for Pete's sake. She can do a lot better than that."

"We're in the early stages of the negotiations. We'll see what happens."

"I could pressure her to up the offer," Greg suggests.

"That worked real well for us in Fort Lauderdale. Didn't it, Greg? Don't do something stupid, and don't do anything until I say so. Understood?"

"I'm just saying, she's got plenty of money."

"And I'm telling you, to let me handle it. End of conversation. Now let's get out of here. This place is depressing."

She gets up and walks out. Greg picks up the twenty Erica left, and replaces it with a ten, before following Lauren out the door.

~ 21 ~

Despite his initial reservations about the nature of the work he'd be performing for Erica Dupree, Curtis has no regrets over taking the job. Not only has it been lucrative, the group he's been keeping tabs on are a really entertaining bunch of people. Gordon, for instance, has enough skeletons in his closet to fill a graveyard. And Lauren is not far behind him. He was able to snap a few photos of Greg and Lauren while they talked inside of The End Zone, and as they were walking out.

"I had a contact in the Bureau run the picture through a facial recognition program to identify him," he informs Erica, the day following her meeting with Lauren at The End Zone. "His name is Greg Smith, AKA Greg Malloy. That's the name he's using currently."

"That name sounds familiar. What's his connection to Lauren?"

"If you remember, when you first hired me, I did a basic background check on Lauren Drake. Her driver's license records show her maiden name as Malloy. When I traced that name, I found a marriage certificate filed in Florida for Greg and Lauren Malloy."

"You're saying this man is her ex-husband. That's interesting."

"I'm not sure he's an ex. There's no record of a divorce. Not that I can find, at any rate. Besides the marriage certificate, I found a record of an arrest for Greg and Lauren Malloy. He was charged with procuring and theft, she was charged with prostitution. The charges were later dropped. From what I read of the police report, it sounds like they were running a con where Lauren, posing as a prostitute lures a John to a motel room. As soon as the John drops his pants, Greg comes out of a closet, and rolls the guy for his wallet. That sort of thing happens all the time, but it seldom gets reported because the John doesn't want it to get back to his wife."

"This gets better and better."

"There's more. I searched for a marriage license for Nolan Drake and Lauren Malloy. There is none."

"They're not married?"

"Not legally, or not legally in this country, anyway."

"I want you to find out more about this Greg Malloy. Meanwhile, I'll find out from Nolan where his wedding to Lauren took place."

~ ~ ~

That evening Erica has a surprise for Nolan when he arrives there after a day at the office.

"I thought we could use a night out. I know of a place where we can enjoy a quiet and intimate dinner. I've scheduled a limousine to pick us up at eight. This place requires a coat and tie. I hope you don't mind."

"Of course not. Putting on a suit is a small price to pay for a night out with a special lady like yourself."

"Oh Nolan, you always say the right thing."

The limousine picks them up on time and drives them to a twelve-story office building in Houston's historic district. The plaque over the entrance reads, 'The Dupree Building'.

They step into an elevator, and Erica uses a special key she's brought along to unlock a panel, behind which is a button that sends the elevator up to the rooftop restaurant.

"This building is where the main offices of Dupree Oil and Gas were located until 1973. The Gusher is an exclusive members-only club on the top floor. My grandfather was a founding member. Originally it was the kind of place where men drank bourbon, cursed and smoked cigars. Women weren't allowed inside until the 1980s. All that aside, the food is spectacular and there is no place in Houston more private."

The maître d', a Caucasian man dressed in a tuxedo who looks to be in his seventies, greets them as the elevator door opens. "Welcome Ms. Dupree. It is wonderful to see you, again. And Mr. Drake, my name is Amos. I am very happy to meet you. Alec will escort you to your table."

A man, only slightly younger than Amos, and also dressed in a tuxedo appears as if by magic. Alec bows deferentially to Erica.

"This way, please, Ms. Dupree," he says, before turning to lead the way to a small dimly lit private room.

A table set for two with a single rose in a bud vase and a burning candle atop a white tablecloth awaits them. Beside it a bottle of Dom Pérignon is chilling in a bucket of ice. Alec uncorks the champagne and pours a sample into Nolan's glass. He sips, then nods his approval to Alec, who fills their glasses before returning the bottle to the bucket and leaving them alone.

Somewhere not far away a pianist begins playing. A few measures into the tune a violinist joins in. The volume of the music is just loud enough to provide ambience without drowning out their conversation.

"Here's to us, darling," Erica says, raising her glass.

"To us," Nolan echoes. They clink glasses. "I take it you come here often, since everyone knows you."

"It's their job to know the members, or at least act as if they do. I haven't been here in years, since before I met Gordon."

"Does that mean you've never brought him here?"

"That's what it means. In fact, you're the first man I've brought here."

"Wow! How is it I'm the first to rate such a privilege?"

"Don't you know? Aren't my feelings for you obvious?"

"You have been open with me, that's true. I guess, I'm still trying to wrap my mind around us. Sometimes it's hard to believe this is really happening to me. You can have any man you want."

"You mean, I can buy any man I want, because of my wealth. Isn't that what you're saying?"

"I wouldn't put it so bluntly. I'm simply stating your wealth is a huge consideration for most people. Throw in the beautiful face and magnificent body, and it's an irresistible combination. I'm not being insecure. It's only natural to wonder, how I got so lucky."

"Being rich is a circumstance I was born into, not one I created, and not something you should feel uncomfortable with. In time, you'll get used to it, the same way I have."

"Can I ask you something, Erica?"

"Of course, dear."

"Why did you marry Gordon?"

"I can't answer that. I guess, it was timing. We met when I was sort of at a low point. I was twenty-nine, coming up on my thirtieth birthday, and had never been in a serious relationship with a man. I know that doesn't sound like much of a reason, but it's the best I can come up with when looking back at the events that led to our marriage."

"Were you at a low point when we met?"

"Don't do that, Nolan. Don't compare what we have to Gordon and me. The answer to your question is no, I was not at a low point when we met. I was feeling very happy. And

113

since you've asked me, I'll ask you. Why did you marry Lauren?"

"For all the wrong reasons, I realize, now. We were in love, or so I believed at the time."

"Where did the wedding take place?"

"In Jamaica, while we were vacationing there. Why do you ask?"

"I was curious to know if it was planned very far in advance, or more spur of the moment."

"The latter. We saw a sign offering to perform a wedding ceremony on the beach and acted on an impulse."

"Did you apply for a marriage license when you got back to the States?"

"No. We talked about it and agreed it wasn't that important. As long as we thought of ourselves as husband and wife, then that was enough."

"Nolan, that means you're not legally married to her. She has no claim to your property, business or money."

"I don't know if that's true. We've lived together as common-law husband and wife. That gives her some legal rights, I would think."

"Would you like me to have my attorneys look into it for you? I mean, just so you have the information, should you need it."

"It might be helpful at some point, but don't talk to them, yet. Let me think about it a little longer."

"I don't mean to be pushy, but with no formal separation, she may still be entitled to half of everything you're earning even though she's shacked up with Gordon, or some other man."

"Maybe you're right. I guess it won't hurt to find out where I stand legally."

~22~

Nolan meets with Karin Hearn, the attorney who came to get him out of jail. Erica is right. There's too much at stake with Lauren to ignore it any longer. Besides, he's not actually filing for divorce, he merely wants to be aware of all his legal options. She takes notes as Nolan answers her questions, then lays it out for him in layman's terms.

"The minute you leave my office, you're going to close all your bank and credit card accounts. Because as soon as she finds out you're considering divorcing her, she'll drain your savings and max out your credit cards. And don't think for a second she won't."

The meeting with Karin Hearn takes place at eleven a.m. Nolan follows her instructions, and the task is completed by twelve thirty. He has every intention of telling Lauren, as soon as he gets back from lunch. She calls him while he's eating at a deli down the block from his office.

"Nolan, I'm at the Galleria Mall. The store is refusing my Visa. Did you forget to pay the bill?" In the background he can hear the store clerk talking, and then Lauren says to her, "I've got my husband on the phone. He's going to call them and get it straightened out."

"Lauren!" Nolan shouts into the phone.

"I'm here. Did you get through to Visa?"

"No, there's no need for me to call them. It isn't their mistake. I cancelled the credit cards this morning. I was going to call you after lunch."

"Just a minute," Lauren says to the sales clerk. Then, in a quieter voice, she asks Nolan, "Why did you do that? Do you have any idea how this makes me look? Why would you embarrass me this way?"

"It wasn't done to embarrass you. I acted on the advice of my attorney and closed the credit card and bank accounts."

"You've hired an attorney, without talking to me first?"

"There's nothing to talk about. I went to an attorney to get her advice."

"Her advice on divorcing me? That's what you're saying, isn't it. You're planning to divorce me. You bastard, Nolan. You selfish bastard."

A few of the deli patrons nearby have caught bits of the conversation and are giving Nolan looks to let him know they feel the same as Lauren does about him.

"Lauren, I'm sorry I didn't tell you sooner," he says into the phone, but Lauren has already disconnected. He wraps the uneaten portion of his sandwich in a napkin, and takes it back to his office to finish.

~~~

When Lauren arrives back at her house—her house for now, that is—she finds Gordon asleep on the sofa. Oprah is discussing weight loss with three other women on the TV. The remote control rests on Gordon's chest and a half-full bottle of beer is wedged between his legs. He's wearing a wife-beater and boxers. He hasn't bothered to shower, shave or comb his hair since yesterday, or the day before that.

Lauren would like nothing more than to toss him out on his ear, but she can't. He may be her last hope. With Nolan cutting her off, Greg being more of a liability than an asset

116

and no other immediate prospects, there's no alternative. She has to accept the offer from Erica. But first, she has to work out the logistics. She rouses Gordon awake.

"What," he grumbles. His breath is stout enough to grow legs and stand on its own.

"We need to talk, but first you need to get cleaned up and dressed."

"Why, where are we going?"

"Nowhere, but that's not the point. I'm worried about you letting yourself go the way you have. It's unhealthy for you and unpleasant for me."

He slowly and begrudgingly goes to shower, shave and dress. Afterward, he takes a seat on the sofa next to Lauren and places his hand on her thigh. She brushes it away, then scoots a few inches away, crosses her arms over her chest and appraises him. It's an improvement, but not by much.

"What is it you want to talk about?" he asks.

"Nolan has cut me off financially. You said you have some money stashed away. I need some help with the bills."

"Everything I have is going to the lawyers for my divorce from Erica. It looks like we're in the same boat. We're both cut off by our spouses."

"I have no intention of supporting you for an indefinite period of time while your divorce drags on. I can barely support myself, now that I'm out of a job and Nolan's not going to help."

"There's no one else I can turn to, Lauren. The divorce should be final in a few weeks, a month at most. I'll reimburse you for everything then."

"What if you get nothing, what then?"

"I'll get something. It may not be the full twenty million I'm hoping for, but I'll get something for the five years we were married."

"I'm taking a big chance. I want more than reimbursement."

"I'll pay you ten percent interest. How's that?"

"Not good enough. Whatever the amount of the settlement, I want half. And, I want you to sign a contract agreeing to that."

"Half? That's a little greedy, don't you think? I'll give you twenty percent, no more."

"Half, Gordon. Agree to it, or get out." He hesitates. She can tell he's considering a counteroffer. She says seductively, "Don't forget, it's more than a place to stay. You're sharing my bed. It's a bargain at twice what I'm asking. Don't you agree?"

~~~

Lauren finds a lawyer who draws up the contract, and makes sure there are no loopholes through which Gordon can escape. In the lawyer's office, Gordon reluctantly signs it in front of a witness and notary. Lauren receives her copy, and is assured the agreement is airtight. That done, she contacts Erica to give her the go-ahead.

"I've decided to accept your offer. I'll agree to divorce Nolan on the condition you give Gordon five million to settle your divorce."

"I'm glad to hear it, but some things have come to my attention, since we last spoke. It seems you're not legally married to Nolan. A divorce isn't necessary."

Lauren starts to deny it, but knows it would be futile to do so.

"That doesn't change anything. You want me out of his life, and I'm agreeing to leave him alone."

"Have you and Gordon set a date?"

"I'm not sure I want to marry Gordon, but again, that changes nothing."

"I disagree. You marrying Gordon will give Nolan closure. He'll know without a doubt you and he are through.

Besides, you can't be certain of getting your share of Gordon's money if you don't marry him."

"I can handle Gordon and his money. What I can't do is marry Gordon before he is officially divorced from you. You see the problem?"

"Yes, the order of things will be tricky to work out. Here's what I propose. Prior to my divorce from Gordon becoming final, you announce your engagement to him. Whether or not you ever marry him, Gordon and Nolan have to believe it's going to happen. Set a date for the ceremony, and wear an engagement ring for everyone to see."

"I can do that."

"Then, we have a deal. As soon as you get Gordon on board, set a date and buy a ring, I'll let my attorneys know. If all goes on schedule, you can plan on having your money in about six weeks."

That's longer than she thought it would take, but it will be worth the wait. This will be the biggest payoff, yet. It will take time to get over losing Nolan. She's really fallen for him, and Gordon is no replacement. But then, Gordon is only temporary. Once she has the money, she won't need him. Actually, she won't need anyone, not Greg, Gordon, Nolan or anyone else. She can take a vacation to somewhere like the French Riviera or Rio de Janeiro. Who knows, she might meet a billionaire playboy and be set for life.

~23~

The fall from grace has been humbling and demoralizing for Gordon. He went from being admired and respected among Houston's social elite, to being ostracized and pitied in the restaurants and nightspots he once frequented. Nolan's house is nice, if you're into middle class digs, but it's a far cry from Erica's estate where he lived like a king for the last five years. The twenty million guaranteed to him by the prenuptial agreement would have set him up nicely, if it hadn't been for his slip up with Lauren.

"I'm worried about you, Gordon. Your self-esteem seems to be sliding lower all the time. It's a combination of things causing it. The divorce, losing the business, and being out of touch with your circle of friends. It has hit you harder than you realize. I want us to go out tonight. Let's go to one of the expensive restaurants where you and Erica used to go. We'll dress up, and look happy to show everyone you're doing just fine without Erica. People talk. It will get back to Erica and Nolan. I don't want them to think they've beaten us down and we've given up."

"I don't know if it will go that way. If any of Erica's friends see us together, it will look like I left her for a younger woman. All it will get us is pity, like I'm having a midlife crisis."

"A few of the women may feel that way, but every man will envy you. They will understand exactly why you chose me over Erica. And when their wives see this engagement ring on my finger, Erica will be the object of their pity, not you."

"Where'd that come from?"

"I bought it at Walmart. It's a cubic zirconia with an imitation gold setting, but it looks real from a distance. I'll confess to you I have an ulterior motive for wearing it. I'm hoping it will get back to Nolan. I want him to think about what he's losing."

"Just don't make him so jealous he comes around picking a fight with me, again. I don't need more bruised ribs."

~~~

Gordon couldn't stop smiling if his life depended on it, as he walks into Luigi's Seafood and Steakhouse Restaurant with Lauren on his arm. She's wearing a black backless evening dress with a hemline which stops midway down her thighs. Her left hand is busy patting her hair, pulling at her earlobe or hiding a yawn. This is done so the ring is in plain sight at all times.

Gordon waves at a couple he recognizes. Lauren points a dazzling smile in their direction. He asks for seating in the rear, so they'll pass by most of the other diners on the way to their table. Someone takes a picture of the couple with their cell phone and sends it to Erica. She and Nolan are just sitting down to enjoy an intimate dinner when the picture is sent. Erica has the phone turned off, which is just as well. It'd be a shame to spoil such a fabulous evening.

"You look sensational, and the food smells delicious. Is this a special occasion?" Nolan asks Erica.

"Each time I'm with you is cause for celebration. So yes, it's a very special occasion."

"What is this we're having?"

"It's a French dish, Coq au vin, with a red Bordeaux. Taste it and tell me what you think."

Nolan cuts a bite of chicken, forks it into his mouth, chews slowly, and then washes it down with the Bordeaux.

"Incredible. My compliments to Phuong."

"Actually, I cooked the meal we're having, tonight."

"Wow! Sexy, gorgeous, filthy rich and she cooks, too. That's some combination."

"And it's all yours for the asking, Nolan."

They go straight to the bedroom after dinner, and couple so intensely Erica weeps, afterward.

"It wasn't that horrible, was it?" he teases.

With eyes still moist, she says, "I love you, Nolan." He doesn't reply immediately. "You don't have to say anything. Whether or not you feel the same, won't change how I feel."

"Erica, I don't deserve you. How can you love me?"

"Nolan, love isn't earned, or taken, or given. It's simply how I feel. It's a good feeling. One I can't describe with words. I hope one day you'll have this feeling, too."

Erica has trouble falling asleep, even though she's exhausted from hours of lovemaking. While Nolan snoozes, she rises and goes to her kitchen for a mineral water. She turns her phone on to check for calls she's missed during the evening, and finds the picture of Lauren in the restaurant with Gordon. It's not the best picture, but the engagement ring is clearly visible, and the couple appears very happy together.

"Good job, Lauren," Erica says to the image displayed on her phone.

In the morning, they have a light breakfast of coffee and scones in the dining nook. Nolan glances at his watch. He has an early meeting with a prospective client.

"What time will you be home this evening?"

"Around six, I think. Do you have something planned?"

"If I did, I wouldn't tell you because that would ruin the surprise." He smiles at the thought. "There's something I need to show you. I've been debating over whether to wait until later, but I don't feel right about keeping it from you until then." Erica brings up the image of Gordon and Lauren on the screen of her phone, and then turns it where Nolan can see.

"Did you take this picture?"

"No, a friend who saw them at Luigi's sent it to me last night while we were having dinner. I didn't see it until I turned my phone on, later."

"I knew they were still seeing one another."

"Lauren has a new piece of jewelry. I think that's why the friend thought I'd be interested in seeing the picture."

"She does?" Nolan says, not understanding the significance of Erica's observation.

"She's wearing an engagement ring."

It's another minute before it registers. His expression is one of astonishment, as he says, "Lauren and Gordon are engaged? Neither one of them is even divorced from you or me, yet. I didn't see this coming."

"I'm sorry, Nolan. I knew this would upset you. Should I have waited for a better time to tell you?"

"No, I'm glad you told me now. And, I'm not upset. Nothing Lauren does should surprise me, but this did."

"There's something more I want to tell you, but it can wait until this evening. Try not to brood on this, today. I'll help you get over Lauren, the same way you've helped me with Gordon. It will bring us closer."

As they cuddle on the sofa that evening, in front of the glowing embers in the fireplace, Nolan asks, "What was it you wanted to tell me?"

"I have a confession to make, concerning Lauren's engagement. I intend to offer Gordon a five-million-dollar settlement, in order to speed up the divorce. My confession to you is, I told Lauren of this, and suggested she might be wise to marry Gordon, so half of it would be hers. I did it for purely selfish reasons. I want you to see her for what she is, an opportunist. I'm hoping you'll get over her and give me a chance to win your heart."

"I do see through Lauren. I have for some time, now. I feel bad that you thought it necessary to win me from Lauren, though I have to admire the clever way you went about it."

"You're not angry with me for doing it, are you?"

"No, I understand why you did it. You weren't being selfish. You were thinking of me. Was there anything else you wanted to tell me?"

"Actually, there is one more thing I wanted to ask you. Would you go away with me for a week? This thing with Gordon has taken a toll on me. It must be the same for you with Lauren. I have a house near the beach in Costa Rica. It would do us both good to get away. Don't you think?"

"A week in a tropical setting, just the two of us. How could I say no?"

"You won't regret it, I promise. Clear your calendar at the office. I'll make the arrangements to have the house ready for us when we arrive. We can leave Saturday morning. How's that?"

"I can't think of a better way to get our minds off our soon-to-be exes."

~24~

The letter from Nolan arrives by registered mail on the following Monday. It is brief, to the point and as impersonal as anything Lauren has ever received from him.

Congratulations on your engagement to Gordon Weston. I hope the two of you will be very happy. Since our marriage was never certified in the USA, a divorce or annulment isn't required. Consider this as notice of the dissolution of our partnership and a request to remove yourself and personal belongings from my house within seventy-two hours.

She calls to give him a piece of her mind over it, but his phone goes to voicemail. Discontent to wait, she calls his main office line and demands to speak with him.

"I'm sorry, Mr. Drake is out of the office this week," the receptionist dryly informs Lauren.

"Where is he?" Lauren snaps.

"I don't know. He didn't tell me."

Lauren calls Greg to tell him, Nolan is kicking her out.

"I told you this thing with Gordon was a bad idea. Now all the time you spent working on Nolan is down the tubes."

She did get a Lexus SUV, manage to stash away thirty thousand in cash and purchase a new wardrobe during their time together, but Greg doesn't need to know that.

"Well, there's no point in fretting over it now. I'm going to need to stay with you."

"Great! At least something good comes out of it."

"Since your apartment just has one bedroom, you can sleep on the couch. Gordon and I will take the bed."

"That's not funny."

"It wasn't meant to be."

"No way. I'm not taking the couch while this old dude sleeps in the bed with my wife. That's where I draw the line."

"We don't have a choice. I have to keep Gordon happy until his divorce is final, and Erica pays me the money."

"What about keeping me happy. I'm your husband."

"You aren't able to provide the things I want. That's how this all got started. I'm the breadwinner in the family, making money the best way I know how. Now, stop being difficult. I'm already stressed enough. Move your things around to make room. Nolan wants me out of here within seventy-two hours."

~~~

The week in Costa Rica with Erica exposes Nolan to a lifestyle he's only seen in movies. They fly by private jet to the Tamarindo Airport, where porters load their luggage into a limousine and a chauffeur drives them to Erica's expansive house overlooking the Pacific Ocean and Playa Grande. For seven days, they enjoy the local cuisine, walk the beach together, bask in the sun beside her infinity pool, and never once think of Lauren, Gordon or Houston.

"You've spoiled me," he tells Erica, one evening as they sit on the edge of the pool with their legs dangling in the water, and gazing out at the Pacific Ocean, while sipping Costa Rican rum from paper cups. "I don't think I'll ever be the same, after this."

"I've told you before, I'm yours for the asking. I mean that. All this," she says, spreading her arms to indicate their luxurious surroundings and the ocean view. "It's all part of the package."

"That sounds like a proposal. We haven't known each other very long. I'd think after Gordon, you'd be slow to rush into that, again."

"It's not a proposal, not like that. I'm offering to share what I have with you, if you'll share yourself with me. There's no obligation beyond that."

"I think you're getting the short end of the stick in that bargain, but I'd be foolish to refuse the offer. This extravagant setting has made a big impression on me. I won't try to tell you otherwise. But just so you know, your gorgeous face, fabulous body and sexual prowess won me over long before now."

"You're saying all this wasn't necessary?"

"I'm saying, it's only the icing on an already delicious cake."

Early the next day, Erica calls Joseph Edgar, the head of the team of lawyers handling her divorce, on his personal phone. He recognizes her number.

"Yes, Mrs. Weston. Sorry, I mean, Ms. Dupree."

"I want to finalize my divorce from Gordon Weston as soon as possible. I'll agree to give him five million dollars. Draw up the papers and have him sign them. Then, bring the papers to my house for my signature next Monday at ten a.m."

"I think five million is too high for an initial offer."

"I'm not interested in what you think, Joseph. Make sure he and his attorneys understand, this is a final offer, and good for a limited time only."

Erica's team of attorneys meet with Gordon's over lunch to pass along the offer. Gordon's attorneys agree to tell him, as soon as they get through gorging themselves at their client's expense.

"Counter at fifteen million," Gordon replies, when he receives the news.

"She's made it clear five is as high as she'll go."

"I was married to her for five years. I know how she thinks. She's bluffing."

"Her people assure me she's not. The offer is only good for forty-eight hours. That's noon, the day after tomorrow."

~~~

Lauren is in the middle of removing Greg's clothes from the closet to make room for her own when Gordon tells her.

"You did what?!" she exclaims. "You idiot! What were you thinking?"

"It's her first offer. You never take the first one. The fact that she made it means something has changed. She's softening, I can tell. This is a long way from being over."

"Is that what your lawyer told you?"

"No, they want me to take the deal. They see a sure thing and they're ready to take the money and run. They don't have the balls to wait it out for the big score."

Lauren massages her temples in an effort to stave off the headache beginning to form in her frontal lobe. Keeping her voice calm and speaking slowly, as she would with a three-year-old child, she says to Gordon, "You really should have discussed this with me, first."

"Relax, I know what I'm doing. A month from now, two or three at most, and you'll be thanking me for holding out for a bigger payoff."

"After two or three months of living with you and my brother in his one-bedroom apartment, you'll be lucky if I haven't killed you both, by then. And while we're on the subject of my brother, don't say anything to him about the money you expect to get from your divorce. Because of his substance abuse problem, the less he knows about it the better."

When Lauren informs Greg their guest might be staying longer than expected, he comes unglued.

"Damn it, Lauren. You've botched this whole thing from the start. First, you screw up things with Nolan, and he tosses you out without a dime. Then, you put all your eggs in one basket with Gordon, and now that's about to go south on you, as well. Either you tell him or I will. He needs to stop stalling and divorce his old lady, so you get your money, or find somewhere else to live."

"You're not going to say anything to Gordon. I'll handle him. You have to trust me. I'll find a way to make this work. I always do."

~ ~ ~

Greg wants to obey Lauren, but after three nights of sleeping on the couch and listening to the sounds of Gordon screwing Lauren in the next room, he's unable to contain himself. Lauren has gone out to run a few errands, or so she said. Truth is, she's had all she can stand of the stuffy apartment with the daytime soaps playing on the TV, dirty dishes in the sink, and takeout pizza boxes stacked in the trash. To makes things worse, the place is beginning to smell like the men's locker room at a gym.

"So, Gordon," Greg says, casually. "What's the plan, here?"

"Plan? What do you mean?"

"Lauren says you owned a big investment business that went under. I'm wondering what's next for you. Are you looking around for a job? The reason I'm asking is, the bills are starting to add up. I can't afford to put you up indefinitely."

"Don't worry, Greg. You'll be reimbursed in full. I have a severance package from the investment business coming to me, soon."

"Oh yeah, for how much?"

"That's not certain, but it will be more than enough to cover your expenses and get us out of your hair." Greg looks skeptical. Gordon attempts to shift the focus off his financial problems. "What about you, Greg? You don't appear to have a job. How do you make ends meet?"

"I do temporary work."

Gordon interprets that to mean he sells drugs, or does small-time cons and petty thefts, in order to support his habit.

"My soon-to-be ex-wife keeps a lot of valuable things at her house. She'd be an easy mark for a burglar."

"Why are you telling me?"

"I thought that might be the temporary work you were talking about."

~25~

Nolan and Erica arrive back in Houston on Sunday, after their time in Costa Rica, to gray skies, drizzle and a temperature of fifty degrees. Because of the slick streets and heavy traffic, it takes two hours to get from the airport to Erica's house in River Oaks. The driver pulls the limousine into her circular driveway, drops them at the front door, and carries their luggage inside. Erica discreetly slips one hundred dollars into Nolan's hand, so he can pay the driver. Hernando comes to whisk the luggage away, leaving Nolan and Erica alone. He pulls her close and wraps his arms around her waist.

"I had a great time in Costa Rica, but it's good to be back. Thank you for inviting me, Erica."

"We can do again, soon. Next time we can stay longer, if you like."

"As much as I like the idea, I can't be away for any longer than a week. My business would suffer and there's no one to look after my house."

"The people who work for you can run your business. You can give them instructions and answer their questions by email. And as far as your house, Lauren is looking after it, isn't she?"

"Not for much longer. I sent her a letter, before we left for Costa Rica, asking her to move out. I need to go by to see if she has, and what condition she left the place in."

"Would you like me to come with you?"

"No, thanks. I know you're tired and besides, if Lauren is still there, I don't want you involved in the confrontation."

"How long do you think you'll be?"

"If she's moved out, I could stay there. It would give you a break from having me around, constantly. As much as we've been together this last week, I'm probably starting to get on your nerves."

"You're wrong about that, but I suppose I can live without you for one night, while you take care of things. Will you come back tomorrow, after work? I'm planning a small informal celebration. I'll be signing the divorce agreement papers tomorrow."

"That's a party I wouldn't want to miss."

~~~

The last thing Nolan wants is to walk in on Lauren in bed with another man, so he calls her before he arrives home. He gets her voicemail.

"It's me, Nolan. I'm on my way over to my house, and giving you a heads-up, in case you haven't moved out, yet."

She doesn't call back, but her car is in the driveway when he gets there. He calls her name as he enters through the front door.

"I'm back here, Nolan," Lauren replies.

He finds her sitting on a stool at the bar counter in the kitchen. She is clutching a glass containing an amber liquid on ice.

"Are you here alone?" Nolan asks.

"Yes, I've moved in with Greg. I got the message that you were coming here and I wanted to talk to you."

"If this is about getting back together, save your breath. That's not going to happen."

"It's not about that, but you don't have to be such a prick. Why don't you fix yourself a drink? It might help take the edge off."

"It couldn't hurt, I guess."

He goes to the freezer for the vodka he keeps there, but the bottle is empty. In the liquor cabinet, which was fully stocked when he moved out, there's only one half empty bottle of scotch. He pours two fingers' worth into a glass, and takes a seat next to Lauren.

"How's Erica?" she asks.

"She's fine."

"She has a beautiful home. What's it like living in the lap of luxury?"

"It's comfortable, and Erica is quite a woman. She told me she's going to give Gordon five million dollars to finalize the divorce. She also said she told you, to give you an incentive to marry Gordon."

"That's true, and that's what I wanted to talk to you about. Gordon isn't going to take the offer. He thinks he can wait her out for a better deal. I think he's going to end up with nothing. You've gotten to know Erica pretty well. What do you think?"

"I was surprised when she told me about the offer. She knows it's more than fair. He's a fool to think he can get more out of her."

"I agree. He is a fool, and will likely come out of the divorce empty-handed. Which puts me in a spot."

"I hope you're not looking for sympathy from me."

"I don't want your sympathy, Nolan, but I would like you to understand why I did some of the things I did. I didn't have anything of value before I met you. The first time you brought me here, I wanted to have the sort of lifestyle that you have. You treated me like a queen and enticed me to marry you with your generosity and gifts. Can you tell me it's

133

not the same with you and Erica? I bet she gives you whatever you ask for. Am I right?"

"I'll admit there's some truth to what you're saying. I gave you things to impress you. Erica does the same with me."

"I know it doesn't excuse me cheating on you. I'm truly sorry for that, but I can't undo what's been done."

"No, you can't."

"I was tempted by the better lifestyle you offered me, and later I was tempted by Erica's money. I wanted both. I thought I could do what it took to get the money and hang on to you at the same time. It turns out I was wrong. I sincerely hope you and Erica will be happy together, but I think Gordon will continue to be a thorn in her side, unless they can come to an agreement on the settlement amount."

"That's between them. I'm not involved and don't want to be."

"But, you care about Erica, don't you? I don't think you want to see her tormented by Gordon. You don't know him like I do, Nolan."

"You can say that, again."

"Alright, Nolan. I probably deserved that, but I didn't come here to argue with you. I'm here because I thought we could help each other. Once Gordon and Erica are divorced, you have her to yourself and I get the money she's promised me."

"You want me to ask Erica to give him more money. Is that where this is leading?"

"The money doesn't mean anything to her. Another five million would probably be enough to satisfy Gordon. She spends that much to throw one of her charity bashes. She'll never miss it."

"As I understand things, you plan to marry Gordon in order to get half of the money he gets from Erica. Is that how it works?"

"That shouldn't concern you. You stand to gain much more than Gordon. For once, think about yourself."

"I'm not bothered about Gordon getting the money or that you're going to profit from the deal, I'm just curious as to how you're going to pull it off. What if Gordon decides he doesn't want to marry you, after he gets the money? What then?"

"Erica told me not to reveal this to you, but since she's already let the cat out of the bag, I guess it won't matter. I made Gordon sign a contract which gives me half of what he gets from her. He's broke and has been sponging off me since she threw him out. I threatened to cut him off, as well, if he didn't sign the contract. Marrying Gordon was never part of the plan. Once he gets the money, we'll split it and go our separate ways."

"Wow! Once again, I'm amazed by how your mind works. I don't know whether to admire or pity you."

"Think what you like about me, Nolan, but talk to Erica. Do it for me, for her and for yourself. Everybody wins in this deal."

"I'll have to think about it. First and foremost, I want what's best for Erica. Everything else takes a back seat to that."

"You're too soft for your own good, Nolan. But I have to say, it's by far your most attractive quality."

"It's only recently I've come to realize that's how you see me, as an easy mark. It's been humbling to find out I'm not nearly as smart as I thought."

"You're looking at this all wrong, Nolan."

"Am I?"

"You're acting as if we were competitors, like I won and you lost. It wasn't that way, at all. We both had something the other wanted. I wanted the things that money can buy, and you wanted to be loved by a beautiful woman. We made an exchange. I think it was a fair trade. Ask yourself, if you had it to do over, what would you change? Do you wish you'd never brought me here and made love to me? Do you wish we hadn't spent the three fabulous nights together in Jamaica, which led to us marrying? Those experiences with you are precious to me. I wouldn't trade them for anything. I'm fairly certain you wouldn't either."

"You're right, I cherish those same memories, but that's all they are, now. Recollections of events from the past. We can replay them in our minds, but we can't relive them. I'm glad we had this talk. It's my fault I didn't try to get to know you while we were together. The truth is, I didn't want to look past your beautiful exterior."

"Now that you've glimpsed beneath the surface, what do you think?"

"Frankly, you're a little scary."

~26~

On Monday, Erica wakes early with a bad feeling about the meeting with Joseph Edgar scheduled for ten a.m. She calls him at seven, only to have her fears confirmed. Gordon has refused the offer.

"I was putting off calling you, hoping he'd change his mind before our meeting at ten, but apparently he hasn't," Joseph explains.

"Well, this is disappointing. Did you make it clear, this was my final offer, and that no counteroffer would be considered?"

"Yes ma'am. And, he was informed through his attorneys the offer was good only until noon this past Thursday."

"Very well, if that's his decision, the offer is off the table. We'll do it the old-fashioned way. End the negotiations, and take the matter in front of a judge for a ruling."

"I'll ask for the first available spot on the docket. With the evidence against him of adultery, the prenuptial agreement will be voided. The court proceeding should be over and done with in less than an hour."

"Good, that's what I want to hear. Let's keep our ten o'clock appointment today. There's another matter I want to discuss."

"What's that?"

"I'm making some changes to my will."

After disconnecting, Erica sits with the phone in her hand, stewing over this latest turn of events with Gordon, and considering placing another call. A voice in the back of her head is telling her to wait until she's had ample time to cool down and regain her composure, but the voice goes unheeded. She punches in Gordon's number and a robotic sounding voice tells her to leave a message.

"Gordon, this is Erica. It seems that every time I think you couldn't possibly get any dumber, you prove me wrong. At a time when I was feeling uncharacteristically generous toward you, I authorized my attorneys to offer you five million dollars. They advised me against doing so, but I didn't listen. And now, I understand you've turned down the offer, thinking if you wait, you can get more. Guess what. You're wrong about that. You'll never get another dime from me. I'll see you in court."

~~~

In the bedroom of the Greg's apartment, Gordon plays the message back over the phone's speaker, so Lauren can hear. He's laughing like a lunatic as he listens to Erica ranting at him.

"We'll see who's looking dumb after this is over," he says, in response to her recorded voice.

Lauren is staring at him in disbelief, and wondering, not for the first time, if he's deranged.

"She sounds perfectly serious to me. I think you've screwed yourself royally, this time. Call her back and apologize. Tell her you haven't been thinking straight since Nolan beat you up. Say you've reconsidered and decided to accept the five million."

"I told you before, she's bluffing. I could hear the desperation in her voice on the message she left."

138

"That isn't what I heard. I heard her calling you an idiot, and I agree with her. I've tried to coach you on what to say and how to act, but you don't seem capable of getting out of your own way. I give up. You're beyond help, and I'm fed up with trying."

"Be patient. I'm telling you, we're winning this battle. Time is our ally."

"Oh, puh-leeze, Gordon. You're delusional, and I've got to get out of here. I can't stand to be around you, right now. When I get back, you'll have either called Erica to salvage this deal, or you'll be gone."

She walks from the bedroom and out the front door, slamming it behind her. He starts after her, but Greg puts a hand on his chest to stop him.

"You better let her go blow off some steam. I've seen her like this enough to know it's senseless to argue with her further. She'll just get madder and madder."

"Yeah, you're probably right. I'll let her go."

"Say, Gordon. While she's gone, I was thinking we could discuss that thing you mentioned."

Gordon has been expecting this conversation, ever since he mentioned the valuables Erica keeps at her house. He saw Greg's eyes light up with interest, when he added they could easily be stolen.

He says coolly, "What thing is that?"

"You know that thing about all the valuable things your ex-wife has at her house."

"I was just commenting on how easy it would be to rob her. I wasn't really suggesting that you or anyone else do it."

"No, I understand. We're talking hypothetically. I bet a woman with her dough has some nice pieces of jewelry. Probably a few thousand dollars' worth."

"Try hundreds of thousands. You're talking fifty-thousand-dollar watches and diamond rings worth twice that."

"That stuff is light, too. You put it in your pocket and go. It's not like trying to steal a car or a refrigerator."

"That's right. The best way to do it, would be to take a few pieces at a time. That way she won't notice it missing right away. By the time she does find out, the stuff is already fenced and the money is spent."

"It sounds like you've given this a lot of thought, Gordon. I bet you've even got an idea or two for the best way to get in and out, don't you?"

"Yes, I do. And, I know where she keeps her finer jewelry, where she stashes cash and the combination to her wall safe. Of course, if she is robbed, I'll be the first person the police will want to question, because of what I know."

"Yeah, the timing will have to be right. When the burglary takes place, you'll need to be far away, somewhere several people will recognize you and can later testify they saw you there."

"Good thinking. I'll need an airtight alibi for the police. I can have dinner at a busy restaurant, where they know me. I'll chat up the hostess and leave a big tip for the waiter, to make sure they remember I was there."

"Yeah, that will work. Uh, about Lauren, Gordon. If you could give me some time alone with her, when she comes back, I'll try to talk to her about giving you more time to work out things with your divorce."

"Hey, Greg. I'd appreciate that. She was pretty mad when she left here."

Lauren has been a block away watching and waiting for Gordon to leave. She sees his car pull out of the parking lot, and then returns to the apartment.

"How did it go?" she asks Greg.

"Exactly as you thought it would. He's going to tell me where she keeps the expensive stuff, how to get in and the best time to do it. He plans to be eating at some busy restaurant when it happens, to have an alibi for himself."

"Don't let on to him that I know anything about this."

"Don't worry, I won't."

"Did you discuss when it's going to happen?"

"No, but the more we talked, the more excited he seemed to get. I'm guessing it will happen soon."

"It couldn't happen too soon for me. The guy is driving me nuts."

"I hear that. I don't know how you've put up with him this long."

"I've put up with worse. He's not so bad in bed, for a guy his age."

"Damn you, Lauren. I wish you wouldn't say stuff like that. You know it makes me insane."

"I'm just teasing you, Greg. Don't pout." She caresses his face and kisses him. He wraps her in his arms and pulls her close.

"After this job and you get your money, I was thinking we could leave Houston, just you and me. We can put Gordon and Nolan behind us and get a fresh start somewhere else. I miss those times when it was just the two of us. Don't you?"

"Not really, Greg. I think we remember those times differently. You remember being young, happy and in love. I remember struggling to get by and doing without the things I wanted. I'm not interested in reliving that."

"It won't be that way, again. We'll have money to blow."

"Only as long as I keep it rolling in, and that will be more difficult as I grow older. I won't always have the same sex appeal and influence over men that I have now. I need to make as much as I can in the next few years."

~27~

Curtis Leyden doesn't understand Erica's obsession with knowing more about this Lauren Drake. He's given her more than enough evidence of Gordon's adulterous affair with the woman to satisfy the courts. Nonetheless, he doesn't say no when asked to look further into her past. She is the client and she pays extremely well for his services. That's as far as he needs to think about it.

Hernando answers the door when he arrives at her River Oaks home, and escorts him to her workout room. She is walking at a fast pace on the treadmill, breathing heavily as he enters.

"What do you have for me?" she asks, without pausing or even slowing the treadmill's speed.

"The woman you know as Lauren Drake is really Lauren Sutcliffe, and currently married to Greg Malloy."

"The woman has been lying to Nolan since the first."

"I believe so. Up until last week, she and Gordon were living in Nolan's house. Then, they moved to an apartment. The name on the lease is Greg Malloy. The three of them appear to be living there together."

"That sounds cozy. Lauren, her husband and Gordon sharing living quarters. I don't think I want to dwell on that image for too long."

"According to the apartment manager, it's a one bedroom. I haven't tried to get a camera inside the apartment, because I didn't see anything to be gained from it."

"Hmm. That would certainly be incriminating if the three of them are sleeping together. But, I agree, it's of no benefit to me."

"It's just a hunch, but I don't think this is a threesome sort of thing going on. I think Lauren Drake is using one or both of them."

"She's definitely not above that."

"It could be they're a team. Lauren and Greg, I mean. He plays a part in whatever scam she's working on, or vice versa."

"The marriage certificate you found for them. What year was it filed?"

"2015."

"Which means they've been married for three years. That's long before Lauren met Nolan. I wonder if Nolan has met Greg."

"Would you like me to look into it?"

"No, I'll ask Nolan about him, tonight."

~~~

In the evening Phuong prepares Peking duck, Mandarin pancakes with plum sauce, and rice pilaf with mushrooms. Nolan and Erica enjoy the meal with a French Pouilly-Fuissé wine.

"Nothing like a good home-cooked meal, is there?"

"Are you making fun of what I selected for dinner? You'll want to be careful you don't get on Phuong's bad side."

"I wasn't making fun of the meal. I was poking fun at you. Dining at the finest restaurant in town is a step down from having dinner here. Do you ever eat a normal meal?"

"That depends on what your idea of a normal meal is."

143

"Meatloaf, fried chicken, spaghetti and meatballs, that kind of thing."

"I don't normally, but if you have a craving for one of those things I'll have Phuong add it to the menu. How's that?"

"That'd be great. I mean, as long as Phuong isn't offended by it."

"You're in a good mood this evening, Nolan. Has something happened at work to boost your spirits?"

"No, nothing has changed there, except everyone has been giving me strange looks all day. I think it's due to this dopey smile I haven't been able to remove from my face since we got back from Costa Rica."

"I know exactly how you feel. I've been troubled by the same problem."

For dessert they have crème brûlée, and afterward they take snifters of warm brandy to sit on the sofa in front of the fireplace.

"I spoke with Lauren when I went to check on my house yesterday. I called her to see if she was still there, but got her voicemail. She was waiting for me when I arrived," Nolan says, as they settle onto the leather cushions.

"Was there an argument?"

"No, not at all. She's moved out, and seems okay with the split. She was there because she wanted to talk to me about Gordon."

"Oh, really."

"She says, Gordon is not going to settle for the five-million-dollar offer."

"It's true. I learned about it this morning from my attorney. He's a fool, but he doesn't seem to want to listen to reason."

"Lauren agrees that he's a fool. She wants me to ask you to up the offer. I told her I would convey her message to you, but nothing more. She believes it's in your best interest to get rid of Gordon, even if it costs another five million."

"What she means is, it's in her best interest, not mine."

"I'm not arguing with you there. Lauren makes no secret of the fact she's after Gordon for his money, and nothing more. Anyway, I delivered the message, and I have nothing more to say on the matter. You do what's best for you, and to hell with everyone else, as far as I'm concerned."

"While we're on the subject of Lauren, something came up earlier today that I wanted to ask you about," Erica says.

"Ask away. For you, I'm an open book."

"Do you know a man named Greg Malloy?"

"Yes, he's Lauren's brother."

"Oh!" Erica exclaims, unable to hide her surprise.

"How did his name come up?"

"The investigator I hired to surveil Gordon before I filed for divorce still keeps an eye on him. Gordon and Lauren were seen with Greg Malloy. My investigator said it appeared like Lauren knew him well. That's why I wanted to ask you about him."

Her gaze drops from his face to her snifter.

"Is there something you're not telling me?" Nolan asks.

"I don't know if I should say more. I honestly don't think it's something you want to hear. Let me wait until some other time."

"From what Lauren says, Greg is homosexual and has a history of drug abuse. Is that what your investigator discovered?"

"Please, Nolan. Let's talk about it later. I don't want to spoil your good mood. I shouldn't have brought it up, now. I'm sorry I did."

"That's okay," Nolan says, but it isn't really. Now it looms over them ominously.

145

She snuggles closer. He wraps his arm around her shoulder, and they remain that way for several minutes, with neither of them speaking.

"This isn't going to work, is it?" Erica says, finally.

"No, it's not. Now that you've implied there's something I should know about Greg, I can't stop asking myself what it could be. You might as well tell me and get it over with. I doubt it will affect me as much as you think."

"I hope you still feel that way after I've told you."

He gives her shoulder a reassuring squeeze and says, "Don't worry about me. I'm tougher than I look. Go ahead and tell me."

"Alright then, here goes. Because I had a suspicion concerning Gordon and Lauren—this is before Grand Cayman—I had my investigator check into her history. According to her driver's license application, her maiden name is Malloy. He searched for other documents filed under that name and found a marriage certificate."

"A marriage certificate for Lauren, or for Greg?"

"Both, actually. Greg Malloy married Lauren Sutcliffe in 2015."

Nolan's first impulse is to say it must be a mistake, or an odd coincidence, but memories of Lauren and Greg are clouding his thoughts. He recalls looks that passed between them, which at the time struck Nolan as too intimate for a brother and sister. Now, he realizes he was right. If this discovery had come a few months earlier, it would have shocked and sickened him.

"Nothing Lauren says or does surprises me, anymore."

"Ms. Dupree," Phuong addresses Erica from the kitchen doorway. She stands timidly wringing her hands, while waiting for permission to speak.

"Yes, Phuong?"

"I'm not feeling well. Would it be alright if I went to my room, now?"

"Of course, dear. Go ahead. We'll be fine for the rest of the evening."

"Thank you, ma'am. And goodnight to you, sir."

"Goodnight, Phuong," Nolan replies.

She crosses the kitchen to enter the servants' wing of the house. Only one room other than hers is occupied. That's where Hernando stays. His door is closed as she passes by it, on the way to her own room. Tung Pham, her boyfriend of six months, is waiting under the covers in bed as she enters. The sheet is pulled down to his waist, exposing his bare chest, and his clothes lay in a pile on the floor. He flashes her a broad smile. She quickly undresses and slides into bed beside him.

"What did you tell your boss?" he asks, as she snuggles close to rest her head on his chest.

"I said I didn't feel well."

"I hope she wasn't upset. I don't want you to get into trouble and lose your job."

"It's okay. Mr. Drake is with her, and she is happy to be alone with him. It won't matter that I left early."

"Will he stay all night?"

"Probably, what does it matter to you? Are you jealous?"

"No, why would I be jealous. The most beautiful girl in all of Houston is in love with me."

"Is she really? And what is this beautiful girl's name?"

"Her name is Phuong Nguyen. One day she will be my wife."

Phuong squeezes Tung, then raises her head to kiss his lips. They've discussed marriage before. It makes her happy to think of a being a wife and mother, but at the same time she worries it will never happen.

"I would like very much to be your wife, Tung, but I wonder if we can ever afford to marry, or to have children. Everything is so expensive."

"You have a good job, and someday soon, I'll have a better job, too. Then, we can afford to marry and have several children."

"Where would we live? We couldn't stay here. Ms. Dupree wouldn't allow it. To rent an apartment would cost as much as I make in a month."

"Let me worry about the money. I have a plan."

~28~

Most Mondays, Nolan feels energetic and eager to set a pace for himself and his staff to keep up with during the long week ahead. This carries through to Tuesday, Wednesday, and sometimes right into Thursday. By the time Friday rolls around, however, his pace is slowing and his energy level is waning. This week has been different. He started it off sluggish on Monday and it got worse with each passing day. He calls Dana to his office on Friday.

"I'm thinking about scaling back my hours, maybe only coming to the office two or three days a week. What do you think?"

"What do I think? Your mind hasn't been on the job, lately. I think without it, the rest of you won't be missed."

"Thanks, I knew I could count on you for an honest opinion."

"What's this about, Nolan? You're too young to retire, even if you could afford to. Are you and Miss Moneybags going to travel the world?"

"Miss Moneybags?"

"Don't play dumb, stupid. You know who I'm talking about. Erica Dupree. Everybody knows you're seeing her."

"Who's everybody?"

"Everybody who works here, and half the city. You're mentioned in the society pages of the Houston Chronicle as someone she's been seen with."

"I can't decide which amazes me more, the fact the Chronicle has a society page or that you read it."

"I don't read it, but people talk, somebody tweets, and someone else puts it on Facebook. Before long the word has spread like a flu epidemic."

"Well, since you already know, I won't deny it. I am spending time with Erica, and it is a factor in my decision to cut back on my hours. I called you in here to ask if you'd keep an eye of things when I'm out of the office."

"You mean, like I've been doing all along?"

"Yes, like that, except now we can make it official, so everyone else in the office knows you're the boss when I'm not here."

"Do I get a title and a raise?"

"Absolutely. I'll give you a small, insignificant raise and you'll be the office manager. How's that?"

"I was thinking more like I'd be vice president and get a very large and very significant raise."

"I'll meet you halfway. You can be vice president, but your salary stays the same as it is now."

"You call that halfway. I'm halfway thinking about quitting if you can't do better than that."

"You wouldn't quit, you like it here too much. Besides, who else would have you?"

"Just for that, I want to be executive vice president with a fifteen percent increase in salary. And that's my final offer."

"Alright, you've got it."

"Wait a minute. You're giving in, just like that? That was too easy. I should have held out for more."

"You said it was your final offer, and I took your word for it. Don't look so surprised, you won. Savor your victory."

"If it's all the same to you, I think I'll go back to my office and sulk over the lousy deal I got."

In spite of her complaints, Nolan knows Dana is pleased with the raise and promotion. And it's a load off his mind to know he and Erica can get away for a week or weekend, without having to worry about things at the office. Erica will be ecstatic to hear he has more time for her. Each day since returning from Costa Rica, there's somewhere new she wants to visit. Soon, she says, while we're still young enough to enjoy it.

~~~

Late Friday afternoon while she waits for Nolan to come over, Erica receives a call from Lauren.

"Hello Lauren," she answers, coolly.

"I've been unable to convince Gordon to take the five million and sign the divorce papers. Would you consider giving him another five million, in order get him out of your life?"

"You mean, in order to get him out of your life. He's already out of mine. My attorneys have assured me the divorce will be finalized shortly, and Gordon will get nothing."

"That isn't fair to me. I've done everything you've asked me to do. Gordon might deserve to come out of it empty-handed, but I don't."

"And you won't, Lauren. Once the divorce is final, which should happen within the next two weeks, I'll pay you the one million dollars I agreed to. Think about it, Lauren. That's a lot of money."

Lauren does think about it, and what she thinks is, one million is a lot, but three and a half million is a lot more.

"Yes, Erica. That is a lot of money to me, but it isn't squat to you. I don't believe you've thought this through. Initially

151

your plan was to get rid of Gordon without paying him twenty million dollars. I helped you with that, in exchange for one million dollars. Then, Nolan entered the picture, and your plan evolved to include getting rid of me, as well. That won't be as easy a task as you might think. Nolan still loves me, and I can take him back anytime I want to."

"You're overestimating your hold on Nolan. He still cares about you, I'll give you that. But, he's becoming more aware all the time of how deceptive you can be. For instance, just the other day he discovered the man he thought to be your brother, is really your husband."

"What are you talking about?"

"Greg Malloy, who you introduced to Nolan as your brother, is the same Greg Malloy who married Lauren Sutcliffe in Florida, in 2015. That's what I'm talking about." Lauren is speechless. "Lauren? Are you still there?"

"You had your investigator checking up on me, didn't you? And you're accusing me of deception?"

"Having my investigator look into your history wasn't deceptive. You were hired to help me with Gordon. I run background checks on all of my employees. One can't be too careful these days."

Lauren struggles to maintain her composure. She'd like nothing more than to tell Erica off, but feels it might be better to feign defeat.

"As much as I hate to admit it, you've won. You're a smart woman, Erica, and I hope you and Nolan will be happy together. I won't try to interfere. Once I've received the payment, you won't hear from me again."

~~~

Despite her bravado with Lauren, Erica isn't at all sure Nolan has gotten over the woman. Last night as their lovemaking approached its climax, Nolan cried out, "Oh,

Lauren!" He immediately realized his mistake, and apologized profusely, but the damage was already done. With only an hour until Nolan will be there, she tries to put it out of her mind.

"Hernando," she calls. He appears from some recess where he's been patiently waiting for her summons. "Draw me an herbal bath. I'd like to soak for thirty minutes or so."

"Yes, ma'am," he replies, before heading to the master bedroom suite.

As Hernando prepares the bath, Erica tells Phuong, "Mr. Drake and I will dine in the master bedroom, tonight. Bring a bottle of champagne on ice to the room before he arrives, which should be about an hour from now."

"Yes, ma'am."

"Dinner can be served at seven. I don't wish to be disturbed after that."

"I understand, ma'am."

"Madam is waiting for you in the master suite," Phuong explains to Nolan, when he arrives near six.

Erica is stepping out of the tub as he enters.

"This is a pleasant surprise," Nolan says. "I'm speaking of the champagne and intimate dinner, but finding you dripping wet and naked is just as nice."

He picks up a towel from beside the tub, and begins patting Erica dry with it. This arouses her, which arouses him. He lifts her into his arms and starts toward the bed.

"No, Nolan. Not yet," she whispers in his ear. "We'll have champagne, and then dinner. After that, you can have dessert, as much as you want, and for as long as you want it."

The evening goes exactly as Erica hopes it will. The sweet anticipation of what it will be like to give themselves to one another, builds to a crescendo. And when they finally make love, it continues for two hours, and then they spoon until falling asleep wrapped in each other's arms.

Nolan wakes once during the night, to finds himself alone in bed. The clock beside the bed says three fifteen a.m. He thinks nothing of it. Erica often gets up in the middle of the night to go to the bathroom, or the kitchen. He soon falls back asleep. The next time his eyes open, the clock says eight twenty. Again, Erica isn't beside him.

If he were home, he could tread into the kitchen in his boxer shorts and bare feet, to grab a cup of coffee or a glass of orange juice, but not here at Erica's house. He showers, shaves and dresses before going downstairs in search of his lover and a cup of coffee. He goes first to the kitchen. There's no one there, and no coffee brewed. Phuong enters from the servants' wing. She acts startled to see Nolan.

"Good morning, sir. Would you like something to eat?"

"I came in here looking for coffee. Have you seen Ms. Dupree, this morning?"

"No, sir. I haven't been in here, before now. I'll have the coffee ready in a few minutes."

"Thank you, Phuong. I'll wait in the dining room."

The kitchen door has barely swung shut behind him when Nolan hears Phuong let out a shrill scream. He reenters the kitchen to see her standing at the doorway to the walk-in pantry, with her hands covering her mouth, and her eyes locked on something inside it. He crosses the room to see for himself. Erica lies on the floor with blood pooling around her head. Without thinking, he rushes to kneel next to her and feel for a pulse.

"Call 9-1-1!" he shouts to Phuong, but she's frozen in horror. "Phuong, snap out of it." Still, she doesn't move. He pulls his phone out and punches in the number.

"What's the nature of your emergency?" the 9-1-1 operator asks.

"My friend has a head injury. I can't feel a pulse. Please, send EMS and the police."

~29~

Erica's house is declared a crime scene by the homicide detectives who arrive after the EMS and responding police officers. They conclude her head wound couldn't have been self-inflicted because of the location and severity of the wound. The three people who were in the house overnight, Nolan, Phuong and Hernando are questioned separately, and afterward are asked to leave. That is, except for Nolan.

"I'd like you to come to the station to answer a few more questions," Detective Ray Brown, says to him. He's a burly African American with a brusque manner and an appearance to match.

This is an area in which Nolan has no experience. It doesn't matter how many times he's seen the same scenario played out on TV. He doesn't know whether to naively go along with it, as if the police couldn't possibly suspect him, or indignantly profess his innocence and demand to speak with his lawyer.

"Is that really necessary? I'm happy to answer all your questions, here."

"We don't want to contaminate the scene any more than we already have. It won't take that long. You can ride with us. Someone will bring you back here for your car, later."

They tell him to get in the back of the squad car driven by the uniformed officers. There's wire mesh between the front

155

and back seats, and no handles to operate the doors or windows from the inside. The back seat feels damp and reeks of vomit. Fortunately the officers flip on the flashing lights and the trip to the station doesn't take long.

At the station they put him in a room reminiscent of the back seat of the squad car. It smells like puke and the door doesn't open from the inside. He sits in the room by himself for an hour before Detective Brown comes in. He sits across from Nolan and looks over his notes before beginning.

"Mr. Drake, what were you and Erica Dupree arguing about, the night before she was murdered?"

"We didn't argue. Who said we did?"

"The way this works is, I ask the questions, and you answer them. How long has the affair with her been going on?"

"Affair?"

"Yeah. How long have you been banging the rich broad?"

"That's it. We're done here. You can treat me like a criminal if you like. I'll write it off to you being ignorant. But show a little respect for the victim. Erica Dupree was a beautiful person. She doesn't deserve to be talked about like she was some prostitute murdered by a John."

Nolan gets up and attempts to leave. Brown doesn't try to stop him. Since the door won't open from the inside, it isn't necessary.

"Sit back down, Mr. Drake. I have a few more questions."

"I have nothing more to say to you."

"I didn't mean to offend you or Ms. Dupree. Now, sit down and answer my questions."

"You can ask my attorney the questions, as soon as I retain one. Unless I'm being arrested, I'd like to leave now."

"Wait here," Brown commands, before leaving the room.

"Do I have a choice?" Nolan asks, but gets no reply.

The second he's gone, Nolan takes out his phone. He scrolls through his call logs for Karin Hearn's number, the lawyer he sought advice from regarding dissolving his marriage to Lauren. He leaves a brief message explaining his dilemma, and then disconnects. A few minutes later, a broad-shouldered Hispanic woman comes into the room. She was at Erica's house along with Brown.

"I'm Detective Gutierrez," she says. "Can I get you a coffee, soda or water, Nolan? You don't mind if I call you Nolan, do you?"

"Call me whatever you like. And, nothing for me, thanks. All I'm interested in is getting out of here."

"I understand, and I'm sorry for your inconvenience." She glances at a paper she's holding. "You told the responding officer you were upstairs in the master bedroom, asleep when Ms. Dupree was murdered. Is that correct?"

"As I told Detective Brown, I'm not answering another question until I've spoken with my attorney."

"That's your right, but you said you'd like to get out of here, and I'm just trying to facilitate that. I need you to verify the information you provided to the officer is accurate, then sign the form attesting to it."

"I remember what I told the officer who first questioned me. The information is correct. I haven't lied to you and I'm not hiding anything from you. I'll be glad to sign your form as soon as my attorney has thoroughly reviewed it."

"Without your cooperation, this is going to take a whole lot longer."

"By this, do you mean asking me the same questions over and over, until you wear me down, and I confess to a crime?"

"What would you be confessing to? Did you and Ms. Dupree have a fight? If she said or did something that angered you, and you reacted to it without thinking, that's different than premeditated murder."

"Are you familiar with the term, tunnel vision?"

"There's no need to take that attitude. It will only delay the process."

157

A knock on the door interrupts the interrogation. The door opens just enough for a man to stick his head through, and say, "His lawyer is here." Behind the man, Nolan catches a glimpse of Karin Hearn.

"Excuse us," Karin says to Detective Gutierrez, as she enters the room.

"You got here quick," Nolan says to Karin.

She holds up her hand to silence him. Gutierrez slowly gathers her paperwork and leaves.

"Before you say anything," Karin tells Nolan, "let me explain a few things. I don't do criminal law. I came to see what I can do to get you out of here. From this point on, don't say anything other than to answer my questions. Understood?"

"Yes."

"First of all, I'm so sorry to hear about Erica Dupree. She was a terrific lady, and I know you two have become close. I scanned the police report. She was found inside the pantry in the kitchen, by a woman who worked for her. Where were you at the time?"

"Nearby, maybe twenty feet away. I'd just walked out of the kitchen."

"The time of death is estimated to be between twelve and five a.m. Where were you at that time?"

"Asleep upstairs in the master bedroom."

"The entire time?"

"Erica and I went to bed before ten. I remember waking once during the night. The clock beside the bed said three fifteen. Erica wasn't there. I don't know what time she got out of bed, or if she ever came back to bed. The next time I woke it was after eight."

"The 9-1-1 call came in at nine fourteen. Where were you between the time you woke and nine fourteen?"

"I showered and shaved, and then I went downstairs to find Erica. I'd only been in the kitchen a minute before

Phuong came in. She said she'd make coffee. I said I'd wait in the dining room. I was walking out of the kitchen when she screamed. It was then I saw Erica and ran to check her pulse. I told Phuong to call 9-1-1, but she was in a state of shock, so I made the call."

"Okay, let's call the detective back in and see if we can wrap this up."

She raps on the door. Detectives Gutierrez and Brown come back in.

"Do you have any questions for my client he hasn't yet answered?" Karin asks them.

Gutierrez speaks up, "Your client refused to answer any of my questions."

Karin whispers something to Nolan. He whispers something back. She says to Gutierrez, "Alright, go ahead. Ask your questions."

"Mr. Drake, did you kill Erica Dupree?"

"Absolutely not."

"There you are, Detective Gutierrez," Karin says. "He's answered your question. Now, if there's nothing more, we'll be leaving." She stands, pulling Nolan by the arm as she does.

"Wait a minute," Gutierrez protests. She looks at Brown, who shrugs his shoulders to say he's out of ideas.

Once they're outside the station, Karin says, "I'll give you a ride to your car. I assume it's at Erica's house in River Oaks."

"Yes it is," Nolan tells her. "And thanks for getting me out of there. I think Detective Brown was considering beating a confession out of me before you showed up. How did you get here so quick?"

"I happened to be nearby when I got your call. It was fortunate for you I was. Otherwise you would have been there for a while."

"I still can't believe it happened. Why would anyone want to hurt her?"

"I can't answer that. It seemed she was respected and liked by everyone who knew her."

He is suddenly overcome with grief. With the EMS and police at her house, and then the trip to the station, he hasn't had a second to reflect on how her loss will impact him. All the things they planned to do together in the years to come. The tears begin to well in his eyes, so he turns his head and pretends to watch the traffic passing by.

~30~

Gordon finds out about Erica's death from the attorney handling his divorce. It's noon when the call comes in. His initial reaction upon hearing the news is to grieve the loss of the twenty million he hoped to get out of her. It renders him so distraught he misses what the attorney says next.

"I'm sorry, Marv. I didn't catch what you just said."

"I said, the police want to talk to you. I've got a phone number for a Detective Brown. You need to call him."

"Why? What do they want from me?"

"It's standard procedure to talk with the victim's spouse, especially in a case like this, where the couple is separated. He's going to want to know where you were last night, at the time she was killed."

"I had dinner at Luigi's. I left there around twelve and went to my fiancé's brother's apartment, where I stayed for rest of the night."

"Alright, call Detective Brown and tell him."

Gordon disconnects, sits down on the bed and buries his face in his hands. "That imbecile," he says aloud, meaning Greg. He wonders how he could botch a simple job like this so badly. And more importantly, what evidence did he leave behind that can be traced back to him? Lauren and Greg left the apartment earlier, saying they'd be back after lunch.

Gordon punches in her number. It goes to voicemail. He hangs up.

~~~

"It's Gordon calling," Lauren says to Greg, and sends it directly to voicemail. "I don't want to talk to him, now."

They're sitting in a booth at a Denny's restaurant near the apartment. Gordon doesn't know Greg has been keeping Lauren informed of their progress in the plan to steal from Erica, and the news of Erica's murder hasn't reached them.

"How did it go, last night?" Lauren asks Greg.

"It couldn't have gone better. I was in and out, and back home in a little over an hour. I took a watch and some other jewelry Gordon says she never wears and probably won't notice is gone. I think we can wholesale it all for around thirty grand, maybe more."

"That's great," Lauren says. "Was Erica and everyone else asleep when you went in?"

"Apparently. All the lights were out."

"Where is the jewelry, now?"

"I stashed it up under the dash in my car, for now. Gordon says he knows someone who will buy it. He plans to take it to them on Monday."

"How is the money going to be split?"

"Sixty-forty, with the forty going to me."

"Do you trust him? I mean, you don't know the guy he's dealing with. If he tells you he only got five thousand for everything, you have no way of knowing if he's telling the truth."

"I don't have any choice. This is what we agreed on, and it's too late to back out. If I don't like how it turns out, I won't do it again."

Lauren's phone sounds. "It's Gordon, again," she tells Greg.

"You better take it. You don't want him to think you're dodging his calls. Like it not, he's our partner until all business is concluded."

"You're right," Lauren agrees. "Hi Gordon. We'll be back in a short while. Would you like me to bring you something from Denny's?"

"No, something's come up. I have to go down to the police station. Erica has been murdered."

He hears a clunk sound coming from Lauren's end of the line. She drops the phone, and stares in dismay at Greg.

"What did you do?" she hisses between clenched teeth.

"Lauren! Lauren! Are you there?" Gordon can be heard shouting into the phone.

Lauren takes a deep breath, and tries to calm herself. With a shaky hand she picks up the phone and speaks into it. "I'm so sorry about Erica, Gordon. This is such a shock. What do the police want?"

"I'm her estranged husband. That makes me a suspect. She was killed last night, sometime. Probably while I was having dinner at Luigi's. The police may want you to confirm I was with you for the rest of the night, afterward."

"Alright, I will."

"Is Greg there with you?"

"Yes, he's right here. Why? Do you need to speak with him?"

"Yeah, I do. Tell him I'll talk to him when I get back from the police station. Explain what's happened to him, and let him know the police may want to come by the apartment and question you both, to see if your story matches mine. Okay?"

"Yes, Gordon. I understand."

~ ~ ~

Gordon has skirted the law for years, in the course of fleecing an investment client, or scamming an unsuspecting

163

widow. He's dealt with the police on many occasions, and he's been accused of wrongdoing, but he's never been convicted of a crime. So, he walks into the police station feeling confident he can hit any pitch they throw at him.

"I'm here to see Detective Ray Brown," he tells the desk clerk.

"Have a seat," the clerk replies.

There's an unwritten rule that applies to every government office, whether it's a police station, post office or the IRS. Which is, don't glance at your watch while sitting in the waiting area, even if you think no one is looking. Gordon breaks the rule at least four times. It's thirty minutes before Detective Brown appears, introduces himself and ushers Gordon back to the interrogation room. Detective Gutierrez is waiting for them.

"This is Detective Gutierrez, Mr. Weston."

"I'm sorry for your loss," Gutierrez says. "Have a seat. This shouldn't take long. Because your wife and you were in the process of divorcing, we need to ask where you were at the time she was murdered. That way we eliminate you as a suspect and focus our efforts on finding the killer."

"I understand completely, Detective Gutierrez. You have my full cooperation in this matter. I'm as anxious as you to see her killer brought to justice. She was a wonderful person."

"So for the record, Mr. Weston," Brown says. "Where were you from six p.m. yesterday, until six a.m. this morning?"

"I had dinner at Luigi's Restaurant on Broad Street. I left there around midnight, and went to the apartment of my fiancé's brother, where we've been staying. I've been there until coming here. Lauren, her brother Greg, and several people at Luigi's will verify what I've told you."

"Do you know anyone who would want to hurt her?"

"I have a theory as to what might have happened," Gordon says.

"I'd love to hear it," Gutierrez tells him.

"Erica and I have been considering reconciling. She was going to break it off with the man she's been seeing."

"Is that man Nolan Drake?"

"Yes, that's him. She had begun to suspect he was only after her money. She was waiting for the right moment to tell him it was over between them."

"She told you this?"

"Yes, those were her exact words, as best as I recall."

"Did Ms. Dupree ever tell you of any incidents where Mr. Drake got angry with her or became physical?"

"He has a temper. I can personally attest to that. He came to my office and assaulted me because he thought I was acting inappropriately with his wife. The man's a lunatic. He's a ticking time bomb."

Brown is furiously jotting notes onto his pad as Gordon speaks, and occasionally exchanging a glance with Gutierrez.

"Was there something going on between you and his wife?"

"There wasn't at that time."

"Meaning there is now?"

"She's not his wife anymore. She's my fiancé, Lauren Malloy."

Several things are puzzling Brown as Gutierrez questions Gordon. He interrupts her inquiry to clear up some things in his mind.

"You said you and Ms. Dupree were going to reconcile. Or in other words, you were going to get back together. But on the night she is murdered, you're still engaged to another woman. You spent the night with her. Have I got that right?"

"Yes, but...,"

"And the husband of your fiancé," Brown continues, "is sleeping with your wife?"

"It's complicated," Gordon says.

"Oh, I can see that. It's the sort of love quadrangle that you read about in the checkout line at the grocery store. Did anyone other than you and Ms. Dupree know about this planned reconciliation? Was this discussion you had with her witnessed by a member of her household staff?"

"I don't recall."

"No, I didn't think so," Brown says sarcastically.

Gutierrez retakes control of the interrogation.

"We'll need phone numbers for Lauren Malloy and her brother. Also, the address for the apartment where you're staying. We'll confirm your whereabouts for the period in question. If everything checks out, we can cross you off our list."

"Will you let me know if you find her killer? She's still my wife, our divorce wasn't final. I have a right to know."

"We'll tell you if we charge someone with her murder. How's that?"

31

After the call from Gordon, Lauren jumps up from her seat and runs out of Denny's without a word or even a glance at Greg. He runs after her, but the restaurant manager stops him, thinking he's trying to leave without paying. He quickly pulls enough cash from his wallet to settle the bill, and then hurries out the door. Lauren is already backing out of the parking space when he reaches the car. He grabs the door handle and manages to open it, but she pumps the accelerator once, knocking him to the ground. Then she shifts into forward, almost running over him as she drives away.

The traffic is heavy, and she's forced to wait for an opening, before she can pull out of the parking lot onto the street. She checks the mirror, expecting to see Greg dazed and struggling to get to his feet, but he's not there. She pivots her head for a better look, and as she does the door beside her flies open. Greg reaches in and wraps a lock of her hair around his hand.

"Put the car in park and scoot over," he commands.

She slides over enough for him to get in, then she tries to get out on the passenger side. He restrains her with a tug of her hair. With his left hand, he shifts into forward and pulls into the street. He drives only a block, turns into another parking lot and kills the engine.

"What the hell has gotten into you?!" he screams at her.

"Why'd you kill her? Why, Greg?!" she hollers back.

"What are you talking about? Kill who?"

"Who do you think? Erica! They found her body, this morning."

"Oh, shit! I can't believe it. Wait! You think I killed her? Why the hell would I do that?"

"I don't know why you would, Greg. I just know you were there in her house to steal jewelry, on the night she was murdered."

"I never even saw her. According to Gordon, she goes to bed around ten most nights. The lights were out when I went in through the service entrance. I assumed she was asleep in bed."

"Okay, let go of my hair, I'm not going anywhere. I'm sorry if I overreacted, but I heard about her murder and knew you were there. The police want to question Gordon, because he and Erica were in the process of getting a divorce. That makes him their prime suspect."

"Do you think he'll tell them I was in the house?"

"No, he wouldn't do that. At least, I don't think he would. I mean, it would look as bad for him as it would for you, maybe worse."

"Yeah, unless he spins it to look like he didn't know anything about it. He could say, he mentioned his ex-wife keeps a lot of valuable things at her house, but the idea of stealing them was all mine."

"I really don't think he would do that, Greg. It's too chancy. It could backfire on him. But just to be safe, you need to cover your tracks. Get rid of the stuff you took. Wipe your prints off it and toss it in a river or somewhere no one will ever find it."

"That's like flushing thirty thousand dollars down the toilet. Besides, what would I tell Gordon? He's expecting half the money from the sale of it. He wouldn't believe me if I told him I threw it in the river."

"What do you care what he thinks. Do what I'm telling you to do. Dump the stuff where it won't be found."

~~~

Lauren and Greg are waiting anxiously for Gordon when he gets back from the police interview. He says, "I told them I was at Luigi's until midnight. They can easily verify that, but they didn't tell me when she died, so I don't know if it will be enough."

"Greg and I will swear you were here all night," Lauren says.

"That will help," Gordon replies. He's looking past Lauren at Greg, as if trying to detect something from his demeanor. Lauren excuses herself, so the men can talk one-on-one.

"I need to run an errand. I'll be back in a while."

As soon as she's gone, Gordon asks, "What happened?"

"I didn't kill her, Gordon. I never even saw her. I went in, took the stuff, and then I left. It went just the way we planned."

"Did you see anyone at all? Phuong or Hernando? Was Nolan there?"

"I didn't see one person. The house was dark like everyone was asleep. I was inside for less than twenty minutes. I swear, I have no idea what happened to Erica."

"What did you do with the stuff?"

"I've got it hidden. I'm thinking we need to get rid of it quick."

"Not yet. Let's see how the investigation goes. If it becomes necessary, we might be able to use the watch to focus the police's attention away from me and onto someone else."

~~~

169

Erica's death leaves Phuong without a job, income or place to sleep. She is forced to stay with her sister, Minh and her family. Minh lives with her husband and four children in a two-bedroom suburban home, northwest of Houston. Phuong sleeps on the floor, next to the oldest of Minh's girls, and performs household chores to earn her keep. She is grateful for the generosity shown her by Minh and her family.

Nevertheless, the living conditions are a huge step down from those at Erica's mansion. There, she had a room, with a bed and bathroom she shared with no one, except for Tung when he came to visit. Erica never scolded or punished her. She treated Phuong kindly, praised her cooking, paid her well, and allowed her time off if she asked for it. Phuong doubts she will ever again be as happy as she was while living there.

She hopes the police will find Erica's murderer, soon. Furthermore, she hopes that person will suffer a slow and painful death. But when the police questioned her that morning, she didn't tell them everything. For instance, she didn't tell them about Tung, and how she warned him to leave before the police arrived. And she didn't tell them about Hernando's lover, who she knew was with him during the night. Now, she fears what will happen if they find out she's lied to them.

Hernando is faced with a similar quandary. He didn't tell the police about his lover, Douglas, or that he was in the house that night. He would have, but Douglas insisted on being kept out of it. He was afraid of it somehow getting back to his wife, or so he said. Hernando wonders if that was his only reason. At one a.m., the night of Erica's murder, Hernando was awakened by the sound of the door to his room opening and closing. A moment later, he felt Douglas slide into the bed beside him. Douglas had left the room sometime after Hernando fell asleep at eleven, and returned at one. Hernando didn't ask Douglas about it then, and there wasn't time to ask about it before the police came in the morning.

He didn't tell the police when they questioned him because he wanted to talk to Douglas, first. Now, he's stuck in limbo waiting for Douglas to call and explain.

~~~

When Karin Hearn drops Nolan at Erica's house to get his car, the crime scene investigators are still there. Before getting into his car, Nolan stands for a moment staring at the yellow tape across the entrance, and the people coming and going from the house. Only twelve hours earlier, he was lying next to her with the fragrance of hair and perfume filling his nostrils.

"Go home. There's nothing more you can do for her, now," Karin tells him, before driving away.

~~~

At home, Nolan paces back and forth, unable to sit or stand still. He can't stop thinking about her. It's unfathomable to him that someone would want to hurt her. Detectives Brown and Gutierrez are going over it, too. But they're looking at it from another perspective.

"Who stands to gain the most from her death?" Gutierrez asks.

"I guess that'd be Gordon Weston," Brown replies. "She's about to divorce him, thereby cutting him off from her money. He kills her to stop the divorce from going through."

"I'm not sure it works that way, but I'm no lawyer. They were legally separated. That in itself may be all that's necessary."

"I like this Nolan Drake fellow for it, but I can't come up with a motive."

"I don't see him doing it," Gutierrez disagrees. "I think you're just jealous because he was logging sack time with a good-looking rich lady."

"Hell, I'll admit it. I hate the guy for that alone, but that doesn't mean he didn't kill her. He had the opportunity, and his alibi is weak. He says he was asleep and didn't hear anything. I don't buy it."

"As far as not hearing anything. Phuong and Hernando's rooms are closer to the kitchen, and neither one of them heard anything."

"Or so they say."

"What, you don't believe them?"

"Not completely. The Vietnamese girl kept looking down at her feet while I was questioning her. Hernando was shaking like a leaf the whole time. I felt like they both knew more than they were telling me."

"Well, so far we've got several reasons to dislike the suspects, but no motive for any of them. I think we need to dig into her phone and bank records, to see who's been calling her, and who she writes checks to."

"That sounds like a plan. I'll take the bank records, you take the phone."

~32~

The memorial service for Erica is held in the First United Presbyterian Church on the Tuesday following her death. Her body is to be cremated, but not until the coroner's office has completed the autopsy, so there's no body lying in repose. In lieu of a casket, a life-size picture of Erica is on display in the sanctuary near the pulpit. Before the service begins, Nolan walks to the front of the nave for a better look. The picture appears to be recent. It was taken in her house with the massive fireplace in the background. Erica is posing for a professional photographer it appears. Her hair is perfectly coiffed and the makeup is freshly applied. She's wearing an elaborate evening gown that looks chic and very expensive. She's absolutely stunning. He stands staring at her picture long enough that people are whispering to one another and starting to wonder about him.

He makes his way back up the aisle and takes a seat in the rear of the nave. Every row of pews is filled to capacity with mourners, by the time the officiating minister starts speaking. One entire section is reserved for her family. They enter after everyone else is seated. Nolan estimates there to be sixty of her relatives in all. Grandparents, aunts, uncles, siblings and cousins, all here to say goodbye to a woman whose life ended much too early. He's never met any of them. The only faces in the crowd he recognizes are those of Gordon and Lauren who are sitting across the center aisle from the family.

The minister is praising Erica for her benevolent nature, and for the contributions and countless hours she gave to several charitable organizations. It's a side of her he didn't really know. He mentions her beautiful singing voice, which Nolan never had the pleasure of hearing. Then the minister says a prayer and the choir sings a hymn. It's a beautiful service, but Nolan finds it depressing. He's not sure why he came. Out of respect for Erica he tells himself, but in truth that's not the reason. He's never been a religious type of man. Nor does he put much stock in the existence of heaven and hell. But if Erica *is* somewhere up there, looking down on her memorial service, she'd want him to be here.

In the parking lot of the church, after the memorial service, Lauren waves to Nolan as he's getting into his car. He acknowledges her. As she starts toward him, Gordon grabs her arm.

"What are you doing?" he asks.

"I want to talk to Nolan. Now, take your hand off of me."

"You're making me look bad in front of her family."

"No, Gordon. You're doing that on your own."

Nolan considers driving away while Lauren and Gordon are arguing with one another, but the parking lot is full and traffic is bumper to bumper getting out of there. So he sits behind the wheel of his car watching Lauren jerk her arm away from Gordon and hurry toward him. She gets into his car.

"I'm glad I caught you before you left."

"Yeah, Gordon looked pretty happy about it, too."

"Screw Gordon. I've told you before, he doesn't mean anything to me. I wanted to tell you how sorry I am about Erica. I know you two were close. She certainly didn't deserve to have this happen."

"No, she didn't."

"What are you going to do now?"

"I'm going to my office, and find something to do."

"No, I mean, what are going to do for companionship? I don't want to think of you sitting home by yourself."

"I don't recall that bothering you while we were together. You never let it stop you from going out on the town whenever you felt like it."

"Nolan, I'm trying to tell you that I still care deeply for you. If you ever need to talk, or if you don't want to be alone, you can call me. I want you to know that. We can get together as friends if you like."

"I don't think so, Lauren."

"Nolan, please don't be this way."

"It looks like your fiancé is getting a bit anxious. You might want to go before he starts to wonder if something's going on here."

"He's not my fiancé."

"Alright, your boyfriend, John, mark or whatever you call him. He's not happy about you talking to me. Does he know about Greg?"

"What about Greg?"

"Does Gordon know he's your husband, and not your brother?"

"That's none of his business."

"Like it was none of mine, when we were together?"

"Oh, knock it off, Nolan. If you'd stop feeling sorry for yourself long enough you might see what we had together was something very special. The good times we had far outnumbered the bad."

"Maybe, I should borrow your rose-colored glasses, because I come up with a different score than you."

"I give up, Nolan. I'll go, but I hope you'll change your mind about me. I'd really love to see you, again."

~~~

175

From the church, Nolan goes to his office, hoping to find a project to work on which will take his mind off of Erica. He's sitting at his desk with the door to his office closed, staring out the window at nothing in particular. A knock sounds.

"Yes," he calls.

Dana enters, wearing an expression of concern on her face.

"Are you alright?" she asks.

"Not really."

"Do you want to talk?"

"Sure, pull up a chair."

"So, how was the memorial service?"

"Depressing. It made me realize how little I knew about Erica. I never met any of her family, or talked to her about the charity work she did. I can't help but feel her killer targeted her because she was rich. Everyone's first impression of Erica is tainted by her wealth, and that's not who she was. That was a condition of birth. That lifestyle was all she ever knew. Sure, she took it for granted, but she didn't flaunt it."

"I think memorial services are intended to be sad and depressing. They're designed to make everyone feel bad they're still alive."

"If so, it worked on me. What about you? Are you seeing anyone?"

"Am I seeing anyone? Where did that come from?"

"You came in here to talk. I shared my feelings about the memorial service with you. Now, it's your turn."

"My turn? Well, let's see. I haven't had a date in four months. My mother says it's because I'm too fat, and if I don't lose weight, I'm going to die an old maid. The problem is I like eating more than dating, and I don't feel like depriving myself of food just to snare a man."

"I've heard certain clothes will make a person appear thinner than they really are. You could try that."

"Yes, I could try that, and it might work for a while, but only until the clothes come off."

"That's far enough, right there. We're venturing into a topic that's probably forbidden in the workplace. I appreciate you coming in to chat. It helped. Do me a favor."

"I know. Shut the door on my way out."

~33~

Nolan's second session with the homicide detectives investigating Erica's murder, comes four days after the first. They call Karin Hearn because she is his attorney of record. She offered her services to Nolan after his first interview with the police.

"I didn't think you took on criminal cases," Nolan said to her, then.

"I don't normally, but I have plenty of courtroom experience, and our firm represents the Dupree family. I can assure you'll be well taken care of."

From what Nolan has since gathered about her, Karin is a sharp and capable, no-nonsense sort of person. He could do worse, no question about it. She arranges for the meeting with the detectives to take place in the conference room at the law firm where she works.

"What time do you want to do it?" she asks Nolan.

"When do they want me there?"

"No, Nolan. That's not how this works. They ask politely for everything they get from us. We give sparingly, when and where it's convenient for us."

"In that case, two in the afternoon works well for me."

Detectives Brown and Gutierrez have been waiting thirty minutes when Nolan arrives at the law offices of Drury, Sutton, Leman and Stovall. That's because Karin told them the meeting was set for one thirty. They don't look happy about being kept waiting. Karin on the other hand, seems quite pleased with herself.

Karin begins by pushing a button on a recorder and saying, "For the record, this interview is being conducted by Detectives Ray Brown and Sylvia Gutierrez in the law offices of Drury, Sutton, Leman and Stovall. They are interviewing Nolan Drake, who is represented by Karin Hearn, regarding the alleged homicide of Erica Dupree. Go ahead detectives."

Brown starts the interview by saying, "I knew there was something not right about you the first time I met you. I just couldn't put my finger on what it was."

"Do you have a question, Detective Brown?" Karin asks.

Gutierrez takes over for him. "How long have you and Ms. Dupree been involved with one another?"

Karin whispers in his ear, "nod your head like I'm saying really smart things. Make them wait for it, and then answer in two or three words."

"Approximately three months," Nolan says, after a beat.

"Three months?" Brown says, theatrically. "The woman was some kind of generous to someone she'd just met."

"If there are no more questions…," Karin says.

Gutierrez takes over, again. "I understand your ex-wife is engaged to Gordon Weston. Isn't that right?"

Karin whispers in his ear, again.

"I've never been married," Nolan says.

"Come on, now," Brown says, gruffly. "You were married to Lauren Malloy, and when she hooked up with Gordon Weston, you lost it and punched him out, didn't you?"

"Detective Brown," Karin says in a condescending tone. "If you can't manage your temper any better, I'll have to ask you to leave. Detective Gutierrez seems in control of her emotions. Maybe you should let her ask the questions, from now on."

179

Brown folds his arms across his chest, presses his lips together and nods at Gutierrez to proceed.

"Gordon Weston said in a sworn statement Lauren Malloy is your ex-wife, but let's skip past that for now," Gutierrez says. "He also states he believes you began seeing Ms. Dupree to get back at him for taking your wife from you. Is there any truth to that?"

Nolan doesn't wait for Karin to coach him.

"None whatsoever."

"Then, would you care to give me your version of how you and Ms. Dupree met?"

Karin gives Nolan a cautious go-ahead nod.

"First of all, Lauren Malloy and I lived together for about nine months. We were never legally married. In fact, she was married to another man during that period, which is something I learned afterward. Erica came to me, when she found out about the affair between Lauren and Gordon. We began seeing one another after she separated from Gordon."

"You spent a day in lockup over the incident in Gordon's office. No charges were filed, but I'm going to assume there's some truth to his allegation you beat him up. Just between the four of us, he probably had it coming. There is one other thing I'd like to ask you about, though. Gordon Weston says he and Erica had been discussing reconciling. Did she say anything about that to you?"

"I'll take that question," Karin says. "The law firm I work for, Drury, Sutton, Leman and Stovall was handling Erica Dupree's divorce from Gordon Weston. As of close of business on Friday, less than twelve hours before her death, Erica's instructions to this firm were to finalize the divorce as quickly as possible."

Gutierrez jots a few things down on a pad, and then reviews her notes, before saying, "I think that's all the questions we have for now."

"Now, hold on a minute," Brown says to her. "What about the will, aren't you going to ask him about that? It's one hell of a motive, and four hundred million reasons to kill her."

Nolan looks blankly at the detectives, and then at Karin. She's eying them smugly, as if she knows something they don't.

"What are you talking about?" Nolan asks Brown.

"Detectives," Karin interrupts. "As a standard practice, the contents of a will are disclosed to all beneficiaries at the same time, when the will is read. In the case of Erica Dupree's will, the reading is scheduled for later this week. In other words, my client doesn't know about his inheritance."

"You don't expect us to believe that malarkey, do you?" Brown says.

"I don't care whether you believe it or not, but it is the truth. Now, Mr. Nolan has answered all of your questions, and you've been unable to establish a motive. Nor have you linked him to her murder with fingerprints on the murder weapon, or anything else that would be considered credible evidence in a courtroom. You have every reason to eliminate him as a suspect. I suggest you do so."

Nolan barely notices the detectives leave the conference room. He sits in stunned silence trying to absorb this latest revelation.

"I didn't mean to blindside you with that. Erica's will is being handled by another attorney in our office. He alerted me the police had asked about it. I'm not at liberty to reveal the details of her will to you or anyone else mentioned in it."

"I don't know why she did that."

"Maybe you'll find out more at the reading of her will."

~~~

The reading of Erica Dupree's final will and testament takes place two days later, in the same conference room.

181

Presiding over the event is Alan Rutherford, the attorney who drew up the document, only a week before she died. Besides him, his assistant and Nolan, there are five others present. They include Erica's brother, Jacob, her younger sister, Caroline, her household helpers, Hernando and Phuong, and Gordon Weston. Gordon and Nolan sit on opposite sides of the table casting evil looks at one another. Alan Rutherford clears his throat before speaking.

"Erica Dupree gave specific instructions for how the disbursement of her estate should be handled. She requested that you, the beneficiaries all be present for the reading of her final will and testament. I'll proceed to do so without further delay.

"To Caroline, my sister, I bequeath the jewelry collection that belonged to our paternal grandmother, Harriet Dupree."

Caroline smiles. It's exactly what she expected. She's wealthy in her own right. Receiving money from Erica wouldn't carry the same significance as the prized jewelry collection.

"To Jacob, my brother, I bequeath my shares of Dupree Oil and Gas."

The shares will strengthen Jacob's influence in the family business. Again, it's a gift far more important than money.

"To my friend and helper, Phuong Nguyen, I bequeath the sum of one hundred thousand dollars."

Phuong buries her face in her hands, and sobs.

"To my friend and assistant, Hernando Perez, I bequeath the sum of one hundred thousand dollars."

Hernando tries to hide his elation at hearing this, but a soft squeal escapes from his lips. Phuong squeezes his hand.

"To my former husband, Gordon Weston," Rutherford says, and then pauses. He sneaks a quick glance at Gordon, who has an ear cocked toward him, eagerly awaiting what's coming. After a beat, Rutherford reads, "I bequeath the sum of one dollar, the last one he'll ever get out of me."

Gordon's disappointment hangs in the air like a foul odor. He grumbles something unintelligible under his breath as his head drops.

"To the man I love, Nolan Drake, I leave everything else."

Nolan is shell-shocked and staring awestruck at the table in front of him. Gordon glares at him with utter contempt.

"That concludes the reading of the will. Mr. Drake, if you'll come with me, I'll go over an inventory of Erica Dupree's assets with you. For the rest of you, my assistant, Mark Sabin will answer your questions regarding the disbursement of your benefits."

Once inside Rutherford's office with the door closed, Nolan asks, "When did Erica have her will drawn up? It must have been recently."

"Her original will was done years ago, but she made changes to it last week. She did so to ensure that Gordon Weston wouldn't have a claim to anything of hers, in the event of her death prior to the divorce being final."

"Had she been threatened by anyone?"

"Not that she told me about. She was always meticulous with the handling of her affairs. She left nothing to chance."

"I'm still struggling to understand why she left the bulk of her estate to me. Did she say anything to you about that?"

"No, but I think you'll find an explanation in here." He gives Nolan an envelope with his name on it. The handwriting on the front is Erica's. "Have a seat, Mr. Drake. There's a lot to go over, and several papers to be signed. This may take a while."

~34~

Shortly after they wed, on a night when she had consumed a bit too much champagne, Erica confessed to Gordon she had revised her will to include him. She never told him what the term 'include' equated to in dollars, but he convinced himself it had to be a shitload of money. So, as he walked into the conference room for the reading of the will, he could barely contain his excitement. Afterward, he took his crisp, new dollar bill and walked out, unable to mask his dismay. It was his last opportunity to come away with something for the five years he was married to her.

Now, Nolan gets it all. And what did he do for it. He spent three lousy months with her. Lauren is going to be livid, when she finds out. Nolan, the man she dumped, is inheriting a fortune, while the man she's with will probably be living on welfare before long. He stops at the liquor store on the way back to the apartment, and buys a pint of bourbon, because he can't stand the thought of facing her sober.

"How much?" she asks, the second he stumbles in the door.

"You don't want to know." His words are slurred, and he's shifting his weight from one foot to the other, as if he has to pee.

"You're drunk. That must mean you have good news, if you've already begun celebrating. Don't keep me in suspense. How much?"

"One whole dollar."

"Stop joking around, Gordon. Tell me. How much did she leave us?"

"I'm not joking around. She changed her will and left me one dollar, just to rub my face in it."

Lauren is speechless. The million dollars she was to get for screwing Erica's loser of a husband is history. The same for the two and a half million she would have received if Gordon had agreed to the divorce settlement. The will was Gordon's last opportunity to get anything from Erica, and Lauren's last chance to get anything from Gordon.

"Get out, Gordon! Right now!"

"Come on, Lauren. You don't mean that."

"I've never been more serious in my life. You've been nothing but trouble to me from the day we met."

"I've had a run of bad luck, that's all. Things will turn around. I'm working on a new idea. It came to me on the way home."

"I've heard all of your brilliant ideas I care to hear. Get the hell out, now, or I'll call the police."

He starts to argue further, but she takes out her phone and hits the 9-1-1 button. He hears the dispatcher answer, and puts out his hands with the palms toward Lauren.

"Alright, I'm going," he whispers.

"I'm sorry. I pushed the button by mistake," Lauren says into the phone and disconnects.

"Just let me get a bag and some clothes, and I'll leave." He begins packing an overnight bag, mumbling under his breath as he does, "This is all his fault. Every bit of it."

"Greg had nothing to do with this."

"I'm talking about Nolan. He screwed up everything. He only knew Erica for three months. I was with her for five years. I should be the one in her will, not him."

"Nolan was in her will? What did she leave him?"

"Everything."

Lauren's lips move in an attempt to speak, but no words emerge. Gordon relishes the moment of silence. It is short-lived.

"But…, but…," she sputters. "That's not true. This just can't be happening to me."

"It not only can be happening, it is. All her money, real estate, stocks and bonds—everything. The only things he didn't get were the two hundred grand she gave to Hernando and Phuong, a jewelry collection she gave to her sister, Dupree Oil and Gas stock she gave to her brother, and the lousy dollar she gave me. Nolan got every other stinking thing she owned."

Lauren slumps into a chair, and sits staring blankly ahead. Gordon waves his hand in front of her face, and then snaps his fingers. There's no response. He shrugs his shoulders, picks up his bag and starts for the door.

Lauren suddenly comes out of her trance. "Wait!" she blurts out. "I want to hear your idea."

Gordon plays dumb. "What idea?"

"You said it came to you on the way here. It's something about the will, isn't it? I want to hear your thoughts on it."

"I want to have my lawyers look into contesting the will."

"On what grounds?"

"I'm still working on that. I could say Erica wasn't in her right mind, or that Nolan tricked her into it."

"It would be tough to prove either of those things. And even if you could, what good would it do you?"

"I don't necessarily have to prove anything. I just have to cast enough reasonable doubt on the legitimacy of the will to stop the disbursement of her assets. If the beneficiaries are faced with it being tied up in court for a year or so, they might be amenable to a settlement."

"When will her attorneys begin disbursement of the assets?"

"I'm not sure. It might be within a week or two, or it could be a few months. I don't know what all is involved."

"It's already after business hours at most law offices. You need to contact your attorney first thing Monday morning to find out. You can tell him you're considering contesting the will, and ask for his advice."

"That might be a problem. I still owe him money for the divorce. I was planning on paying him once I got the settlement from Erica, but that isn't going to happen, now."

"We have at least until Monday to figure it out. Nothing will happen over the weekend."

"Does this mean I can stay?"

"You can stay for now. Think of it as a probationary period. The first indication this plan of yours isn't going to work, and you're history. Is that understood?"

"Don't worry. I've got a good feeling about this."

"I wish I could say I felt the same. One other thing. The agreement we made over the settlement from Erica, covers this too. I get half of whatever you get out of it."

~35~

Before leaving his office to attend the reading of Erica's will, Nolan mentioned where he was going to Dana.

"Miss Moneybags included you in her will?!" Dana replied. "And all along you've been saying you two were just friends. Apparently that was a load of crap."

"Please, don't call her that. She was a great lady who never had anything bad to say about others, except maybe for her estranged husband. I have no idea why she included me in her will. I'm sure it's just a token gesture on her part, to thank me for being there during her separation from Gordon."

Knowing Dana will tell everyone in the office where he's gone, Nolan doesn't feel like returning there, afterward.

"I'm not up to coming back to work, today," he tells Dana, by phone.

"Don't worry about it. We've been so busy, I'd forgotten you weren't here. How'd it go with the will thing?"

"I'll tell you about it later, okay?"

"That bad, eh?"

"Worse that you can imagine."

~~~

He goes straight home, eager to read the letter from Erica which he hopes will answer a few of the many questions swirling around in his head. Before breaking the seal on the envelope, he fills a tall glass with vodka, takes it along with the letter to his breakfast table. He sits himself down, pulls the page from the envelope, unfolds it and reads Erica's handwritten words.

My dearest Nolan,

I honestly hope you never read this letter. Our short time together has made me feel extraordinarily blessed, and more than anything I want it to continue for many years to come. However, if something were to happen to me, you'll want an explanation for what I have done. In a world where people are murdered over the change in their pocket, someone with my wealth is always a potential target. That reality combined with the divorce proceedings is what influenced my decision to remove Gordon from my will. I cannot explain why I am choosing at this time to designate you as the primary beneficiary. I thought of all the charitable organizations I have supported over the years, my other friends and relatives, and then I thought of you. The best days and nights of my life have been spent with you. If I precede you in death, it is my sincere hope to live in your memory forevermore. I will end this letter with one final request. Please spread my ashes on the hillside overlooking the Pacific Ocean, at my home in Costa Rica. The week I spent there with you was the happiest of my life.

With all my love,
Erica

Alan Rutherford told Nolan it would be a minimum of four to six months before Erica's assets were distributed to the beneficiaries. Fortunately, that gives him plenty of time to consider what he'll do with it all. Besides the house in River Oaks and the one in Costa Rica, she owned several other properties. It must have required an army of people to manage her properties and other investments. She was apparently a shrewd businesswoman, which is something else he was unaware of.

The mention of the divorce proceedings in her letter seems to imply she felt Gordon might harm her. Or maybe it was someone else who stood to lose money once the divorce was final. A creditor of Gordon's, perhaps. The police will probably be interested in getting a copy of the letter, but before he talks to them Nolan wants to run it by Karin Hearn.

~~~

In another part of town, Curtis Leyden is trying to decide whether to tell the police about the cameras he had installed in the servants' wing of Erica's house. Before the installation was performed, he asked Erica if she wanted the live feed from the cameras monitored by a security company, or simply recorded to be viewed later, as necessary. She chose the latter. However, with an app for his smartphone, he can still view everything the cameras record. He had things set up that way so he can check the cameras from time to time to make sure they're working properly. The cameras record activity inside the rooms within the servants' wing and in the hallway leading to the service entrance. As far as he knows, only Erica, the installers and he are aware the cameras are there. He was at home watching the nightly news on TV when he heard about the murder. His wife was pointing the remote toward the TV, about to switch channels, when Erica's face filled the screen.

"Turn the volume up!" he shouted.

"She was found dead in her River Oaks home. According to a police spokesperson, her death is being investigated as a homicide," the newscaster said. "She and her husband were in the process of divorce. A male friend of Ms. Dupree's was in the house at the time. The police would not comment on the cause of death or any suspects because of the ongoing investigation."

There's no question the police will want to see the camera footage recorded on the night she died. It may contain key pieces of evidence crucial to their investigation. But before he hands over anything to the police, he wants to thoroughly go over what the cameras captured on the night in question. There's no telling how much it could be worth.

~36~

Gordon Weston calls his attorney, Marv Feldman early Monday morning, to insist Marv cancels all other appointments to take an emergency meeting with him. Even though the only thing he has scheduled is an estate planning consultation at ten thirty, he acts as if it's a huge imposition.

"What's so important it can't wait until tomorrow, Gordon?"

"I'll tell you when I get there. Trust me, this is bigger than anything else you have going."

"Where have I heard that before?"

Marv's office is in a circa 1970s strip mall whose tenants come and go as frequently as jets at George Bush Intercontinental Airport. It's scheduled for demolition in three months, but Marv is hoping for a major lawsuit to drop into his lap before then, so he can afford to move his operation into some fancy digs in one of those shiny new high-rise office buildings. Like Gordon, Marv has been a little down on his luck as of late. It's the glue that binds the two of them together. Marv motions Gordon into his office as he arrives.

"I usually don't berate my clients when they make a mistake, but I'm going to make an exception in your case, Gordon. You really screwed the pooch by turning down the settlement offer from Erica. Tell me you're not kicking yourself over that."

"I've been able to get over it and put it behind me. That's what a smart man does, Marv. They forget the past and focus on the future."

"So, tell me smart guy, does that future you're focused on have me getting paid what you owe me, anytime soon?"

"If you're half the lawyer you claim to be, you'll get what I owe you and a whole lot more."

"I'm listening."

"I want to contest Erica's will, and I want you to file an injunction, or whatever it's called, to stop the executor of her estate from distributing the assets to the beneficiaries."

"Hmm, interesting. On what basis would you be challenging her will?"

"The guy she was seeing somehow tricked her into taking me out of it, and putting him in."

"That's the ex-husband of your so-called fiancé, isn't it? I'm fairly certain any judge would say she took you out of her will because she was divorcing you. Do you have any evidence this other guy coerced her into including him in the will?"

"What if he's suspected of her murder?"

"That might delay things, but only until he's cleared or the DA decides not to indict him. At which time, the executor will have to give him whatever is specified in the will as his."

"How long does it usually take after a person dies until their estate is distributed to the beneficiaries?"

"That depends on several things, of course, but with an estate the size of Erica's, I'd say anywhere from six months to two years."

"Alright, that gives us plenty of time."

"It gives you time, but without a basis to challenge the will it won't do you any good. You have to prove her signature was forged, she was somehow coerced, or she wasn't mentally capable of handling her own affairs at the time she changed the will."

~~~

Gordon only has a vague notion of how to accomplish the task. The plan beginning to take shape in his mind revolves around Nolan Drake. If he can present credible evidence of a plot by Nolan to steal Erica's fortune, that might do it. He places a call to Greg Malloy.

"Greg, Gordon here. I've been thinking about the watch. We should get rid of it. After what happened to Erica, it's too risky to keep it around."

"Yeah, I've been thinking the same thing. I could toss it and the rest of the jewelry off the bridge into the ship channel, where no one would ever find it."

"Hang on to the jewelry. We can take the stones out of the settings. Those are untraceable. The watch is a different story, it's engraved on the back plate, and easily identified. If we were to put the watch somewhere it was sure to be found by the police, it might be better for us."

"I'm not following you there."

"For instance, if it was found in the possession of someone who was known to be in Erica's house at one time, it would draw suspicion away from us and put it on them."

"You mean, like the maid or a gardener, someone like that?"

"I don't know where to find anyone who worked for her. I was thinking more along the lines of Nolan Drake."

"I don't know, Gordon. I've got nothing against Nolan, and I don't think Lauren would like it."

"Lauren doesn't need to know. This is in her best interest. Make up a reason to stop by Nolan's house. Tell him Lauren left something there. Once you're inside his house, say you need to use the bathroom. Then, hide the watch in the vanity cabinet."

"How are the police going to find it there?"

"An anonymous tip. The police already suspect him. To be honest, I do, too. They don't need much encouragement to go after him."

"You really think Nolan had something to do with Erica's murder?"

"He stands to inherit the bulk of her estate, which is probably worth around four hundred million. That's enough to tempt the pope into killing Mother Teresa."

"I think she's already dead."

"You're missing the point, Greg. Hide the watch at Nolan's like I'm telling you. Do it for Lauren."

~~~

Monday evening Nolan is sorting through his stock of microwave dinners in his freezer, trying to decide between Szechuan chicken and spinach ricotta ravioli. His doorbell sounds, but because he's not expecting anyone he figures it's a visit from Jehovah's Witnesses, and doesn't answer. It sounds a second time. Looking through the peephole he sees Greg standing there, and opens the door.

"I didn't expect to see you again, Greg."

"I know, but I felt bad about my part in things with you and Lauren. I came by to apologize, and try to explain. Can I come in?"

Nolan steps aside for Greg to enter. "You want a beer?"

"Sure, that'd be great."

Greg follows Nolan to the kitchen where he grabs two beers from the refrigerator. They sit on stools at the bar to talk.

"I've got to ask you something, Greg. How does a man sit idly by while another man takes his wife?"

"Lauren is a different kind of woman. You must know that by now. We don't have a conventional marriage."

"That much is obvious."

"I really am more of a brother than a husband to her. That's how we think of each other. I love her like a sister. Her happiness is more important to me than my own, even if that means she has other men in her life. That's the sort of sacrifice a brother makes for his sister."

"Maybe, but it's not the sort of sacrifice a husband makes for his wife. Lauren uses men to get what she wants. She's told me as much. Does Gordon know you're not her brother?"

"No, I don't think so. At least, I've haven't told him. You won't tell him will you?"

"It's of no benefit to me. Besides, I have no need or desire to speak to either one of them."

"I'm sorry you feel that way about Lauren. She really does care about you, man."

"Her kind of caring, I can live without." Nolan swallows the last of his beer, and sets the bottle on the bar. He doesn't offer Greg another.

"That's all I wanted to say. Do you mind if I use your bathroom? Beer seems to go straight through me."

"Go ahead. You know where it is."

Greg goes into the bathroom down the hall. He waits for a minute, then flushes the toilet, and turns on the sink faucet. With the water running to mask the sound of the vanity cabinet door opening and closing, he sticks the watch in a corner behind a container of cleaning solution.

"Thanks for the beer, Nolan," Greg says, before leaving.

"You're welcome. You and Lauren have a great life."

~37~

All the larger cities in the USA have an anonymous tip program. Typically it involves a phone number anyone can call to report a crime without giving their identity. It's a controversial program because the information is difficult to verify. It often results in people being falsely accused, and occasionally falsely arrested. It is the perfect means for Gordon to implicate Nolan in Erica's murder.

"I say we get a warrant to search his house, and go over there today, before he has a chance to get rid of the evidence," Detective Brown tells Detective Gutierrez.

"If we don't let him or his attorney know before we go in, they're going to raise hell with the DA. Any evidence we find might get thrown out."

"And if we do tell them in advance, the evidence will be gone by the time we get there. I'd rather have it in my hand and let the lawyers argue about whether or not it's admissible, than not have it at all."

They find the watch exactly where the anonymous tipster said it would be. Erica's sister, Caroline identifies it as part of the jewelry collection which belonged to their grandmother, Harriet Dupree.

"Erica bequeathed the collection to me. I just found out a few days ago when her will was read. She wouldn't have given the watch or any other piece from the collection to anyone. It has to have been stolen. There's no other explanation."

"Let's go," Brown tells Gutierrez, after Caroline leaves.

"Where?"

"To arrest that slick bastard, that's where."

"His lawyer isn't going to like that."

"I don't give a damn. I want a few minutes alone with him. I think I can get a confession out of him. There's nothing she can do for him, after that."

"Why do you hate this guy so much? What did he do to you?"

"He didn't do anything to me, but he killed that rich broad. That makes him a murderer, and I hate all murderers."

Nolan is in the conference room going over the plans for a new medical building. Two representatives of the building's owner and Dana are there, as well. They're all leaning over a set of plans laid out on the table when the door bursts open. He recognizes the two detectives.

"Nolan Drake," Brown says, loud enough to be heard throughout the architectural firm's offices. "You're under arrest for the murder of Erica Dupree. Read him his rights."

"You've got to be kidding," Nolan says.

Brown cuffs Nolan's hands behind him while Gutierrez takes a card from her pocket and reads what's written on it.

"You have the right to remain silent. Anything you say can and will be used against you in a court of law. You have the right to an attorney. If you cannot afford an attorney, one will be provided for you. Do you understand the rights I have just read to you?"

"Yes, I understand my rights, and I'd like to call my attorney, now."

"You can call her from the station."

Nolan doesn't try to resist. He doesn't want to give Brown the pleasure of throwing him to the ground and stepping on his head. Dana and the clients watch in stunned silence as they march him out. A uniformed officer puts him in the back of a marked squad car with the same putrid odor of urine and vomit as the last one he rode in. Twenty minutes later, Brown half drags him through a side door of the station and into an interrogation room. He seats Nolan at a table, leaving the cuffs on, and sits across from him. It's just the two of them in the room.

"That was pretty stupid to steal her watch like that," Brown begins. Nolan gives him a puzzled look, but doesn't speak. "You thought you'd committed the perfect crime. And, you almost pulled it off, until you got greedy and took the watch."

"These cuffs are pretty uncomfortable," Nolan says.

"Not nearly as uncomfortable as a jail cell. Would you prefer I throw you in lockup?"

"What I'd prefer is to call Karin Hearn, so I can get out of here."

"It's not going to work that way this time around. Before, when you were here, you weren't under arrest. It's different now. Your lawyer is not going to waltz in here, and walk you out. You're going to be processed. You'll go in front of a judge who will set bail, and if you can afford it, you pay and go home. Now, how long all that is going to take, depends on how cooperative you are."

"Detective Brown. I don't know who killed Erica Dupree. I only know that it wasn't me. And, that's all I've got to say to you."

"We'll see how you feel about that in a few hours. Get up."

Brown pulls Nolan up from his chair and takes him to be processed. Nolan knows what to expect because he went through it after he beat up Gordon. They fingerprint and photograph him, take his phone, wallet and clothes, then issue him a jailhouse jumpsuit. He's placed in a holding cell with three other inmates. There's no bed, toilet or chair in the cell.

That's because it's designed to confine prisoners for an hour or two while they're waiting to be transported somewhere else.

Nolan sits on the cold damp floor with his back to a wall and knees folded against his chest, wondering how things reached this point. With his eyes closed and head resting against the wall he looks to be sleeping when Brown appears at the cell door to rouse him.

"Hey Drake!" Brown shouts. "How are you doing in there?" Nolan doesn't believe Brown really cares how he's doing, so he doesn't reply. "You think this is bad, wait until you get to the county jail. That's where they take you next, unless you're ready to start talking to me."

~~~

Nolan finds out for himself how bad it is at the county jail, when they transport him there an hour later. He spends a sleepless night listening to his fellow inmates screaming, cursing and fighting. It's not until the next morning when he gets to speak with Karin Hearn for five minutes before being taken into a courtroom.

"Your arraignment hearing is in twenty minutes. You're being charged with capital murder in the death of Erica Dupree. The charges will be read aloud in court, you'll enter your plea, and the bail amount will be set. The whole thing takes less than five minutes. I'm assuming you'll want to enter a plea of not guilty. Am I right?"

"Yes, of course. I don't understand why I'm being charged. What evidence have they got?"

"We don't have time to go into that now. Once the bail is set, I'll go to work on getting you out on bond."

"Good, I don't want to spend any more time than absolutely necessary behind bars."

Karin's expression changes from that of the strictly business attorney Nolan is used to seeing, to one of concern.

She says, "Nolan, there's something I need to prepare you for. Erica Dupree was well known as a socialite and philanthropist. Her murder is national news. The trial will be high profile, which means lots of time in front of the cameras for the police, judge, district attorney, you and me. It's a career maker for a DA. They're going to pull out all the stops to win this one. Win or lose, this is going to be an expensive and lengthy ordeal for you. I wish I could tell you otherwise, but those are the hard facts of the matter."

"Karin, I didn't do it. There can't be any credible evidence against me for something I didn't do. What are they going to do, fabricate some?"

"It's not beyond the realms of possibility. The police will be setting other cases aside to free up time and man-hours for the purpose of finding more evidence. They'll spare no expense to come up with DNA or forensic evidence to implicate you."

"I can't believe this is happening."

Karin takes a sheet of paper from her satchel and places it along with a pen in front of Nolan.

"This is a form giving me power of attorney. I'll need it to access your bank account or place a lien on your house and business." Nolan signs it and pushes it back to Karin, who returns it to her satchel. "They'll take you into the courtroom in a short while. I'll see you there."

~38~

The instant Nolan is brought into the courtroom, cameras begin to click and flash. The district attorney himself along with two others from his office stand on one side of the center aisle striking their most photogenic pose for the assembled news media. Karin Hearn stands on the opposite side of the aisle. She has a woman and a man beside her. Nolan has never met either of them, but presumes them to be a part of her legal team. A court officer leads Nolan, who is still handcuffed, to the center of the room, where he'll face the judge with Karin on his right and the officer on his left.

The judge presiding over the arraignment hearing is Juliet Franklin, an African-American woman Nolan guesses to be in her fifties. She appears to be in no hurry to begin. Instead, she seems to be enjoying the buzz of activity in the courtroom. Finally, after the camera clicking subsides some, Franklin picks up her freshly oiled gavel, made of walnut hardwood with brass trim, and raps it on the sound block to hush the crowd. The case number is read aloud, along with Nolan's name as the defendant, and then the show begins without further delay.

"Mr. Drake," the judge says, theatrically. "You're charged with one count of murder, one count of felony theft and one count of failure to render aid, in the death of Erica Dupree. How do you plea?"

Karin prompts him with a nod. "Not guilty to all charges," he says.

"On the matter of bail, Mr. Hardwick?" Franklin says to the DA.

"We request the defendant be remanded without bail, Your Honor. He has inherited an enormous sum of money from the estate of the deceased and we believe him to be a flight risk."

"Your Honor, my client hasn't received a dime from Erica Dupree or her estate. He has a home and business, both of which are heavily mortgaged. We can supply his financial records to prove this. Furthermore, the state's case is extremely weak. The only evidence they have was obtained during an illegal search of Mr. Drake's home. It's obvious this whole thing is nothing more than a self-promotional sham on the part of Mr. Hardwick."

"I object to that slanderous accusation," Hardwick says loudly.

The judge's gavel comes down to stop the bantering. "Save it for the trial you two. Bail is set at five hundred thousand dollars."

"Your Honor," Hardwick protests.

The gavel comes down, once again. "Next case," Franklin states, sternly.

It's midafternoon when Nolan walks out of the county jail. Somehow the news media has been alerted he made bail. Karin is there to escort him through the throng of reporters and photographers, responding with, "No comment," to every question shouted in their direction, before shoving Nolan into a car and driving away.

"They may be camped out around your home and office while the trial is going on. My advice to you is don't talk to them. There's nothing to be gained from it. Hardwick held a press conference after the arraignment. There was a lot of posturing during it, and promises of getting justice for Erica and the Dupree family. He's up for reelection in the fall. To convict you in court, he needs evidence, which he doesn't have. He hopes to sway public sentiment against you, to make it look as if he's duty bound to prosecute you."

"The judge seemed okay. If the DA had gotten his way, I'd be sitting in jail until the trial started. So, what's our next step?"

"It's a waiting game, now. A trial date will be set. Between now and then, I'll try to negotiate with the DA, but he won't be very flexible. Not at first, anyway. He's hoping the investigating detectives can pull a rabbit out of their hats, and link you to her murder. As the trial draws nearer, and his case is still looking weak, he might be willing to make a deal."

"By deal, you mean he might accept a guilty plea from me in exchange for a lighter sentence. Isn't that right?"

"That's usually how it works, but we're getting ahead of ourselves, now. For the time being, I want you to keep a low profile. I'll call you whenever I have something to report."

~~~

That evening Nolan calls Dana at home, to update her on his status. She already has one version of it from the media.

"It's on every news channel, even CNN. All the sordid details are out there for public consumption. I don't know what to say to you, Nolan. I thought I knew you."

"What are you saying, Dana? Do you think I killed Erica? Christ, Dana. I loved her."

"I don't know what I think. The reporters are saying you inherited something like four hundred million dollars from her. I'm not sure what I would do for that kind of money. You never told me about that, or anyone else, for that matter. You've been secretive about your relationship with her. You never said you loved her, before now."

"Dana, don't believe what you hear on the news. I haven't been any more secretive about Erica than you are with the men in your life. It's not something we talk about at the office, that's all. And I didn't know about the inheritance until the will was read, last Friday. Would you tell me about the money, if our positions were reversed?"

"I don't know, probably not."

"That's right, probably not. You'd be afraid it would look like you were gloating over your good fortune."

"Yeah, that's true."

"Look, Dana. I'm sorry I wasn't more forthcoming, but everything has happened so quickly, and there's still a lot going on. I called to tell you I won't be in the office this week."

"That might be best. None of the others in the office or any of our clients have had a chance to absorb the news. It's impossible to say what their reaction will be."

~~~

Nolan doesn't have the time or opportunity to worry about his business. The next day, Karin calls with a double dose of bad news.

"This morning, Gordon Weston's attorney filed a suit contesting Erica Dupree's will."

"Can he do that?"

"He can and he has. But, that's not all I have to tell you."

The tone of her voice gives Nolan a sinking feeling in the pit of his stomach. "What?" he asks.

"I have to resign as your attorney in the murder trial."

"Why?"

"It's a conflict of interest. The outcome of the trial will directly affect the outcome of the lawsuit. The firm represents Erica Dupree's estate. It would be unethical for the firm to represent any of the beneficiaries at the same time. I can recommend a good criminal defense attorney. His name is Frederick Pollard. He's with Nelson, Lubick and Wallace."

Nolan arranges a meeting with Pollard the following day.

"Karin Hearn called to tell me she was referring you because of a conflict of interest. I've reviewed what information she has on the case. District Attorney Aaron Hardwick has appointed himself as head prosecutor. He'll be pressing hard for a conviction."

"Yes, Karin has explained that to me. How do you like your chances against him?"

"He doesn't scare me. Like the rest of us, he's human and capable of making mistakes. However, he has a lot of resources at his disposal. He can turn this into a lengthy trial, if he decides to. So before we even begin to discuss your case, I'll need a retainer in the amount of one hundred thousand dollars."

Nolan waits a beat, hoping Pollard will start laughing, and then say he was just kidding. He remains stone-faced.

"I don't have it. The bail bondsman has a lien on my house to cover the five-hundred-thousand-dollar bail amount and my checking account is tapped out. Can I do it in payments?"

"If you can come up with fifty grand, you can pay the rest out over the next couple of months."

"Sorry, I don't know how I could come up with fifty, much less the balance."

"Well, if you figure something out, I'll be glad to take the case, but don't wait too long to decide."

~39~

Lauren awakens late afternoon. Gordon is lying in bed next to her with one arm draped across her stomach. Greg and Gordon arrived back at the apartment an hour earlier, after stopping off somewhere for a few rounds of cocktails. They walked into the apartment acting all buddy-buddy, with drunken grins on their faces.

Gordon declares, "We're celebrating."

"I can see that," Lauren says. "Does this have something to do with Nolan being arrested?"

Lauren saw the news report of Nolan being charged with Erica's murder on TV. It included video of him in handcuffs standing in a courtroom before a judge. It was difficult to watch. The Nolan she knows is proud and confident. The man in the courtroom was slump-shouldered with his gaze cast downward. He looked broken and defeated.

"Yes, it does have to do with his arrest. It provided us with the grounds to challenge Erica's will. My attorney filed the suit, today."

This news excites Lauren enough to make her forget about Nolan's troubles, and allow Gordon to take her to bed for a celebratory romp. He begins to snore. She raises his arm to slip out from under it, then gets out of bed and begins dressing. He stirs.

"Hey, where are you going?"

"Nowhere, but it's too early to sleep. It's not even dark, yet."

"Okay, I'll get up, too. You want to go out to dinner, tonight?"

"We probably shouldn't splurge like that, since not one of us has any money coming in, right now."

"That's going to change in a big way, once Erica's current will is tossed and the previous one with me as the primary beneficiary is reinstated."

"Did Marv Feldman say how long that would take?"

"He needs the money as much as we do, so he'll push it through as quickly as possible."

"But the bottom line is we're probably looking at a few months, at least. Isn't that right?"

"Yeah, probably. But look at it this way, things have turned around for us. If Nolan gets a speedy trial and conviction, it's a sure thing Erica's will is going to be overturned. We're finally beginning to see light at the end of the tunnel."

~~~

That light is only growing dimmer for Nolan. He makes a few phone calls to lawyers he finds in the Yellow Pages. They're all familiar with the case. It's all over the TV and online. Every one of them is willing to take the case, but only for a substantial fee paid in advance, because he's already been convicted by the public, and getting money out of someone on death row is nearly impossible.

The court will appoint an attorney to represent him, but only if he can show proof of his inability to pay. The problem with that is he *can* pay, just not the tens of thousands of dollars the decent lawyers are demanding. He finds the number for the courthouse and places a call to the judge.

"Judge Juliet Franklin's office," the voice on the other end answers.

"I'd like to speak with Judge Franklin, please."

"She's in court. If you'll give me your name and the purpose of your call, I'll see that she gets it."

"I'm Nolan Drake. I'm a defendant in a trial she's presiding over. My attorney has resigned due to a conflict of interest. I'm going to be representing myself. I thought I should notify the judge, so she'll know to contact me directly if need be."

"I'll let her know."

Next, he calls the District Attorney's Office, to leave the same message. That call is returned in thirty minutes by an assistant.

"I'm ADA Rita Sanchez. District Attorney Hardwick would like to know if you intend to change your plea."

"Absolutely not."

"Then, there's nothing to negotiate."

"I didn't call to negotiate. I called to inform your office I'll be representing myself. You're required to give me a list of the witnesses you intend to call, so I can prepare my questions ahead of time."

"Mr. Drake, things are much different in an actual courtroom than you've been led to believe by the way it's depicted in the movies. My advice to you is to reconsider your decision to represent yourself. The charges against you are extremely serious. If you're found guilty, we'll be asking for the maximum penalty. In Texas, that means lethal injection."

"As I've already stated, Ms. Sanchez. The only reason for my call is so your office knows to contact me directly, if necessary. Have a nice day."

Late in the day, the call to Judge Franklin's office is returned by the same woman Nolan spoke with earlier.

"Mr. Drake, Judge Franklin will assign you an attorney. They will contact you within forty-eight hours."

"I don't know if I qualify for an appointed attorney, and even if I do, I believe I'll be better off representing myself."

Fifteen minutes after that, the judge herself calls.

"Mr. Drake, what part of *I will assign you an attorney* did you not understand? Do you have a law degree? You are on trial for capital murder. It is not a laughing matter, and I will not have you making a mockery of my courtroom by acting as your own attorney."

"With all due respect, Your Honor, no one knows better than me the seriousness of my predicament. I think you know as well as I do, someone who doesn't feel they're being paid fairly for their service, is not going to give their best effort. I may not be schooled in legal procedure, but of everyone in or out of the courtroom I'm the only person who is one hundred percent certain of my innocence."

"Stop right there, Mr. Drake. I've returned your call to urge you to use a court-appointed attorney. I cannot discuss the specifics of your case with you outside of the courtroom, and that includes whether or not you're guilty of the crime."

"Fair enough. I understand, and I won't take up any more of your time. Please have your office contact me directly for scheduling and all other matters concerning the trial."

"Very well, if that's the way you want it, Mr. Drake. I will allow you to act as your own attorney, for now. But be advised, I am not a exceedingly tolerant person. You'd better read everything you can find on courtroom procedure during a criminal trial, between now and the date your trial begins, because no one, including myself is going to cut you any slack. Good luck, and good day sir."

As Nolan ends the conversation with Judge Franklin, his doorbell sounds. Looking through the peephole he sees a FedEx delivery guy holding a large envelope. Nolan warily opens the door a few inches.

"I have a special delivery for Nolan Drake, from Founders Mutual Life Insurance. It requires a signature."

Nolan scribbles his name on the electronic pad, and takes the envelope to the kitchen bar counter to open it. The first sentence of the letter inside informs him that Erica named him as sole beneficiary on a twenty-million-dollar life insurance policy. This is followed by a lengthy paragraph of legal jargon explaining the company's right to withhold payment in cases where the insured is murdered by the beneficiary.

"Great," he says aloud. "Twenty million more reasons for the prosecutor, judge and jury to believe I did it."

~40~

Gordon's day in court comes before Nolan's. In the hearing to determine if his challenge of Erica's will is legitimate, the parties on both sides are eager for a ruling. Nolan is sitting in the back of the room as it begins, and not only because of his interest in the outcome. As of late, he's been attending one or two criminal trials each day as a spectator. It's an excellent way to see the attorneys in action, and pick up a few pointers.

Lauren is the only woman in the courtroom. She and Greg are sitting on the opposite side of the aisle, in the first row, right behind the plaintiff's table. Nolan came in after them. Greg turned his head and spotted him, then whispered to Lauren. She hasn't acknowledged Nolan.

In front of Lauren, Gordon is sitting beside his attorney, Marv Feldman, who is shuffling through a stack of papers in front of him. Alan Rutherford and Joseph Edgar are at the table across from Gordon and Feldman. They're representing Erica's estate, and looking as if they would rather be anywhere else but here. Judge Irvin Reynolds is presiding. A clerk reads the case number and states the reason for it, as if everyone there doesn't already know. Then Judge Reynolds speaks.

"Mr. Feldman, your client, Gordon Weston, is contesting the will of Erica Dupree, his estranged wife."

"Yes, Your Honor. My client believes...," Judge Reynolds holds up his hand to stop Feldman halfway through the sentence.

"The basis of your claim is one of the beneficiaries named in the will is being tried for her murder. Is that correct?"

"Yes, Your Honor."

"Although some states have a so-called slayer's law, Texas does not. Murder does not exclude the murderer from inheriting from the murderer's victim. Are you aware of this?"

"Yes, Your Honor. We believe Erica Dupree was coerced in an unlawful manner by Nolan Drake to change her will. We believe her previous will reflects her true intentions at the time of her death."

"Do you have indisputable evidence of this coercion?"

"Yes, we do."

"Mr. Rutherford, would you care to respond?"

"Erica Dupree conveyed to my colleague, Joseph Edgar, the changes she wished to make to her will. I drew up her final will and testament, and was present when she signed it. Two other witnesses besides myself were there as well. The witnesses and I signed a statement saying we believed Erica Dupree to be of sound mind when the will was signed and appeared to be acting of her own free will, without outside influence. All signatures were notarized."

"If I may, Your Honor," Feldman says.

"Go ahead."

"Mr. Rutherford's judgement and that of the witnesses he mentioned was based on the five or ten minutes it took to sign the papers. My client was married to Erica Dupree for five years. He's more capable of determining whether or not she was under emotional duress during the period leading up to the changing of her will."

Rutherford speaks out, "Erica Dupree has been a client of our firm for her entire adult life, long before she met Gordon Weston."

"You knew her as a client. It was a business relationship. You just said so. That's not nearly as close as being married to someone," Feldman says.

"I've heard enough," Judge Reynolds interjects. "I have copies of the contested will and the one which preceded it. I'll review those and rule on whether or not the claim merits a trial. That's all."

Nolan rises and leaves the room ahead of everyone else. He stops Alan Rutherford in the hallway outside the courtroom. Rutherford glances around as if he's worried about being seen talking to Nolan.

"Do you think this thing will go to trial?" Nolan asks him.

"I'm not going to speculate on what the judge will decide. No offense Mr. Drake, but I really shouldn't be discussing this with you, right now."

He moves around Nolan heading for the elevator. Nolan watches him go. Then, Gordon, Lauren and Greg emerge from the courtroom. Nolan and Gordon lock eyes for a moment, but neither is eager for a confrontation. Greg looks nervous and anxious to leave. Lauren calmly examines her nails. Then, Gordon turns and walks toward the stairwell. Lauren and Greg follow him. Feldman stops to talk with Nolan.

"I heard you're planning to represent yourself in the murder trial."

"That's right," Nolan replies, coolly.

"I could recommend somebody, if you're interested."

"Thanks just the same, but I have a whole page of recommendations."

"Suit yourself," Feldman says, before walking away.

The time spent in the various courtrooms as a spectator has taught Nolan two things. The first of those is, the judicial system has nothing to do with justice. Those who are a part of the system, the judges, prosecutors and defense attorneys, are protective of their turf. They like having the home-field advantage and resent outsiders playing in their ballpark. It's a classic us-and-them mentality. His guilt or innocence won't be a factor to the judge and prosecutor in his trial. It's all about winning or losing to them. His only hope for an acquittal lies with his ability to elicit sympathy from the jurors. The second thing he's learned is, the longer you're around those who look at you as a criminal, the more you start to believe it yourself.

~41~

Nolan's trial begins with the jury selection. Between one hundred and one hundred twenty people receive a summons to appear for jury duty. On average, eighty or ninety of them show up, and out of those, twelve jurors and two alternates are selected. Nolan was able to view the process take place at two other trials, while waiting for the calendar to roll around to his own court date. The attorneys for both sides seem to place a great deal of importance in choosing the right twelve individuals. While they are trying to decide, there's a lot of whispering between the attorneys and their jury consultants. The whole process seems to boil down to a shared belief that all people of the same gender, race, income or age think alike.

Nolan isn't confident he'll be able to make the best selections based on the questions asked and what he gleans from their mannerisms. He would probably do just as well to flip a coin. At the same time, he doesn't feel it's that important. The jury members are outsiders like himself. They're more likely to empathize with him rather than with the prosecutor. His game plan is to play on his inexperience and ignorance of procedure. The prosecution will call a dozen witnesses, while he calls none. The DA will want him to take the stand. Hardwick will badger him, hoping to make him slip up somehow, and come off as a bully in the eyes of the jurors, as a result.   Unless Hardwick can present indisputable evidence Nolan killed Erica—and Nolan is certain no such evidence exists—the jury will have no choice other than to acquit him.

The prospective jurors occupy all the seats in the gallery. They're called in groups of twelve to take seats in the jury box, so Nolan and the DA can take turns posing questions. They can ask the question of the group as a whole or direct it to one person. All the while this is going on, three people assisting the DA are taking notes as they watch the reaction of the prospective jurors, both in the jury box and in the gallery.

"Have you or anyone in your immediate family ever been convicted of a violent crime?" Hardwick asks Della Jimenez, one of the jury candidates. She's a Hispanic woman, age fifty-four, who has three grown children and works as a hotel maid, according to her profile sheet. Being singled out for that particular question offends her.

"No, sir," she answers, indignantly.

Then, it's Nolan's turn to ask a question. "Have any of you seen my picture in the paper, online or on TV in connection with the murder of Erica Dupree?"

All twelve raise their hands.

"Have any of you formed an opinion as to my innocence?"

All twelve shake their heads to indicate they haven't.

"Will it bother you to listen to witnesses describe in graphic detail how the victim was bludgeoned to death?" Hardwick asks Grace Farrell, a fair-skinned and petite, thirty-something woman. She gives Hardwick a puzzled look, like she doesn't fully understand his reason for asking her.

"A little, I guess. I mean, most people are, aren't they?"

Nolan doesn't understand Hardwick's reason for asking the question, either. It seems his intention is to promote the upcoming trial as spectacular and gory. Maybe he does it to get the jurors fired up, and emotionally invested in the outcome, ahead of time.

By four o'clock that afternoon, twelve jurors and two alternates have been selected from the pool of prospects, and the rest are sent home. Judge Franklin decides to adjourn for the day. She speaks to the jurors before dismissing them.

"You are not to discuss the trial or anything that happens in this courtroom with anyone, not even your immediate family. I want you all back here, promptly at eight a.m. Mr. Hardwick, be prepared to give your opening statement at that time."

Nolan exits the courtroom through a side door that leads to the stairwell, in order to avoid the cameras and reporters' questions. As he descends the stairs to the lobby, he removes his jacket and tie, then dons a ball cap and sunglasses. Meanwhile, Hardwick is heading toward the courthouse steps where the media is gathered to capture a sound bite or two for the evening news. He smiles for the cameras and promises those watching to bring Erica's killer to justice.

"How long do you expect the trial to take?" one of the reporters asks.

"We're certain we have the right man, and I believe the jury won't deliberate long before coming to the same conclusion. I expect it to be over in two or three days, unless Drake decides to change his plea and confess."

"How likely is that?"

"I think there's a good chance of it happening. Once I start calling witnesses, he's going to know there's no way out."

~~~

Hardwick's opening statement was prepared weeks in advance. Actually it's a version of one he's used before. He just changes the names, tweaks it some and recycles it. Nolan works on his until late into the night, and still isn't satisfied with it when he arrives at the courthouse the next morning.

"Mr. Hardwick, are you prepared to give your opening statement?" Judge Franklin asks, as things get under way.

"Yes, Your Honor."

He stands, straightens his posture and strides purposely toward a pre-selected spot where every member of the jury and everyone else in the courtroom can see and hear him. He is dressed impeccably in a finely tailored dark gray suit, with a tie the same shade of blue as a policeman's uniform, and freshly shined black oxford shoes. This is his stage, and the jury is his audience.

"Erica Dupree was an heir to the Dupree Oil and Gas financial empire. She used her wealth to help thousands of people in need. As a philanthropist she was legendary. She was only thirty-five when she was brutally bludgeoned to death in her home, by that man sitting right there." He turns theatrically to point an accusing finger at Nolan, before continuing. "I will prove his guilt beyond any shadow of a doubt. I will carefully explain how he planned the killing. His motive for doing it was the oldest one on the books. He wanted her money. I will walk you through the crime scene, and tell you how, where and when Erica was killed. I will place Nolan Drake there at the time of the killing and show you the weapon he used. You will hear testimony from the officers who responded to the 9-1-1 call, the detectives who investigated her murder, the medical examiner and two members of her household staff. We all concur that only one person could have done it." He does the thing with the accusing finger, again. "That man right there, Nolan Drake. The only thing I cannot do is render a verdict. Only you, the jury, can do that. And after I have presented the evidence, you will conclude as I have, he is guilty."

With a humble-servant-of-the-people expression affixed to his face, and his head bowed slightly, he slowly moves his gaze from one juror to the next, imploring them with his eyes to believe what he is telling them. Then, he returns to his seat.

"Mr. Drake, you may give your opening statement, now."

Nolan's sport coat and slacks are ill-fitting and mismatched. His brightly colored tie gives the ensemble a bit of comic relief. He elicits looks of disapproval from Judge Franklin and pity from Hardwick. He rises with a sheet of paper in hand, which he carries with him to the same spot where Hardwick stood to address the jury.

"Good morning. I'm Nolan Drake. I'd like to thank you members of the jury for donating your time to be here. I'm not sure whether or not Mr. Hardwick believes what he just told you, but it isn't true. He can't prove the existence of something which isn't there. Why would he lie? The second oldest reason on the books, selfishness and greed. He likes his job and the perks that come with it. It's an elected position. Winning a high-profile murder case will go a long way toward getting him reelected this fall. Since it is logistically impossible to present indisputable evidence of me committing a crime which I didn't, I have to assume Mr. Hardwick intends to dazzle you with smoke and mirrors. Don't fall for his tricks. As he presents the so-called evidence against me, you might have to sift through a lot of innuendo and illusions to reach the facts. That may not be as easy as it sounds. Mr. Hardwick is a capable and experienced prosecutor with a lot of resources he can call upon. This is his arena. You and I, we're new at this. I'm trusting you to judge me fairly, based on the facts presented and not the illusion."

Nolan returns to his seat, and Judge Franklin doesn't waste any time moving things along.

"Mr. Hardwick, you may call your first witness."

~42~

The first witness called by Hardwick is Officer Gary Young. He was the first policeman to arrive at Erica's house in response to the 9-1-1 call. It is clear Hardwick intends to use his testimony to set the stage. No doubt he's been coached on what to say and what not to say. Hardwick walks Young through Hernando letting him in the front door and leading him to the kitchen where Erica's body lay in the pantry.

"Where was the defendant, Mr. Drake when you entered the kitchen?"

"The defendant was kneeling next to the body of the victim."

"Was he checking her pulse, or attempting to resuscitate her?"

"No. He was just looking at her."

"Did he appear to be in a state of shock, like you would expect from someone who only minutes earlier found their lover unconscious and lying in a pool of blood?"

Franklin glances at Nolan in anticipation of an objection, but he's more focused on the jury than on Young's testimony.

"He looked pretty calm to me. I thought it was odd. I mean, there was a lot of blood. Most people are disturbed by that."

"Did he speak to you, or you to him while he was kneeling beside the victim's body?"

"I asked him if he was okay. He acted like he didn't hear. Then, I told him to move away from her. I did so because I was afraid he might throw up or something and contaminate the crime scene."

"That was the proper thing to do, Officer Young. Your witness," Hardwick says to Nolan.

"I have no questions for Officer Young," Nolan replies.

Hardwick calls the medical examiner, Phillip Uric, to testify, next. He's a heavyset man in his sixties, with gray hair and beard.

"What caused Ms. Dupree's death, Doctor Uric?"

"Her death was the direct result of blunt force trauma to the head. She was struck on the right rear section of her head, hard enough to crack her skull, causing her brain to swell. She also lost a significant amount of blood."

"Could her injuries have been caused by bumping her head or falling and striking her head against a hard surface?"

"It's very improbable the blow could have happened by a fall or an accidental bumping of her head. The impact from either of those wouldn't have been enough to do that sort of damage to the skull."

"What was the time of death?"

"She died between twelve and two a.m., Saturday."

"Given the severity of the injury, would you say her death was immediate?"

"It's more likely she was knocked unconscious and died from the loss of blood, anywhere from thirty minutes to three hours afterward."

"Is it possible her life could have been saved if the person who hit her had called 9-1-1, immediately?"

"Taking into consideration her age and condition of health, if the blood loss had been slowed, and she was rushed to a hospital, it's very likely she would have survived."

"Apparently, the person who hit her did so with the intention of killing her. Is that what you're saying?"

"It would seem so."

Franklin glances at Nolan, again. He's jotting notes onto a pad.

"I have no more questions for this witness."

"Do you wish to question this witness, Mr. Drake?"

"No, Your Honor."

As Uric vacates the witness stand, Hardwick takes a minute to discuss strategy with his team. They seem to be trying to determine who to call next.

"We're waiting, Mr. Hardwick."

"I'd like to call Detective Ray Brown," he says, after a beat.

Brown rises from his seat in the first row behind the prosecution's table and trudges forward. He glares at Nolan as he drops his bulky frame onto the witness seat.

"You're the detective in charge of the investigation into the murder of Erica Dupree. Is that correct?"

"Yes."

"What led you to suspect Nolan Drake, initially?"

"At first it was just a feeling. When a person has been doing this sort of work for as long as I have, he develops a sixth sense about people. Of course, that in itself isn't enough to arrest someone over. But as the investigation progressed, everything we looked at kept pointing back to Drake."

"You say everything you looked at. Could you be more specific?"

"For instance, he was already in the kitchen when the maid, Phuong Nguyen got there around nine a.m. She told me he seemed startled when he saw her. She also said that Ms. Dupree and Drake were the only ones in the house that night, and we found no signs of forced entry on any of the doors or windows. Two days later in our investigation, we discovered Ms. Dupree had recently changed her will, and named Drake as a beneficiary."

"Did Ms. Nguyen say what the defendant was doing in the kitchen the morning Ms. Dupree's body was found in that same kitchen?"

"She said it was unusual for anyone other than her or Hernando Perez, Ms. Dupree's assistant, to be in the kitchen so early in the morning."

"Did you ask Mr. Drake why he was in the kitchen?"

Yes, I did. He said he was looking for Ms. Dupree. He went on to say that although they went to bed at the same time, he didn't see her during the night."

"What did you make of that?"

"It sounded to me like they might have had a quarrel over something, and he or she went to sleep in a different bed."

"Let's back up for a minute. Did the maid say when Mr. Drake arrived at the house the previous evening?"

"Yes. She said it was six p.m. Ms. Dupree left instructions with her to send Drake to her bedroom when he arrived. She took their dinner to the bedroom at seven, and then had the rest of the night off."

"So, she didn't see or hear anything of Ms. Dupree and Mr. Drake until she discovered Ms. Dupree's body at nine the next morning?"

"That's correct."

"It's entirely possible Ms. Dupree and Mr. Drake quarreled, as you suspected they did, and that Mr. Drake killed her and carried her body to the kitchen. Isn't that so?"

Because Nolan doesn't seem inclined to object, Judge Franklin feels duty bound to do so for him. "Don't lead the witness, Mr. Hardwick. Just ask the questions, and leave it to him to provide the answers."

"Yes, Your Honor. Since Phuong Nguyen left after serving dinner at seven, she wouldn't have been able to hear them arguing upstairs in the bedroom. Isn't that right?"

Franklin slams her gavel down hard for emphasis. "Turn the page, Mr. Hardwick. I'm not going to warn you again."

"Yes, Your Honor. I have no further questions for this witness, now, but I may want to recall him, later."

Brown starts to step down as Hardwick prepares to call the next witness.

"Your Honor, I have a question for the witness," Nolan says.

"It's about time," Franklin replies, which draws a few chuckles from the jury box. "Go ahead Mr. Drake."

"Detective Brown, I'd like you to clarify something for the jury. In your testimony you said Phuong was off work at seven p.m. and came into the kitchen the next morning at nine a.m. Where was she between those times?"

"Objection!" Hardwick cries out. "Ms. Nguyen is not on trial here."

"Overruled, sit down, Mr. Hardwick. The witness will answer the question."

"I believe she was in her room."

"You mean her room, thirty feet down the hallway off the kitchen. Isn't that right?"

"I'm not sure of the distance. It's probably closer to fifty feet."

"Erica referred to that section of the house as the servants' wing. Phuong and Hernando both stayed in the wing between their shifts. Isn't that correct?"

"I couldn't say what they do when they're not working. I didn't ask because it wasn't relevant to our investigation."

"Isn't it misleading to the jury to say Erica and I were alone in the house at the time she was killed?"

"I was referring to the main part of the house."

"It's all one structure Detective Brown. Your crime lab people went over the entire house inside and out, didn't they?"

"Yes."

"Did they find any signs of a struggle in the master bedroom?"

"That's hard to say."

225

"What's hard to say, yes or no?"

"It's sometimes hard to determine, I should say. There was no broken furniture or vases, but that doesn't necessarily tell the whole story."

"Let me ask it another way. Was there anything, anything at all, found in the master bedroom suite that could be considered credible evidence of an argument, struggle or disagreement of any kind?"

"Not yet."

Judge Franklin grows impatient with the witness stalling and says, "Detective Brown, this trial is taking place as we speak. Do not allude to evidence you might stumble across at some time in the future while you are under oath in this courtroom. Is that clear?"

"Yes, Your Honor."

Nolan notices a few of the jurors are amused by Brown's reprimand from Judge Franklin. The big detective presses his lips together tightly enough to snap a pencil in half.

"Mr. Drake, do you have any more questions for Detective Brown?"

"One or two more, if you don't mind."

"Go ahead."

"You testified your people found no windows or doors that had been tampered with, or in other words there was no forced entry, correct?"

"Yes, which means the killer was inside the house."

"Really, it that what it means? Can't a person with a key enter through a door without damaging it or forcing it open?"

"I suppose so."

"Did you attempt to find out who else might have a key?"

"There's no way of getting that information."

"In other words there could be dozens, maybe hundreds of spare keys floating around."

"I wouldn't know."

"That might be the first truthful answer you've given, today."

Brown leans forward and starts to reply, but Judge Franklin cuts in.

"Watch yourself Mr. Drake. Is that all of your questions?"

"Yes, Your Honor."

"Detective Brown, you can step down. The Court will recess for lunch, and reconvene at one o'clock. Members of the jury, I'll remind you not to discuss the case outside of this courtroom."

~43~

Nolan finds the jury much more difficult to read than he thought would be the case. As they return to the jury box after lunch, he unsuccessfully attempts to make eye contact with a few of them. The prosecution team is doing exactly the opposite. They're scanning through paperwork, ignoring everyone else in the room.

"Mr. Hardwick, call your next witness," Franklin says, to begin the afternoon session.

He calls Phuong Nguyen to the stand. She appears nervous as the court registrar holds the bible in front of her and asks her, "Do you swear that the testimony you are about to give is the truth, the whole truth and nothing but the truth, so help you God?"

"Yes," she replies, timidly.

"Ms. Nguyen, please speak up so the jury can hear you," Franklin instructs.

"Ms. Nguyen, how long have you worked for Erica Dupree?"

"Two years and four months."

"Did you enjoy working for her, was she a fair employer?"

"I liked it there very much. She was good to me. She was my friend."

"I know this is hard to talk about, but I need to ask you about the morning you found her dead. Would you tell us in your words about that morning from the time you left your room, until the police arrived?"

"I left my room at about nine, and went to the kitchen for my breakfast. When I opened the service door to the kitchen, Mr. Drake was standing there. His back was to me, and he was startled by the door opening, I think, because he turned around quickly. I asked him if he wanted me to make breakfast for him. He said he would like coffee and that he would wait in the dining room while I made it. Then, I opened the pantry door."

She drops her gaze for a moment. When she looks up again, her eyes are moist with tears. She has the full attention, as well as the sympathy of every juror. It's the first show of emotion Nolan has seen from them.

"That's when you found her body, isn't it?" Hardwick prods.

She nods in response.

"We need for you to reply verbally," Franklin tells her.

"Yes, that is when I found Ms. Dupree."

"Where was Mr. Drake at that moment?"

"He wasn't in the kitchen. When I saw her, I screamed. I guess he heard me, because he came back to the kitchen very quickly."

"Did it seem to you as if he was waiting just outside the door, knowing what you'd find inside the pantry?"

"I don't know."

"He apparently was very close by, wasn't he?"

"I think so."

"Detective Brown testified earlier that you left work at seven on the evening before. Is that correct?"

"Yes. Ms. Dupree told me to bring the dinner to her bedroom at seven, and after that I was not to disturb her."

"Did you go directly to your room?"

"I made dinner for myself, first. I took it to my room to eat."

"If Ms. Dupree and Mr. Drake had a loud argument, would you be able to hear it from your room?"

"Objection," Nolan says. "He's leading the witness, again."

"Sustained," Franklin replies.

"Ms. Nguyen, what was Mr. Drake's reaction to seeing Ms. Dupree lying in a pool of her own blood inside the kitchen pantry?" Phuong is puzzled by the question. "Did he scream or cry? Was he emotional or was he calm as if he wasn't surprised to see her there?"

"He shouted at me to call 9-1-1."

"Shouted? As if he was angry at you?"

"No, more like he wanted me to hurry."

"Did you call 9-1-1, as he told you to do?"

"No."

"Who did make the call? Wasn't it Mr. Drake himself who eventually took the phone from his own pocket and made the call?"

"Yes."

"Why do you think he wanted you to make the call, instead of himself?"

Nolan considers objecting, but the jury has already picked up on Hardwick's innuendo. To object now might give the appearance of him trying to suppress damaging evidence.

"I don't know," Phuong answers, and Hardwick tells Franklin he's done with her.

"Mr. Drake."

"Phuong, how many times have I been to the house to see Erica?

"I'm not sure."

"I've been there around eighty times. Does that sound about right?"

"Yes."

"Have you ever seen Erica and me argue with one another, raise our voices or get mad?"

230

"No."

"When you come or go from the house, do you use the service entrance close to your room?"

"Yes."

"Other than you and Hernando, is there anyone else who comes or goes through that door?"

She hesitates long enough to indicate she's unsure of whether or not to tell the truth.

"The caterers use that door when Ms. Dupree has a party."

"Do you know if the catering service has a key?"

"It isn't necessary. There's a keypad on the outside. You have to enter a code to unlock the door."

"On the night Erica was murdered, did you see or hear anyone come through that entrance?"

She hesitates again, this time even longer.

"The witness will answer the question," Franklin says.

"Not that I remember," Phuong says, finally.

"Thank you, Phuong. I don't have any more questions."

The next person to testify for the prosecution is Detective Sylvia Gutierrez. Of the two detectives who questioned him, she seems more even-tempered and somehow less threatening.

"Detective Gutierrez, you work for Detective Ray Brown, and took part in the Erica Dupree murder investigation. Correct?"

"Not quite. Detective Brown works under me. I'm the lead investigator on the case."

"Oh, I'm sorry. I apparently was misinformed on that matter."

"There's no apology necessary."

"At the beginning of this murder investigation, did you have other suspects besides Mr. Drake?"

"Yes. Initially, it appeared there were others who had more motive and opportunity. We interviewed or investigated about a dozen suspects. Her estranged husband, former employees of Ms. Dupree and a few others."

"But, you eventually came back to Mr. Drake. Can you tell us why?"

"My partner, Detective Brown had a strong feeling about Mr. Drake from the first. I didn't agree, but sometimes I'm wrong about people, so I let him keep digging. He discovered that Mr. Drake is mentioned in Ms. Dupree's will, and would receive a substantial amount of money if she died. That gave us the motive. He had no alibi, because the only person who might have provided him with one for the time of the murder was the victim herself."

"How much money was he to receive, according to her will?"

"The executor of her estate gave us a rough estimate. Those are his words. It comes to a little less than four hundred million dollars."

The noise level in the courtroom rises as people gasp and whisper to one another. Franklin brings her gavel down to silence them.

"Did Mr. Drake think to mention that to you during your first interview with him?"

"His attorney at the time, Karin Hearn claimed he didn't know until the will was read six days after she died."

"Do you believe her?"

"I think, she believes what she's telling us, but we'll never know what Ms. Dupree told Mr. Drake before she died. My job is to follow every lead until it either doesn't pan out or produces a conviction."

"Your witness, Mr. Drake," Hardwick says.

"Detective Gutierrez, you allude to the possibility that I may have known I was included in Erica's will before her death. In fact you stated it was my motive for killing her. Do you have any physical evidence, a witness, sworn statement or anything else to support your belief I knew of it ahead of time? Or, was it just a hunch?"

"We obtained a copy of her will. That's the physical evidence. It was a solid lead, and we followed it as our job requires us to do."

"You're evading the question, Detective. Can you prove to the jury that I knew what was in Erica's will before she died? Yes or no."

"No."

"Thank you. Did you and Detective Brown obtain and execute a search warrant for my residence?"

"Yes, we received a tip concerning jewelry stolen from Ms. Dupree's house, and acted on the information."

"While you were there, did you find anything to connect me with the murder of Erica Dupree, like a murder weapon or bloodstained clothing?"

"We found a watch, which Ms. Dupree's sister identified as a part of a jewelry collection that had belonged to their grandmother. It's a family heirloom that she wouldn't have sold or given away, according to her sister."

"And from what the sister said, you surmised I must have stolen the watch. How did you make the leap from theft to murder?"

"If Ms. Dupree discovered the watch missing and confronted you, it could have led to a physical altercation that got out of hand."

"Isn't the real reason you pursued and eventually arrested me, because the DA's office pressured you to find someone to blame for Erica's murder?"

"Objection, Your Honor," Hardwick says.

"Sustained. Do you have any more questions, Mr. Drake?"

"Yes, I do. Detective Gutierrez, the tip you received that led to the search of my house. Where did that come from?"

"It came from a phone call placed to our tip line."

"You're referring to the anonymous tip line? The one where people call with information regarding a crime, but aren't required to give their name or how they acquired the information."

"Some people who call the tip line choose not to give their name, but all information is verified."

"That's all the questions I have for Detective Gutierrez."

"You can step down, Detective Gutierrez. Mr. Hardwick, call your next witness, please."

"At this time, I'd like to call Gordon Weston to testify."

~44~

Nolan isn't aware Gordon is in the courtroom until Hardwick calls him to the witness stand. He's curious if Lauren is here as well, but isn't going to turn to look, because at the moment he's more curious about what Gordon will say. The man has no qualms over telling lies if he thinks it will benefit him somehow.

"Mr. Weston," Hardwick begins. "How long were you and Ms. Dupree married?"

"It would have been six years in September."

"Is it true she filed for divorce in November of last year?"

"Yes, she began seeing another man and thought at the time she wanted to be with him more than me."

"The man she was seeing, did she say who it was?"

"Yes, it was the man who murdered her, Nolan Drake."

"Mr. Weston, confine your testimony to answering the questions asked, and nothing more. The jury will disregard his last statement," Franklin says.

"During the period between your separation and her death, did you speak with her at all?"

Yes, we spoke often. We were very close, even after we separated. She would call just to talk. In the week preceding her death she was beginning to have second thoughts about the divorce. She and Mr. Drake weren't getting along. We were discussing a reconciliation two days before she died."

"She told you they weren't getting along? Did she elaborate on what she meant by that?"

"He has a volatile temper. She wanted to break it off with him, but was afraid of what he might do."

"That's a blatant lie!" Nolan shouts at Gordon.

Franklin slams her gavel down. "One more outburst like that, Mr. Drake, and you'll be watching this trial from a jail cell. Continue, Mr. Hardwick."

"Did Ms. Dupree ever tell you about Mr. Drake striking her or getting physically violent with her?"

"Not in those words, but I know firsthand that he is capable of physical violence. He attacked me in my office. I was afraid he was going to kill me. He punched and kicked me, while I begged him to stop. If someone hadn't called security, I might not be alive, today. He was arrested for that incident, and I was hospitalized."

"That sounds like a traumatic experience. What was it that set him off that day?"

"I was in my office with a woman who was working for me at the time. We were in the middle of discussing investment strategies when Drake starts banging on my office door, calling the woman's name. As it turns out, he has a history with her. He came to my office to confront her because he convinced himself the woman and I were romantically involved. Once inside my office, he unleashed his rage on me."

"Are you saying he appeared delusional, as well as enraged?"

"Yes. He totally lost control."

"A moment ago, you said Ms. Dupree wanted to break it off with Mr. Drake, but was afraid to do so. Did she ever express fear that he might harm her?"

"Yes. The day before she died she called to talk. She had decided to tell him that evening when he came to her house. I asked her if she wanted me to be there, in case he went off

236

the deep end when she told him. She said no. I wish now I had insisted. If I'd been there, maybe she'd still be alive."

Hardwick ends the questioning of Gordon on that note. Nolan can see from the expressions on the faces of the jurors, Hardwick has scored points in their minds with Gordon's testimony. Never mind that not one word of it was true. He decides against questioning Gordon. He would just tell the same lies over again, and the jury would hear them for a second time.

Hardwick calls Hernando Perez, next. He looks even more apprehensive than Phuong did during her testimony.

"Mr. Perez, how long did you work for Ms. Dupree?"

"Four years."

"The room where you stayed was near Phuong Nguyen's room. Isn't that right?"

"Yes, across the hall."

"On the night Ms. Dupree was murdered, did you hear anyone coming and going in the hallway outside your room, or using the service entrance?"

Hernando's eyes dart to one side for an instant, before he says, "No."

It's doubtful anyone on the jury noticed, but Nolan clearly did.

"How did you learn about Ms. Dupree?"

"Phuong told me. She came to my room and said the police have been called because Ms. Dupree is badly injured."

"Mr. Drake didn't call to you for help?"

"No."

"Where was he when you entered the kitchen, after Phuong told you Ms. Dupree was hurt?"

"He was inside the pantry closet, squatting beside Ms. Dupree."

"And this is before the police or EMS arrived. Is that right?"

"Yes."

"Was he attempting to resuscitate Ms. Dupree, or trying to determine if she was still alive?"

"No, not that I could see."

"Thank you, Mr. Perez. I have no more questions."

"Mr. Drake," Franklin prompts.

Nolan has a hunch about what caused Hernando to hesitate when asked if he heard anyone outside his room. Phuong reacted in the same way when asked a similar question.

"Hernando, you said you didn't hear anyone in the hallway outside your room that night. Was there anyone in your room with you? Did you have a guest staying with you on that night?"

Hernando fidgets nervously, but quickly denies there was anyone with him.

"No, I was alone in my room. I never have overnight guests."

Nolan looks at the jurors, letting his gaze linger, and asking with his eyes if they also are skeptical of what the witness is saying, but he doesn't press Hernando further. Franklin tells him to step down.

"The Court will adjourn for the day," Judge Franklin declares, and instructs the jury once again to not discuss the trial outside of the courtroom.

The room empties out, with Franklin and the jurors leaving through a secure passageway. Hardwick and the spectators exit into the main hallway, and Nolan goes out the side door next to the stairwell. Halfway down the first flight of stairs a reporter catches up with him.

"Mr. Drake, do you intend to change your plea?"

"No, why would I? I didn't kill or harm Erica in any way."

"The DA is telling the media his case is rock solid. He thinks you'll realize it and ask for a deal. Would you care to comment on that?"

"Not really."

"Mr. Drake, you've been avoiding the reporters, while the DA is always accessible. The public might interpret that to mean you're guilty."

"Right now, I'm only worried about what the jury thinks."

"You don't think they're watching the evening news, like everyone else?"

"They're smart people. I think they can see through the smoke screen the DA is presenting to the press. I trust them to treat me fairly."

~45~

Nolan knows he won't get much sleep tonight. Hardwick will call his last witnesses in the morning. Then, it will be his turn to present a defense. At the outset of the trial, he believed—or hoped rather—it wouldn't be necessary to call any witnesses to testify on his behalf. He was counting on the prosecution's case being so weak, all he would have to do is request the charges against him be dismissed for lack of evidence. The DA and his team have surprised Nolan. At least a few of the jurors seem to be buying into his version of how Erica died.

As Nolan is considering a strategy for his defense, his doorbell sounds. All lights are off in the rooms in the front part of the house by the entry. He quietly steps up to the entry door to look through the peephole. A man he doesn't recognize is holding an official-looking photo ID at eye level for Nolan to read. He flips on the outside light, and opens the door a crack.

"Mr. Drake, my name is Curtis Leyden. I recently helped Erica Dupree with a few matters. I have some information which may be helpful to your defense. May I come in, so we can talk privately?" Nolan is unsure he wants to trust the man. "I understand your apprehension, but I can assure you I have something you need to see."

"Okay," Nolan consents, finally. He opens the door wider and steps aside. Once Curtis is inside, Nolan shuts the door and asks, "What did you do for Erica?"

"Ms. Dupree first contacted me to investigate her husband, Gordon Weston."

"You're the investigator that took the pictures of Gordon and Lauren, aren't you?"

"Yes, but this has nothing to do with that. She also asked me to have some hidden cameras installed at her home."

Nolan immediately understands the significance of this. "Where are the cameras located? Would they have captured video of her being attacked?"

"The cameras I had installed are in the servants' wing. As far as I know, there are no cameras elsewhere in the house. I've viewed the video feed from that night, and Erica isn't on it. If there's someplace I can set up my laptop, I'll show you what is on it."

Nolan leads Curtis into his office, where he sets the laptop on Nolan's desk and turns it on. It takes a minute to warm up and come to life. Then, Curtis clicks a few keys to bring up the first file.

"There's a hidden camera in each room, and one covering the service entrance. This video I'm about to show you is in the Vietnamese girl's room. She had her boyfriend over that night."

Curtis starts the video forward. It shows Phuong enter the room at seven twenty carrying a tray with two plates of food and two glasses containing a beverage. There's a man waiting there for her.

"I've viewed the feed from the camera pointed at the service door. He came in about thirty minutes earlier, and went straight to her room. At eight fifteen, she takes the tray and dishes back to the kitchen. She returns to the room eight minutes later. They watch TV in bed for the next few hours, then it's turned off and the camera doesn't record anything more for a while. That's because the cameras are motion sensitive. At one-oh-five a.m. the boyfriend leaves the room and goes through the door to the kitchen. He comes back fifteen minutes later."

"Have you told the police about this? I'm pretty sure Phuong hasn't told them about the boyfriend."

"I talked to a Detective Ray Brown. He said they had plenty of evidence against you and didn't need any more, which I took to mean the DA didn't want anything popping up that might mess up his working theory on what happened that night. Let me show you a couple of other files."

He clicks on a second one and plays it forward.

"This is Hernando Perez's room. As you can see, he had a guest in his room that night, too. This is him entering the room at ten-oh-five. He came in the service door and went straight to Hernando's room. I'm going to skip past this part with these two in bed. At eleven fifty, Hernando's guest leaves the room and goes through the door to the kitchen. He comes back to the room at five minutes before one."

"The medical examiner put her time of death between twelve and two a.m. He thinks the attack might have taken place as much as three hours before. This guy must be her murderer."

"Maybe not. I've got one more to show you." As Curtis is bringing up the next file, he comments, "This guy came in the service entrance at eleven twenty-five and went through the kitchen door. He left by the same way at eleven forty-five, just five minutes before the other guy comes out of Hernando's room."

"That means it could have been either of them. Or both for that matter. They could have been working together."

Curtis starts the next file forward and says, "Do you recognize him?"

The image is grainy, and the person has their head down, but as he comes nearer the camera, Nolan identifies him.

"Greg?!" he exclaims.

"That right. It's Greg Malloy, Lauren's husband."

"What was he doing there?" Then, Nolan remembers the last time he saw Greg, and how not long afterward his house was searched because of an anonymous tip. "The watch."

"Pardon me?"

"The police accused me of stealing a watch from Erica. They received a tip, searched my house and found it. That must be what he was doing there, stealing the watch. Gordon would have told him how to get into the house and where the watch was. He came to my house under false pretenses, and while he was there he planted the watch. Two days later the police find it right where their anonymous tipster told them to look."

"That's not uncommon for local law enforcement agencies to use an anonymous tip to do a search when they have nothing else to justify a warrant. I'm a retired FBI agent. We ran across that sort of thing all the time."

"Curtis, this has been eye opening for me. I suspected there was something Hernando and Phuong were hiding, but I never in a million years would have figured Greg was involved. The video files might be enough to convince the jury to acquit me. That is, if I can afford them. I mean, I assume they're for sale."

"I'll admit that when I heard about her death, and remembered the cameras, my first thought was how much the video might be worth. Then, my conscience got the better of me. That's when I contacted Detective Brown. Apparently, Brown wasn't bothered with the same conflict of conscience. If the judicial system worked as it was designed to, these files would have been enough to make the DA reconsider charging you. Anyway, what I'm trying to say is, you'll have to call me as a witnesses to get this stuff admitted as evidence. I'm the only one who can verify the authenticity of the video files. Under cross-examination the DA will ask if you purchased the files from me. It's not illegal to pay for evidence, but it could taint my testimony in the eyes of the jury, and you don't want to chance it."

"I don't know what to say, Curtis, other than I'm in your debt for bringing this to me."

"After the trial is over, and you get the money from Ms. Dupree's estate, if you feel a small gift would be an appropriate way of showing your gratitude, I'll gladly accept it. For now, I'll take a beer. And, you might want to grab one for yourself. We've got a lot to cover. The courthouse reporters are saying you begin presenting your defense tomorrow."

~46~

Although he initially hoped it wouldn't be necessary to call any witnesses to testify on his behalf, Nolan did submit a witness list as required, prior to the start of the trial. It included friends, family and coworkers, people he could call on to serve as character witnesses if need be. No doubt, Hardwick will protest the last minute addition of Curtis Leyden, but with a little luck, Judge Franklin will allow it.

"Your Honor, before I call my first witness, today, I'd like to object to Mr. Drake's last minute addition to the witness list. The Court cannot be expected to make allowances for him, due to his ignorance of procedure."

"Your Honor, I only met Curtis Leyden yesterday at six thirty p.m. He contacted me with crucial evidence I'm certain will vindicate me of all charges in this case."

"Stop right there, Mr. Drake. Don't say another word. Both of you approach the bench." When Nolan and Hardwick are near enough to discuss the matter without being overheard by the jury, Franklin says, "Don't make statements like that in front of the jury. Who is this Curtis Leyden, and what is the evidence he has?"

"Mr. Leyden is a retired FBI agent who does security consulting. He worked for Erica recently. His testimony is necessary to authenticate video recorded on hidden cameras inside a wing of Erica's house on the night she was killed."

"Your Honor, the prosecution has the right to see the video ahead of the jury, and to have it validated by our own experts beforehand."

"And I have the right to a fair and speedy trial."

"Mr. Hardwick, how long do you need to view and validate the video?"

"I guess that depends on how long the video is."

"It will only be necessary to show selected images. My presentation will take five minutes or less."

"How many more witnesses do you intend to call, Mr. Hardwick, and when do you expect to complete that?"

"I have only one more witness, I'll be done by ten thirty."

"Alright, here's what we're going to do. We will break for lunch after you're done with your last witness. During the long lunch you'll view the video and have an expert look at it. When we reconvene at one, Mr. Drake will present his defense. Now step back, and Mr. Hardwick call your final witness."

Nolan and Hardwick return to their respective tables. Nolan sits. Hardwick remains standing to say, "The prosecution calls the defendant, Nolan Drake to the stand."

Nolan has been expecting this. Hardwick will use his courtroom experience, and exploit Nolan's lack of it, during this one-on-one exchange. When Nolan said to Franklin he planned to call a witness who would exonerate him, it swung the jury momentum in his favor. Now, Hardwick will try to regain most of what was lost.

"Mr. Drake, before meeting and becoming involved with Erica Dupree, what did you do for a living?"

"I'm an architect, and I own an architectural design company."

"Your federal income tax return for last year showed your personal income to be eighty-six thousand dollars. Ms. Dupree's investment income for the same period was more than twenty million dollars. How did that make you feel?"

"I don't understand the question."

"Were you envious of her wealth? Did you feel inadequate? Hers was a flamboyant lifestyle. Something you weren't accustomed to. It must have made you uncomfortable at times, like you weren't worthy."

"I wasn't envious of her, and I was never uncomfortable around Erica. Our relationship didn't revolve around her wealth. She told me she was a Dupree when we met. It was never discussed afterward. She didn't hide the fact that she was rich from me, but she didn't flaunt it or try to impress me with it, either."

"You said, she told you she was a Dupree when you met her. What were the circumstances of that meeting?"

"Erica came to my office to inform me of an affair between her husband, Gordon Weston and Lauren Malloy, the woman who was living with me at the time. She showed me pictures of them together."

"And, that's when you began seeing Ms. Dupree?"

"No. We didn't begin seeing one another until later, after she had separated from Gordon and I had ended things with Lauren."

"Ms. Dupree became very fond of you in the short time you knew her. In fact, she fell in love with you, didn't she?"

"Yes. When it started out, we were just friends. We had both come out of a relationship that didn't end well, and we enjoyed each other's company. It evolved into something more."

"Was it mutual? Did you love her?"

"Yes."

"She was also very generous to you, wasn't she? She left you almost four hundred million dollars in her will, besides naming you as the sole beneficiary on a twenty-million-dollar life insurance policy."

"Yes, that's true, she did those things."

"And yet, you stole a watch from her, a precious heirloom valued at fifty thousand dollars."

"That's not true. The watch was stolen by Greg Malloy." As he says this, Nolan quickly scans the gallery for Gordon, and sees him sitting beside Lauren, two rows back. He is leaning forward in his seat, listening attentively for what is coming next. Lauren is pale-faced and wide-eyed. From the smile creeping onto Nolan's face, Hardwick senses something unexpected ahead. He switches to a different line of questioning.

"Where were you between eleven p.m. and one a.m. that night?"

"I was in Erica's bed asleep."

"Where did you believe Ms. Dupree to be while you were sleeping in her bed?"

"Until I woke around three a.m., I thought she was beside me."

"What did you do when you discovered she wasn't there?"

"I didn't think anything of it. It's wasn't unusual for her to get out of bed during the night and go to the bathroom or the kitchen. I fell back asleep."

"And you didn't wake again until nine, is that what you're telling us?"

"I woke at eight twenty. I showered and dressed before going downstairs."

"So, from three a.m. until nine a.m., six hours, Ms. Dupree, the woman you loved, wasn't in bed with you, you didn't know where she was, and it didn't concern you. Is that what you'd like us to believe?"

"That's what happened."

Hardwick keeps sneaking glances at the jurors. He's not getting the reaction he hoped for. He's also worried about the video Nolan intends to introduce into evidence after lunch. He decides on impulse to end his questioning of witnesses, and let Nolan present his defense. No matter how effective it is, he can still sway the jury with his closing statement.

"I have no more questions for the defendant. At this time the prosecution rests."

"Very well, Mr. Hardwick. The court will recess until one 'o clock. Mr. Drake, if you will bring the video files, and Mr. Hardwick, if you will bring your expert, we will go to my chambers to examine them there."

~~~

Curtis sets up his laptop on a table in the judge's chambers. Everyone positions their chair to see. He clicks on the first file.

"Before I begin," he tells those in the room, "I should explain what you're looking at. Erica Dupree instructed me to install hidden cameras in the servants' wing of the house. As far as I know, only she, I and the tech guys who installed them knew they were there. They are positioned to record inside the servants' rooms and in the hallway outside the rooms. I am not aware of any cameras like these anywhere else in the house. As per Ms. Dupree's instructions, these cameras were not monitored by a security service. The camera feed is transmitted to an IP address, which I access to monitor the camera activity remotely. I only do that once a month, for the purpose of making sure all cameras are working as they should and none have been tampered with or disabled. When I heard Ms. Dupree had been murdered, I went back to see what the cameras captured."

"Why wasn't this video made available to the police?" Hardwick demands. "You could be charged with obstructing the investigation for withholding this evidence."

"I contacted Detective Ray Brown and told him about it. He said they already had plenty of evidence against Mr. Drake."

"I don't believe you."

"And I don't care what you believe. Do you want to see the video now, or would you rather wait until it's shown to the jury?"

"Let's watch it, now," Franklin says. "We'll deal with any issues concerning Detective Brown turning these down, later."

Curtis plays all the pertinent video files, and narrates what is happening in each one, in the same order and manner as he did the night before at Nolan's house. When he comes to the clip of Greg entering and exiting through the service entrance, he stops to identify him and explain his connection to Gordon.

"This is Greg Malloy. Ms. Dupree hired me to surveil her husband, Gordon Weston. Greg is the husband of Lauren Malloy, who Gordon was having an affair with. That's only pertinent to this case because of their connection. Gordon knows the passcode through the service entrance, and Greg was at Nolan's house a day before the search turned up the watch."

"You can't be sure that Gordon knows the passcode, or that he gave it to Greg Malloy. These videos prove nothing," Hardwick says.

"They may not offer proof of my innocence, but they definitely offer significant reasonable doubt," Nolan counters.

"We'll see how the jury feels about that."

Judge Franklin addresses Curtis and the prosecution's expert.

"Would you gentleman please excuse yourselves, so that Mr. Hardwick, Mr. Drake and I can discuss this privately. As soon as they have left the room, Franklin says, "In light of this new evidence, I'm going to consider dismissing the charges against Mr. Drake."

"Your Honor," Hardwick starts to protest, but Franklin stops him.

"Furthermore, I'm going to suggest that your office investigate this incident, and determine if the omission of this evidence was intentional or merely an oversight."

"May I say something, Your Honor?" Hardwick asks.

"What is it, Mr. Hardwick?"

"These videos do not clearly exonerate Mr. Drake of all the charges. I think we should proceed and let the jury decide."

"Mr. Drake, do you have anything to say?"

"Even before seeing the videos, I thought Mr. Hardwick's case against me was weak. I'll begin my defense by asking that the charges against me be dismissed for lack of evidence."

"Very well. That gives me eighty-six minutes to consider how I will rule on your motion to dismiss. I'll see you both at one. Have a nice lunch."

~47~

Judge Franklin rules in Nolan's favor, and at one fourteen the charges against him are dismissed. The courtroom erupts as the reporters begin shouting questions. In an effort to save face, Hardwick offers Nolan his outstretched hand and congratulates him while the cameramen snap photos.

"You may have missed your calling, Mr. Drake," Hardwick says. "You handled yourself well, here."

"Thanks, but I'm just glad it's over. Now, if you'll excuse me, I'm going to try and slip out the side door to avoid the reporters."

When he reaches the stairwell he finds it blocked by an officer.

"You'll have to use the elevator, sir," he instructs Nolan.

He's unable to dodge the news media gathered outside the courtroom exit. They crowd in close to slow him and get his comments.

"How does it feel, Mr. Drake?" one of the reporters asks.

It's one of those pointless questions reporters are prone to asking when they can think of nothing else. Nolan repeats his earlier comment to Hardwick.

"I'm just glad it's over."

"What are you going to do with the money?" another reporter shouts.

In the midst of the trial, he'd all but forgotten about it.

"I have no idea."

"District Attorney Hardwick," the reporters all shout at once, as the prosecution team leaves the courtroom. "Are you satisfied with the outcome? Is there a new suspect in the Erica Dupree murder?"

"Justice was served here today, which is always our ultimate goal. As far as other suspects, Erica Dupree's murder is still an open investigation, and I can't comment on it, at this time."

While the media group's attention is directed at Hardwick, Nolan escapes. He pauses in the hall, short of the elevator when he sees Gordon and Lauren waiting there. They're about to step on when Detective Gutierrez comes up behind Gordon and grabs his arm. His first inclination is to jerk his arm free, but Gutierrez's grip is firm, and two uniformed officers are standing behind her with no-nonsense expressions on their faces to discourage any resistance.

"You'll have to come with me, Mr. Weston. I'd like to ask you some questions."

"Now is not a good time for me," Gordon protests.

To which Gutierrez replies, "That's a shame, because it's a damn good time for me."

She shoves him into the elevator with the officers loading on behind her. He instructs Lauren to call Marv Feldman, as the elevator doors close and it descends to the main lobby. Those who were waiting to board the elevator when the real-life police drama unfolded are awestruck by what has transpired. But, none more so than Lauren. She doesn't notice Nolan approach, until he speaks.

"This hasn't been your day, has it? First, the guy your fiancé tried to pin Erica's murder on is cleared of it. Then, he's arrested for it, instead. I'd say your chances of getting any part of Erica's money just vanished."

"What do you mean by saying Gordon has been arrested for her murder? They didn't arrest him, they took him for questioning. They know he didn't do it, because he wasn't there that night. There are plenty of witnesses who saw him at Luigi's at the time she was murdered."

"Gordon became a suspect two hours ago, when the judge and the DA viewed a video taken by cameras hidden in the servants' wing of Erica's house. The cameras captured Greg coming and going through the service entrance at the time Erica was murdered. Gordon knew the passcode for the service door, and Erica's routines. Those police detectives may not be the brightest of people, but they'll put two and two together, and come up with Gordon and Greg. If they conspired to kill Erica, one is as guilty as the other."

Several people are crowding in behind Nolan and Lauren as the elevator nears their floor. Lauren pulls Nolan to the side to let them by.

"You can't believe Greg would have anything to do with this. Or Gordon either, for that matter. Gordon is no boy scout, but he would never murder anyone."

"You don't know that and neither do I. Besides, it doesn't matter what I believe. I won't be in the courtroom for their trial, and I couldn't care less what happens to either one of them."

"Oh no, I've got to warn Greg. They'll be coming for him, next."

She takes her phone out and starts punching in his number.

"I would imagine you're too late. Greg is probably already at the police station being questioned. The police will question them separately, and give each of them a chance to rat out the other for a lighter sentence."

~~~

In fact, that's exactly what they'll do. At that very moment, Greg is sitting across a small table from Detective

Ray Brown in an interrogation room at the police station. Only an hour earlier Brown was royally reamed out by ADA Rita Sanchez, for his failure to bring the video files to the attention of the DA's Office. It almost cost him a suspension, and may yet, if he is unable to redeem himself by coercing a confession out of Greg Malloy.

"I'm through messing around here, Malloy. You murdered Erica Dupree. We have you on the security video entering her home through the service entrance and going directly to the kitchen, where her body was found. The only thing that will save you from the death penalty is a full confession. I can talk to the DA about reducing the sentence to life in prison, but only if you tell me everything, right now."

The discovery of the security cameras catches Greg off guard. He needs time to think this through before saying anything, but this big detective won't let up.

"I didn't kill anyone."

"So, you're saying you just happened to break in to her house on the night she was murdered. You can't expect me to believe that. If her death was an accident, that could change things. If she surprised you, for instance, and you struck her intending to knock her unconscious. That's a whole different story. That would be manslaughter, which takes the death penalty off the table. But, you've got to get out in front of this, now."

"I didn't kill Erica Dupree, or anyone else," Greg reiterates.

"Right now, your partner, Gordon Weston is being brought to the station to be questioned about this. We know the two of you planned this. We just need you to fill in some of the details for us. If he comes in and says this was all your idea to go there and kill her, that's going to look pretty bad for you. That's why I say, you've got to get out in front of this, now."

There's a rap on the door, before it opens a crack. A hand sticks through to gesture for Brown to come out.

"His lawyer is here," another detective from his squad informs Brown.

"He didn't ask for a lawyer."

"Lauren Malloy called me on his behalf," Marv Feldman says. "Has Greg Malloy been mirandized?"

"He hasn't been charged with anything, yet."

"You're saying he hasn't been informed of his right to an attorney. Which is why he hasn't asked for one. Now, I'd like to speak privately with my client, and to be present when he is questioned further."

While Feldman speaks with Greg, Gutierrez comes from another interrogation room to confer with Brown.

"Did you get anything out of Malloy?" she asks.

"No, I didn't have time. What about Weston?"

"Same thing. I had barely gotten him into the room when Feldman showed up."

"I'm Marv Feldman," he says to Greg, once they're alone in the interrogation room. "Lauren called to tell me you and Gordon were here. I don't have any of the details on why you're here. What have they told you, so far?"

"They say they have me on a security camera entering Erica's house the night she was murdered."

"Were you there?"

"Yes, but I didn't kill her."

"Tell me why you went there, and what happened. This is all privileged communication between attorney and client."

"I went there to steal a watch. Gordon said it was one she never wore and wouldn't miss."

"He told you how to get in and where the watch was. Is that right? Did you see Erica or anyone else while you were there?"

256

"Yes, Gordon told me about the service entrance and the keypad. And, he told me where she kept the watch. I didn't see or hear anyone while I was inside the house."

"Okay. Here's what you're going to tell the detective. Following Gordon's instructions, you went to the house to retrieve a watch that Erica had given to Gordon. The rest of your story you can tell them what you've told me. You didn't hear or see anyone else while you were there."

The detectives question Greg and Gordon for another hour. After being embarrassed during Nolan's trial, the DA is reluctant to hold them.

"Let them go for now. Bring Hernando Perez and Phuong Nguyen in for questioning. I want to know more about those men in their rooms."

~48~

The judge overseeing Gordon Weston's legal action contesting the validity of Erica's will, put the matter on hold, pending the outcome of Nolan's trial. Nolan assumed his being cleared of Erica's murder would negate Gordon's claim, but it didn't work out that way. Gordon's attorney, Marv Feldman, was able to persuade Judge Reynolds to grant a hearing on the matter, in spite of Nolan being exonerated.

"Your Honor, whether or not Nolan Drake murdered Erica Dupree has no bearing on the state of her mental health at the time she changed her will. Mr. Weston has the right to be heard in a court of law."

Nolan, on the other hand, has no rights whatsoever regarding it. He can sit in the gallery and watch the proceedings, but it's tantamount to watching paint dry. Even the most trivial of issues requires expert testimony and hours of debate, before either side is willing to move on. At its current rate of progress, the hearing could last for months. Nolan's opinion of the judicial system has become so cynical, he believes the attorneys for both sides and the judge are part of a conspiracy to take Erica's money from him and divide it among themselves.

Feldman calls a psychiatrist, Dr. Helen Nisman to testify. She's a tall thin woman with gray hair in a bun and thick eyeglasses.

"Dr. Nisman, how long was Erica Dupree a patient of yours?"

"I saw her once a month for approximately ten years."

"Can you describe the type of treatment she received during this time?"

"She received therapy and medication for depression stemming from a mild bipolar disorder."

"Were you able to cure her?"

"That isn't the terminology we use. A condition like hers isn't cured as a virus would be. It's always there. The therapy is designed to help her detect an oncoming episode, and deal with it before it gets out of control. The prescribed medications are used to manage the mood swings which accompany the episodes."

"Would the average person, like me, notice a difference in her behavior during one of these episodes, if they weren't trained to recognize the symptoms?"

"Probably not. The personality change is often very subtle, and many of those who suffer from bipolar disorder learn to hide it from others."

Dr. Nisman's testimony continues for two hours. It covers in detail Erica's bipolar depression and the different medications prescribed to her. By the time she is done, Judge Reynolds is questioning if she was mentally competent at any time in her life, not to mention at the time the will was drawn up. Alan Rutherford declines to cross-examine Dr. Nisman.

They recess for lunch. Gordon and Feldman taunt Nolan with smirking faces as they pass by him on their way out of the courtroom. Walking beside Gordon, Lauren chooses to ignore Nolan. As Alan Rutherford and Joseph Edgar exit Nolan attempts to speak with Rutherford.

"Why didn't you question Dr. Nisman's credentials? How do you know she's really a psychiatrist or that she ever as much as met Erica?"

"We can't discuss this with you Mr. Drake."

"Since I have more at stake than anyone else involved, I think I have a right to know why you're not honoring Erica's wishes by defending her legal will."

"No, Mr. Drake. You have no legal rights whatsoever in this matter. Now, if you'll excuse us, we'd like to eat lunch before we return to court in an hour."

"You don't mind if I join you, do you? After all, you're billing the lunch to the estate, so ultimately, I'm paying for it."

"I'm sorry, Mr. Drake. We're having lunch at the Baron's Club. It's members only."

Nolan literally has to bite his lip to keep himself from voicing objections during the afternoon session. Feldman questions Deidra Crowley, who claims to be Erica's closest friend and confidant, though Nolan never heard Erica mention her.

"When was the last time you spoke with Erica Dupree, Mrs. Crowley?"

"I spoke with her by phone on the day she was murdered."

"So, only hours before she died, you spoke with her. How would you describe her mood during the conversation? Did she sound happy?"

"No, I'd say she was sort of pensive. She was undecided about the divorce, like she may have acted too hastily. Norton was coming to her house that evening, and she was planning to break it off with him."

"You mean Nolan, don't you, Mrs. Crowley?"

"Yes, that's right. Nolan was coming over that evening. I'm sorry, I have a poor memory for names."

"What else did you talk about during that conversation?"

"We discussed her medication. She had stopped taking the one for her bipolar depression. Tulata, I think it was called."

"I think you mean, Latuda, don't you, Mrs. Crowley?"

"Oh, yes. That sounds right."

"Did her will come up in this conversation?"

"Her what?"

"Her will and testament. Didn't she tell you she'd mistakenly changed her will and intended to correct her mistake?"

"Yes, that's right. She put Norton in her will, but she made a mistake and wanted to change it. She was going to give everything to Jordan."

"I think you mean, she intended to remove Nolan from her will and put Gordon back in. Isn't that correct."

"Alright, if you say so."

"Your Honor!" Nolan shouts from three rows back in the gallery. "How can you allow this sham to continue?"

"Who are you?" Judge Reynolds asks, tersely.

"I'm Nolan Drake, the beneficiary named in Erica Dupree's will."

"Mr. Drake, you are neither the plaintiff nor respondent in this litigation. Sit down and be quiet, or I'll have you removed from the room."

"Don't bother," Nolan says, and walks out.

The litigation is too painful to watch, anyway. Nolan is more convinced than ever there are some kind backroom dealings at play that will eventually determine how this thing ends. The witnesses and their testimony is all for show. That's the only reason Nolan can think of for Rutherford to sit idly by and watch Gordon pilfer Erica's estate. The fix is in. The outcome has been predetermined.

~49~

Hernando knows in his heart Douglas isn't capable of a vicious crime such as the murder of Ms. Dupree. Yes, he has lost his temper on a few occasions, and twice, he's slapped Hernando. They weren't hard slaps. Afterward Douglas would cry and apologize. If he could have kept Douglas out of it, Hernando would have, but it wasn't an option. The police had a video which showed Douglas going from his room and through the kitchen door into Ms. Dupree's house.

"Douglas Pruitt was your lover. We understand that, and we're not judging either of you. Alright?" Detective Gutierrez tells Hernando.

Brown began the session with him, but the burly detective intimidated him. Hernando broke down and starting sobbing when Brown showed him the video of Douglas entering Ms. Dupree's kitchen at midnight. That's when Gutierrez brought him a Dr. Pepper and sent Brown out of the room.

Gutierrez continues, "Did you know Douglas had left your room during the night?" Hernando shakes his head no. "You didn't wake during the night as he was getting out of bed?" Another head shake. "We're going to need to talk to Douglas. Where can we find him?"

"I don't know where he lives."

"Well, how do you contact him when you want to get together with him? Do you call him?"

"No, I never call him," Hernando lies. "He calls me."

"Let me see your phone. Maybe his number is on your call log."

"I don't have it with me," Hernando lies, again.

"Now, Mr. Perez. I'm a fairly patient person, but the man that was in here before, Detective Brown, he's not."

Hernando starts to tremble and his eyes dart toward the door, expecting Brown to burst through it any second. Gutierrez holds her hand out, palm up, silently demanding the phone. He pulls it from his pocket and hands it over. Gutierrez scrolls through the calls received.

"It looks like you have a lot of friends, or a big family. Should I just start calling these numbers, or would you like to tell me which one is his?"

She holds the phone so he can see the display, and scrolls backward from the most recent calls. Finally, Hernando says, "It's that one."

"This number right here?" Gutierrez asks, and Hernando nods, yes.

~~~

Phuong cooperates fully when the detectives contact her about Tung. She tells them where Tung works and lives, without any hesitation. She does so because she is certain beyond any shadow of a doubt he would never harm Ms. Dupree or steal from her. Tung himself is just as cooperative when the police show up at his job.

"Mr. Pham, we understand you were with Phuong the night Ms. Dupree was murdered. We'd like to ask you some questions about that. I already explained to your boss that you're not a suspect, so he wouldn't get the wrong idea. Would you mind coming with us?" Detective Gutierrez asks.

263

"Of course," Tung replies. "I understand."

Gutierrez places Tung in the same room where Hernando, Gordon and Nolan were questioned previously. She asks if he would like coffee or a soda. He requests tea. While she searches through drawers in the break room for a teabag, Brown observes Tung through the one-way glass. He's calm, too calm given where he is. He sits with his back straight and both hands resting palms down on the table in front of him, staring straight ahead as if in a trance. Gutierrez returns with a steaming cup of tea for Tung and black coffee for herself.

"You can take your coat off and make yourself comfortable, if you like," Gutierrez offers. Tung is wearing a turtleneck shirt and a jacket. The temperature inside the room is close to eighty.

"I'm fine."

"Mr. Pham, on the night Ms. Dupree was murdered, you stayed with Phuong Nguyen in her room." Did you leave her room at any time during the night?"

"No. I believe it was ten when we fell asleep. I didn't wake again until the next morning around seven thirty."

"Recently, we became aware of hidden cameras in the area of Ms. Dupree's house where Phuong's room is. A camera in the hallway outside her room captured you leaving her room at one-oh-five a.m. You went into the kitchen and returned fifteen minutes later."

"Oh yes, that is right. I was very tired, and because of that I didn't remember until now. I woke in the night feeling very thirsty. I don't know what time it was, but if you say it was one a.m., it must have been. I went to the kitchen for a glass of water."

"Did you see or hear anyone else in the house when you went into the kitchen to get the water?"

"No, not that I remember, but like I say I was kind of out of it."

"Would you be willing to take a polygraph test to verify what you're telling me is the truth?"

"If it will help with your investigation, I'll be glad to. I never met Ms. Dupree, but Phuong was very fond of her. She would like to see the killer caught and punished."

The polygraph test has critics among prosecutors and defense attorneys alike. It is not likely the DA's Office would use the results of a test given to Tung, even if he failed it badly. The only reason Gutierrez suggests it is to gauge his reaction to the idea. But since he's so willing, it won't hurt to go ahead and see what it nets. One of the crime lab techs, David Nelson, sets up the equipment in the interrogation room, and attaches sensors to Tung's fingers.

"Is your name Tung Pham?" he asks, first.

"Yes," Tung answers. Nelson watches the graph on the screen respond.

"Are you twenty-three years old?"

"Yes."

"Have you ever lived in Moscow, Russia?"

"No." Now a basic range of emotional responses has been established.

"Do you know Phuong Nguyen?"

"Yes."

"Were you with her on the night Erica Dupree was murdered?"

"Yes."

"Were you with her all night?"

Tung hesitates for a minute, because he's unsure of what qualifies as all night. They already know he left the room at one a.m. He decides to answer, "No."

"You were not with Phuong Nguyen all night. Is that right?"

"Yes."

"Did you leave her room during the night?"

"Yes."

"When did you leave the room and where did you go?"

"I left the room at one-oh-five a.m. and went to the kitchen."

"Did you kill Erica Dupree?"

The sudden change of tactics catches Tung off guard, but he quickly recovers. "No."

"Did you strike Erica Dupree on the head?"

This time he's more prepared. "No."

"Did you witness someone striking Erica Dupree?"

"No."

"Do you have any knowledge of who killed her?"

"No."

"Have you answered truthfully to every question I've asked you?"

"Yes."

Afterward, Nelson gives the results of the polygraph to Gutierrez while Brown listens in.

"The guy is unflappable. He didn't appear to be nervous about the test at all. His pulse, blood pressure and breathing remained steady throughout the questioning."

"We have no choice but to cut him loose," Gutierrez says. "What time is Douglas Pruitt going to be here?"

"His lawyer is bringing him in at two, this afternoon."

~~~

The phone number for Douglas, which Gutierrez obtained from Hernando is answered by a voice saying, "Connelly Funeral Home. May I help you?" Douglas is a mortician there. They found him the previous day in the embalming room, working furiously to prepare the corpse of an auto accident victim for her open casket service, later that day. He's a tall, thin man with a meek manner and pasty white skin. He is so far removed from the profile they've worked up for the murderer, Brown was ready to rule him out before asking him a single question.

"We have to question him, just so we can tell the DA we did, if for no other reason," Gutierrez tells him.

"If we take him in now, who's going to fix that poor girl's face, so the family can look at her during the service?" Brown protests.

So they give him a day to contact his lawyer and make arrangements to come down to the station.

"For the record, my client is appearing voluntarily to answer your questions," Douglas's lawyer, Walter Dahl says. "He is not suspected of a crime and will not be characterized as such to the news media, his employer, his family or anyone else. Agreed?"

"That's right, Mr. Dahl. Your client Douglas Pruitt is fully cooperating with our investigation, and we appreciate him being here," Gutierrez says. "Mr. Pruitt, where did you go when you left Hernando Perez's room, on the night of Erica Dupree's murder?"

Douglas confers with Dahl before answering, "After I left Hernando, I went home."

"No, Mr. Pruitt. When you left Hernando's room at eleven fifty p.m. and didn't return to the room until five minutes before one a.m. Where did you go for one hour and five minutes?"

"Uh..., I'm afraid I don't know what you're talking about."

Gutierrez explains about the hidden cameras, and Dahl requests a few minutes alone with his client. Gutierrez leaves the room for ten minutes.

"Are you ready to explain what happened that night, Mr. Pruitt?" she asks, when she returns to the interrogation room.

Douglas looks tentatively at his lawyer, who gives him a go-ahead nod.

"I went from Hernando's room to the kitchen for a glass of water."

"Mm-hmm," Gutierrez utters, skeptically. Douglas pauses.

"Go ahead," Dahl encourages his client.

"It's such a magnificent room, the kitchen. The cabinetry, all the appliances and counter space. As I drank the water, I fantasized about what it would be like to live in a place like that. I wanted to see more of it, so I opened the door leading into the main part of the house, to take a peek. All the lights were off, and there was no sound of a TV or stereo playing. I could tell no one was there, so I went in, just to see it for myself."

"You didn't go back to the room until an hour later. Are you saying you wandered around her house during that time?"

"Not exactly. I went into a big room, and sat down in an easy chair beside a fireplace. I dozed off. I didn't mean to, but I did. When I woke, I didn't know where I was or how long I'd been sleeping. Then, I remembered I was inside the house, and went back to Hernando's room. I didn't see or hear anyone else in the house during that time."

"Is there anything else you'd like to add to your statement, anything that might help our investigation?"

"No. I wish I could be more helpful."

"You and me both, Mr. Pruitt."

"It won't be necessary to speak to my wife, will it? I'd really rather she not be involved."

"We don't have any reason to speak with her at this time. If I have any more questions for you, I'll call you at work."

ADA Rita Sanchez has been watching through the one-way glass alongside Brown as Douglas tells his story. She asks, "Did the crime scene guys turn up anything to confirm or refute what he's saying? Maybe he left fingerprints on the chair, or on a glass in the kitchen."

"There were hundreds of sets of fingerprints in every part of the house. It would take years to sort through them, and even then, I'm not sure what good it would do."

"So far, you don't have a murder weapon or a suspect you can place with Erica Dupree at the time of her death. The different guys going into the kitchen tells us nothing. They could all be innocent, or it could be a conspiracy involving Douglas Pruitt, Tung Pham, Greg Malloy, Gordon Weston and Nolan Drake, for all we know."

"Yes ma'am. That pretty much sums it up."

~50~

Three weeks after Nolan's trial ends with the charges against him being dismissed, he receives a notice from Founders Mutual Life Insurance of their intent to release the hold on the twenty million dollars from Erica's life insurance policy. He elects to have it wire transferred directly into his bank account. That account has never had a balance above ten thousand dollars, so when the wire transfer is completed, it sets off all kinds of bells and whistles within the bank. Ten minutes later, he gets a call.

"Mr. Drake?" the caller inquires.

"Yes, I'm Nolan Drake."

"I'm Wayne Dickinson, with Union Commerce Bank. How are you today, sir?"

"I'm fine, Wayne, but I don't believe that's why you're calling."

"Yes, of course. I'm the vice-president in charge of our investment advisory department."

"I didn't realize Union Commerce had an investment advisory department."

"Oh yes. We have an excellent staff, capable of designing and implementing a personal investment strategy for your specific needs. I was notified of a large deposit transferred into your account, and wanted to call to offer my services."

"I've got to be honest with you, Wayne. The fact that news of a large deposit gets passed around the bank like a saucy office rumor, doesn't make me feel warm and fuzzy about doing business with Union Commerce."

"Oh no, Mr. Drake. It's not like that at all. The information came directly to me from our accounting department. You see, the money deposited into your checking account earns no interest. If it were invested where it earned two percent interest, for instance, that sum of money would earn four hundred thousand dollars annually. That's more than a thousand dollars a day."

Up until now, Nolan hasn't considered the earning potential of the money. It was only two hours earlier he learned Founders Mutual was going to pay him.

"Look, Wayne. I haven't had a chance to think about this. I need a few days to decide, even if it means losing a few thousand bucks. How about I call you back if I've got any questions."

"Certainly Mr. Drake. That's Wayne Dickinson, with Union Commerce Bank. I'll email you with my direct line, so you'll always be able to contact me immediately. Thank you for your time, Mr. Drake."

~~~

The phone call is likely the first of many to come, and a harbinger of what lies ahead for Nolan. His life has quite possibly just changed, forever. While in Erica's presence it was impossible not to notice how everyone called her Ms. Dupree, and never Erica. It will be tough to get used to people calling him Mr. Drake. He calls his office. The receptionist picks up.

"Hi, Trisha."

"Hi, Nolan. I'm glad you called. People have been calling here, asking to talk to you. I've got a ton of messages for you."

"Give them to Dana, and let her sort through them. Is she there?"

"Yes, I can see her from my desk. She's talking on her cell phone."

"Would you mind interrupting her? Tell her it's important."

She puts Nolan on hold to do as he asked. After a minute Dana picks up.

"Is everything okay? Trisha said it was important."

"Everything is fine. I have something to tell you I think you'll want to hear. Which is, I won't be coming back to work, there."

"What are you saying? You won't be coming back, soon, or you're not coming back at all?"

"The latter. Erica Dupree named me as sole beneficiary on a life insurance policy. Bottom line is, I no longer have to work for a living."

"Uh..., I don't know what to say. I mean, I'm happy for you, but what about everyone here. Are you going to let us go?"

"It's not up to me. I've made a spur-of-the-moment decision to give the company to you. It's out of my hands, now." The line is quiet for a long moment. "Dana, are you still there?"

"Nolan, if this is a joke, it's not very funny."

"It's no joke. You've been running things without my help. I no longer need the money or grief that comes with owning the business. I'm giving it to you. Unless you don't want it. And if that's the case, I'll shut it down and everyone there will be out of a job. Then, it will be on your conscience, and not mine."

"I can't believe you're doing this, Nolan. I mean, I wasn't expecting anything like this to happen."

"Give it a few days to sink in. You'll adjust to owning the company before long."

"What about you, Nolan? Are you going to be able to adjust to being rich? I hear it's lonely at the top, although I have no personal experience."

"I'll adjust to it eventually. Meanwhile, if you have any questions, you know where to reach me. Good luck, Dana."

~~~

At the end of his first day as a multi-millionaire, Nolan can't decide whether to go out and paint the town, or stay home and get drunk. Neither holds much appeal. He's been out of touch with friends and coworkers for months, so there's no one to go out on the town with him. He told Dana he'd adjust to being rich, eventually, but in truth he's not confident of that.

His doorbell sounds as the sun is setting. It comes as no surprise to see Lauren looking back at him as he glances through the peephole. The woman has an uncanny ability to sense when a man comes into a large quantity of money. She dons an apologetic expression as he opens the door.

"What brings you here?" Nolan asks.

"I came to talk to you. Can I come in?"

He steps aside. She brushes past him and heads toward the kitchen for the bottle of vodka in the freezer. Nolan takes two glasses from the cupboard, and sets them on the bar counter. Lauren pours the glasses half full, sits on a barstool and gestures for Nolan to sit beside her. She's wearing a black bandage dress, so short her thighs are exposed up to her crotch.

He hesitates. It's a dangerous combination, Lauren so close, mixed with vodka-impaired judgment. Finally, he slides onto the stool next to her, careful not let his legs touch hers, or the scent of her perfume reach his nostrils. His apprehension amuses her. A coquettish smile plays on her lips.

"So, talk already," he says.

"Oh Nolan, don't be that way. We used to thoroughly enjoy moments like these. Is there any reason we can't enjoy it, now?"

"Lauren, I don't really want to talk about the past. Do you?"

"Fine, let's talk about the future."

"Your future or mine?"

"Both. I think they're connected. In fact, I think there will always be a connection between us, whether you choose to believe it or not. I'll always love you, Nolan. Nothing is going to change that."

"You and I have different ideas of what love is."

"Be that as it may, I know you still have feelings for me, and I wish you would stop trying to convince yourself otherwise. But, that isn't what I want to talk to you about. Gordon and his attorney are going to try every trick in the book to get Erica's will thrown out."

"That's not exactly news. Gordon is a cheat and a liar. It's what he does. Besides, what difference does it make to you? You get half of anything he gets, don't you?"

"He signed a contract which says I get half of anything he gets from Erica, but knowing Gordon he'll try to weasel out of it. If he wins the case, and can get his hands on the money, he'll tie it up in court until I agree to settle for a lot less. That's the kind of person he is."

"If you're looking for a shoulder to cry on, you've come to the wrong place. You were willing to sit by and let me be convicted of Erica's murder when it looked like you might benefit from it."

"That's not completely true, Nolan. I was helpless to do anything about the outcome of your trial. I wasn't a witness to anything, and I couldn't provide you with an alibi. Gordon didn't care if you were convicted of her murder or not. He wanted your character tarnished enough to bring Erica's will into question. That's all. For what it's worth I was thrilled to see the murder charges against you dropped. And initially, I was happy Gordon got a hearing to overturn her will."

Lauren gets up from her stool to retrieve the vodka from the freezer, and returns to refill both of their glasses.

"Initially? I hope you're not going to tell me your conscience started bothering you."

"No, my conscience had nothing to do with it. I don't trust Gordon. Our arrangement is nothing more than business, and I can't stand having a business partner who can't be trusted. I trust you, Nolan. I'd rather have you as a partner."

"I seem to recall that didn't work so well the last time we were partners."

"We were lovers, not partners. And it wasn't that it didn't work out well. It didn't work out the way you planned. Sometimes things don't. If we work together we can beat Gordon. I'm sure of it. That's what I came here to tell you. Let's team up against him, so you can get the money Erica wanted you to have. What do you say?"

"Exactly what are you suggesting here, Lauren. Lay it out for me in simple terms."

"The witnesses they've called, like the psychiatrist who said she's been treating her for ten years, and the woman claiming to be Erica's best friend, they were bogus. Neither one of them ever met her. They were well paid for their testimony. And Feldman has others like that lined up to testify. I can be your inside person. They won't know I'm feeding you information until it's over. Which will be too late to do anything about it."

Nolan has suspected some kind of backroom deal taking place with the hearing, and now he's got confirmation of it. But doing something about it, is another thing altogether.

"I don't like the idea of Gordon walking away with Erica's estate, but the legal system is intentionally tough on outsiders. The attorneys representing the estate won't talk to me. And they don't seem eager for things to end. The longer the hearing goes on, the more they can bill the estate for their time."

"You're a brilliant man, Nolan. I'm not just saying that. I was impressed with your intellect from the very first. I know you can figure a way to keep Gordon from winning if you put your mind to it."

"Let's say we can swing things in my favor, and after the dust settles I get the estate. What do you expect out of it?"

"I'll make the same deal with you that I have with Gordon. You give me half of whatever you get."

"When you made that deal with Gordon, you thought it was for half of the five-million-dollar settlement he was getting from Erica. Now we're talking about her whole estate. I'll give you the two and a half million you would have gotten if Gordon hadn't turned the offer down. How's that?"

"No way! The estate is worth four hundred million. Two and a half is less than one percent."

"Four hundred million is a number the media has been throwing around. By the time estate taxes are paid, and the lawyers take their fees, it will be far less. Maybe less than one hundred million, and it won't be liquid. It will be in the form of real estate, stocks, and things like that."

"Well, that may be true, but you can still do better than two and a half million, a whole lot better. Take a day or two to think about it. You may feel differently about things by then."

~51~

Even though the hearing seems to be going well for Gordon, he's not content to leave its outcome in the hands of fate, alone. Marv Feldman has presented a convincing argument for overturning Erica's will, but still, the final decision will be made by Judge Reynolds. If it was up to a jury, Gordon might be able to read something in their faces. Not so with Reynolds. His years on the bench have taught him to mask his emotions behind a stern poker face.

"How much would it take to buy the judge?" Gordon asks Feldman, as they're having cocktails at a downtown bar, after the hearing has adjourned for the day.

Feldman glances from side to side before saying, "I didn't hear that."

"We're speaking hypothetically. I'm not suggesting you break the law. I'm just curious as to how much money would be required to buy a favorable decision from a judge."

"I've heard things—unsubstantiated rumors, nothing more. One concerns a lawsuit involving food poisoning at a popular fast food restaurant. Most in the legal community thought it was a frivolous suit that would get tossed, but it went the distance. The judge ruled in favor of the plaintiff and awarded her three million. Supposedly, the plaintiff's attorney paid fifty grand for the ruling and bragged about it later to some buddies."

277

Gordon uses the calculator on his phone to run the numbers.

"That's a little more than one and a half percent. At that same rate, a favorable ruling in my case would cost about six and a half million."

"The rumors about judges accepting bribes are only rumors because it's rare for a judge to be charged with accepting a bribe. On the other hand, there are plenty of true stories about people attempting to bribe a judge. Those stories all end the same way. They lose their case and go to jail."

"I understand what you're saying. I'll have to be extremely careful."

"No, what I'm saying is this. We didn't have this conversation."

"That goes without saying," Gordon confirms.

"Because if we did have a conversation concerning a certain judge," Feldman continues, just above a whisper. "I would mention that he's sixty-one and has been married for three years to his third wife, who is forty-two. She's something of a social butterfly, likes to dine out at trendy restaurants, and has expensive taste in clothes. Besides his younger wife attempting to bleed him dry, Reynolds has two kids from his previous marriage who are both attending Ivy League universities. The guy is stretching his judge's salary to its absolute limit. But like I said before, we didn't have this conversation."

~~~

Gordon arrives back at the apartment well after dark to find Greg there alone. Greg appears to be texting someone, but he's not. He's using an app to track the location of Lauren's iPhone, and recognizes the address where she is as Nolan's. She's unaware he occasionally monitors her movements this way. He glances up at Gordon, and then back at his phone without speaking. Things have been a little tense between them, lately. Part of the reason for this involves the jewelry Greg stole from Erica's house. Gordon promised to split the money from the sale of it with Greg. Instead, it's being used to fund the litigation contesting Erica's will. Or so Gordon says.

"Where's Lauren?" Gordon asks.

"Don't know," Greg replies. "She didn't say where she was going."

"Did she say when she'd be back?"

"Not to me."

Lauren didn't tell Greg or Gordon she was going to see Nolan, because she doesn't want them to know. What happens between Nolan and her is nobody else's business.

"There's something I could use your help with, Greg."

"Yeah, what's that?"

"Things are looking good with this hearing. I think there's an excellent chance we can win, but you never know. There's no sure thing in court. With all the money I've invested, and what's at stake, I'd hate to lose because the judge wakes up on the wrong side of the bed one morning."

"Yeah, Lauren would hate to see you lose, too. She's really counting on a big payoff from this."

"That's where I could use your help. I want to offer the judge an incentive to rule in my favor. The trouble is, I can't be seen talking to him outside the courtroom. I'd like you to act as an intermediary."

"An intermediary?"

"Yeah, like a go-between."

"I know what the word means, Gordon. Why me? That sounds like something more suited to your skill set than mine."

"I disagree, Greg. You're perfect for this. You're the quiet sort. The kind of guy who comes off as slow or dim-witted."

"I'm not stupid, Gordon."

"Of course, you're not. That's what I'm saying. On the surface you appear that way, but underneath that, the wheels are always turning. That's why I think you're the right person to get close to the judge without making him nervous."

"I don't think so, Gordon. I won't bribe a judge or do anything else that will get me arrested. That thing with Erica's murder was enough to scare me straight. Count me out, this time around."

"I had your back there. When the image of you on the hidden camera was discovered, I told the police it was my idea. Same thing here. If something goes wrong, I'll take full responsibility. And if it goes as I think it will, I'll make it well worth your time. How does a hundred grand sound?"

"There isn't enough money worth going to jail for."

"No one is going to jail. I can promise you that. We'll do it smart. In order to charge you with bribing a judge, they need a recording of you making the offer, or a picture of you handing over the money. I want you to approach Judge Reynolds away from his home or office, to be sure you won't be recorded or photographed."

"If he accepts the bribe, how will I know he's not setting me up? He might say, yeah I'll take the money. Then, when it comes time to make the payment, he has the police waiting to arrest me."

"The money can be delivered in an inconspicuous package by special courier, after the hearing is over."

"He's not going to do that. He'll want the money beforehand."

"Maybe not. If we offer him five million dollars, to be given to him after the disbursement of the estate, he might go for that."

"I think we should run this by Lauren. She has a lot at stake, too."

"That's not a good idea. The fewer people who know about this the better. Let's keep it strictly between you and me. It will be easier to control things that way."

Before Greg can reply, his phone alerts him of an incoming text message.

"That's Lauren, now," he tells Gordon. "She's shopping and will be here in a couple of hours."

"What's she shopping for this late?"

"Who knows?"

"Well, I don't want to wait until then to eat. I'm going to grab a bite somewhere. You want to go with me?"

"No. Go ahead without me. I've got part of a sandwich left over from lunch in the fridge."

Once Gordon is gone, Greg sends a text to Lauren, telling her Gordon went to eat, and have fun shopping.

~~~

"That's probably Gordon, wondering where you are," Nolan says.

She rolls over away from him to reach for her phone on the bedside table. He can't resist running his hand over her bare back and ass, while she reads the message.

"No, it's Greg. He's letting me know Gordon isn't there, right now."

"Does Greg know you're here, with me?"

"I don't think so. I didn't tell him where I was going."

"Do you need to leave?"

Lauren rolls back to face Nolan. "No. Do you want me to leave?"

He pulls her closer, then says, "Not really."

"Not really?! What kind of answer is that? Nolan, if you want me to stay, tell me so. I haven't heard those words from you in a long time. Far too long. I need to hear you say it."

"Lauren, don't leave, yet. Please stay. How was that?"

"Much better."

Sometime in the two hours following that, Nolan dozes off. He didn't mean to. Erica's death, the murder trial and the contesting of her will have left him sleep-deprived. Coupling passionately with Lauren nonstop for an hour pushed him to the breaking point. When he wakes at eleven, she is gone. She left her panties lying on the bed beside him. Whether the purpose was to mark her territory, or to have an excuse to come back, he can't say.

It would be like Lauren to call and ask, "Did you happen to find my panties? I seem to have lost them somewhere." Yeah right, like there's nothing unusual about a grown woman forgetting to put on her panties while getting dressed.

The thing is, he wants to see her again, and more than he cares to admit. He's never really gotten over her. The mere sight of her stirs something inside him. Once this hearing over Erica's will is done, he'll have to make a hard decision. Either leave town, and leave her behind in the process, or try to win her away from Greg, Gordon and whoever else.

~52~

In the morning following Lauren's visit, Nolan prepares to spend part of the day at the courthouse. His reason for going is twofold. He wants to be there to witness any new developments, and he hopes to see Lauren. She'll be there, ostensibly giving Gordon support. She won't speak to Nolan, probably won't even look his way, because that might arouse suspicion, and further erode the trust between Gordon and herself.

Nolan needn't be so careful when looking at Lauren. It's expected of him to sneak a glance. Men's eyes are naturally drawn to her. He's curious to see if she'll dress with him in mind, after the night before. As he considers the possibilities, his doorbell sounds. He hurries to answer it, not bothering to look through the peephole, thinking it must be her.

"Hello, Mr. Drake. I am sorry to disturb you," Phuong says.

She stands on his doorstep with her hands clasped and head slightly bowed, as if she's unsure she should be there. A Nissan Sentra that rolled off the assembly line two decades before, idles at the curb in front of Nolan's house. A woman who looks a lot like Phuong waits behind the wheel.

"You're not disturbing me, Phuong. I'm surprised to see you, that's all. Would you like to come in?"

"Yes, thank you."

She glances back at the Sentra driver, silently conveying her intention, then steps inside. Nolan shuts the door. Her eyes scan the room and what she can see beyond it, warily.

"Is something bothering you, Phuong?"

"Yes, Mr. Drake. Something happened, and I don't know who to talk to. It is about Ms. Dupree's murder."

"Phuong, if you have suspicions over who might have done it, you should take that information to the police."

"I'm afraid to tell them. They are not likely to believe someone like me. They might put me in jail, and I have no money for a lawyer."

"If they find out you're keeping something from them, they could put you in jail for that. Why did you come to me?"

"Ms. Dupree was very good to me. She didn't deserve for this to happen. I had to do something, and I thought you would help. She loved you, very much. You will do what's right to honor her memory."

"Phuong, do you know who killed her?"

"I think it was Tung."

"Tung? Is he the man who stayed with you, on the night Erica was killed?"

"Yes, Tung Pham. He is my boyfriend. Or at least he was. He has left Houston. He didn't say where he was going. The police questioned him about the murder. Afterward, he told me I should not say anything to the police about the bag if they questioned me."

"What bag is that?"

"He brought a plastic bag with him that night. I thought it held his clothes and toothbrush. After I found her...," Phuong pauses to take a deep breath and compose herself. "After I found her, I went back to my room to tell Tung he should go. He quickly dressed, took the bag from beneath my bed and left. I thought nothing of the bag until he told me not to say anything about it to the police."

"What do you think he was hiding in the bag?"

"Whatever it was Ms. Dupree was hit with. Why else would Tung want me to keep it secret?"

Nolan tries to recall if the bag was evident in the video images of Tung, as he came and went from her room.

"What reason would Tung have for killing her? He had nothing to gain. She was your employer."

"One time, a few days before that night, I looked at his phone to see the numbers he was calling, because I thought there was someone else he was seeing. I found a number he had called twice that day. I pushed redial, expecting to hear a woman answer, but it was a man. One whose voice I recognized. It was Mr. Weston."

"Gordon Weston? You're saying Tung and Gordon knew one another. Did you ask Tung about the calls?"

"Yes. He said Mr. Weston asked him to look at his computer. That's what Tung does. He repairs computers. I believed he was telling me the truth, then. Now, I'm not sure."

It isn't evidence of a crime, Nolan realizes, but it is something the police might find interesting, only he is just as wary of them as Phuong. She turns suddenly and starts toward the door.

"I have to go, now. My sister is waiting for me," she says.

"Wait. What you've told me isn't enough by itself. I'd like to find Tung, to learn what he knows."

"He is gone. He won't be back."

"Maybe you can get a message to him, through a friend of his. Tung had no reason to kill Erica, but he may know who the killer is. The DA wants to convict someone for her murder. I'm sure he'd be willing to make a deal with Tung for any information he has that would help."

"You mean he wouldn't have to go to jail?"

"That would depend on what his part in it was. Take my phone number. See if you can get a message to Tung. Tell him he can call me, and I'll try to help him. I can arrange for

285

an attorney to speak with him, to explain his rights. Would you do that?" He takes a business card, scratches out the office number and writes in his personal phone number. "Here."

"Okay," Phuong says, taking the card and putting it in her pocket. She slips out the door without another word, and is driven away in the Nissan Sentra a moment later.

~~~

Nolan places a call to Curtis Leyden.

"Curtis," Nolan says when he picks up. "I need your assistance with a project. How busy are you?"

"Very. I'm working six days a week just to keep pace with what's coming in. What's the project?"

"There's some new evidence in Erica's murder. It's not solid enough to take to the police, and I'm sure they wouldn't act on it fast enough to suit me. How much would you need to set everything aside to work on this?"

"Uh…, you've caught me unprepared. I'd have to think about it."

"Can you start immediately if I pay you a thousand dollars a day, plus expenses?"

"That's very generous, but I have obligations to my clients."

"What about fifteen hundred a day, plus expenses?"

"That's going to be difficult to turn down."

"Good. I'd like you to come to my house as soon as you can. And bring the video files from that night. There's something we might have missed."

~53~

On weekends when trials are not in session, Judge Irvin Reynolds loves to spend time with Patton, his aging overweight bulldog, named after the famous general. They take walks, during which Patton stops often to rest. The dog is ten, and weighs seventy pounds, too old to be rushed, and too heavy to be carried. There's a park a couple of blocks from Reynolds's house where he can sit on one of the benches while Patton rolls in the grass, or naps under a tree. That's where Greg decides to approach the judge, on a bench at the park.

"He's a good-looking bulldog. What's his name?" Greg asks, as he takes a seat beside Reynolds.

"Patton. He's not good-looking though, he's old and fat, like me. Aren't you Patton?" The dog lets out a muffled bark in response.

"He knows his name. Does he do any tricks?"

"He comes when he's called to eat. That's about it." Reynolds turns his head to look at Greg. "I've seen you before, in my courtroom. The Erica Dupree will contest. You're an associate of Gordon Weston, aren't you?"

Greg expected Reynolds would recognize him, and realize this is not simply a chance encounter. The next few seconds will be telling. Reynolds will either get up and leave, or subtly invite an offer.

"That's right. Gordon is engaged to my sister. I'm Greg Malloy." Greg offers his hand, but Reynolds declines to take it. Instead, he scans the area around them for anyone watching.

"I can't discuss the case with you, Mr. Malloy. That could get us both in trouble."

"I understand. I don't want any trouble for either of us. But, it must be hard for you as a judge to have to sit through this trial. After all, it's two parties squabbling over money that neither one of them deserves. In the end, the lawyers get rich, regardless of which side wins, and all you get is your wages, which I'm sure isn't that much."

"No it's not. A judge's salary is a lot less than what the average plaintiff attorney makes."

"How do you make a decision?"

"I have to decide a case based on the facts presented to me."

Reynolds doesn't seem eager to leave, or uncomfortable with the mention of his salary, so Greg takes it a step further.

"I overheard Gordon telling someone it would be worth a lot of money if he were to win this case. However, the attorneys representing the estate, make the same amount whoever wins."

"That's true. A favorable decision is worth substantially more to Mr. Weston than it is to the law firm representing Erica Dupree's estate."

"The figure I overheard Gordon mention to someone is five million."

"Mr. Malloy, this meeting never happened. You can tell Mr. Weston five million dollars will buy him the outcome he desires. Here is a number for a second phone of mine. When Mr. Weston has the money together, call that number and ask for John Smith. That way I'll know it's you."

"Gordon won't have the money until the trial is over and he gets the funds from the estate. But, I'll personally guarantee payment."

"No offense, Mr. Malloy, but your personal guarantee isn't worth much. My decision is irreversible. I don't believe I want to render it based on a promise of payment."

"Give me a chance to talk it over with Gordon. Maybe he can come up with part of it."

"I'll give you until Monday. Call that number when you know."

With that Reynolds gets up from the bench, gives Patton's leash a tug, and the two stroll away toward home. Greg calls Gordon from his car as he's leaving the park.

"He wants the money in cash, beforehand," he tells Gordon.

"I can't come up with that sort of cash. He won't get anything out of the estate attorneys. I can't believe he'd turn down that kind of money."

"I asked him to give me time to talk with you. I said maybe you could come up with part of it. He gave me until Monday."

"Alright, I'll find a way to make this work."

"Where are you, now?"

"I'm running down a lead on an investment. Why do you ask?"

"Is Lauren with you?"

"No. I haven't seen her since early this morning."

Greg disconnects wondering if Gordon is as confident as he sounds, or if this is just more of his BS. Besides his skepticism of Gordon's tactics, his distrust of the man continues to grow. The guy always seems to think he's on the verge of winning. He's like the gambler who doubles down after every loss, telling himself it's only a matter of time until he wins and gets back to even. He isn't thinking ahead.

Even if he gets the will overturned, his expenses are mounting by the minute. The estate lawyers will take their fees, then there will be federal taxes and other expenses deducted. Once Gordon receives the balance of the estate, Feldman will take a healthy cut of it. Lauren's half of his share might shrink to little or nothing before all is said and done. Same with the hundred grand Greg was promised for his part in bribing the judge. So far, Lauren has been able to anticipate Gordon's moves and stay a step ahead of him. That's why Gordon wants to keep her in the dark about the judge.

~54~

With the hidden camera images of Tung Pham enhanced, Nolan and Curtis can make out the plastic bag tucked under his arm, but there's no way to tell what's in the bag. It's too soon to contact the police with this new information. Tung has left the area, and so far, either Phuong's message hasn't reached him, or he's ignoring it. Nolan has no choice but to wait and see if Tung comes forward.

"Tung is the only one who can tell us what was in the bag," Nolan tells Curtis, after viewing the enhanced video.

"Those are two big question marks, finding him and getting him to talk."

"Curtis, I'd like you to try to talk to some of the people he worked with, and his roommate. I'll leave it up to you, if you feel it's worth surveilling any of those people to see if they lead you to him. If he has or had a bank account, you could check it for a large deposit near the time of her death."

"If I do find him, but he doesn't want to talk to me, there's not much I can do about it."

"I understand. My theory is that he ran because he's afraid of the law. I'm willing to hire an attorney to help him negotiate with the DA. If he has information they want, maybe they'll offer him immunity."

Nolan always suspected Gordon's involvement, alibi or not. In the note she left, Erica hinted it was a possibility someone might kill her for her money. In that same note, she stated it was the reason for taking Gordon out of her will. Greg was in the house that night. Gordon admittedly sent him there. Although he doesn't want to believe Lauren has any knowledge of what happened to Erica, he can't rule it out completely. Greg seldom does anything without telling her.

~~~

Nolan is spot-on with that thought. Even though Gordon said not to, Greg informs Lauren of his conversation in the park with Judge Reynolds.

"Greg, don't be an idiot. Can't you see what he's doing? He's having you take all the risk. If it backfires, and the judge has you arrested, Gordon can deny he had any part in it."

"I know that, but I know how much you're counting on the money from this deal. I did it for you. Everything I do is for you. You know that."

"Yes, I know, Greg. And it's what I love most about you. I can always count on you." She kisses him and squeezes his hand. "So, tell me about it. How did the judge react when you mentioned the five million dollars?"

"He didn't flinch. It was like he was expecting it, like it's something that happens every day. The only snag was when I told him Gordon wouldn't have the money until the estate was disbursed."

"What did Gordon say to that?"

"He said he'd find a way to get the money, but you know him. It's probably just more of his BS. Lauren, if he blows this, all three of us are going to be in dire straits. It's all I can do to make the rent, and Gordon hasn't contributed a dime."

"It's true he's been more of a burden than anything else, but let's not give up on him, yet. He's smarter than you give him credit for. Don't let on that you don't trust him. For

292

now, go along with him like everything is going exactly as planned."

"I'll do it for you, if that's what you want."

"That is what I want, and thank you for understanding. Now, when are you supposed to tell the judge whether or not Gordon can get the money?"

"He wants me to call him on his personal phone, Monday at the latest."

"Give me the number."

"Lauren, what are you going to do?"

"I have a backup plan, in case Gordon can't come up with the money."

Greg thinks about it for a minute, but in the end decides he trusts Lauren more than Gordon. He hands her the piece of paper with the number.

"Ask for John Smith, when he answers. So he knows what it's about."

"Don't tell Gordon I know about this. Alright?"

~~~

Meanwhile, Gordon is scrambling to come up with the five million promised to the judge. His line of credit with conventional lending institutions is exactly zero. He fenced the stolen jewelry, and the money from that is already gone. There's a lien on the title to his car, so he can't borrow anymore against that. In a last ditch effort to secure the cash before Monday's deadline, he makes a call to the very last person on earth he'd dare to borrow money from. Jacques Boudreaux. Boudreaux is reputed to be a high-ranking member of the Dixie Mafia.

"Mr. Boudreaux, this is Gordon Weston." Gordon waits for him to concede he knows the name.

"Yee-aah," he says, after a beat.

293

"You may have heard that my wife, Erica Dupree died recently."

"Erica Doo-pree? Where do I know that name from? Oh, now I remember. She's that rich oil heiress who got herself killed a few weeks back. And you say you were married to her. I saw her picture on the news. She was a fine-looking lady. It's too bad she got herself killed."

"Yes it is. The timing of it was unfortunate as well. The man who I believe killed her, coerced her into changing her will. I'm contesting it in court. That's why I'm calling. I need to borrow money to pay legal expenses and keep things going. The estate is worth a few hundred million."

"A few hundred million? Sweet! How much do you need for your legal expenses?"

"I'm looking to borrow five million. I'm willing to pay back the five, and another five on top of that, once the estate is disbursed which should take place a month after the trial ends."

"That's a whole lot of money to loan to someone I don't know, Mr…, what'd you say your name was again?"

"Gordon Weston. Yes, it is a lot of money, but how often do you get an opportunity to double a sum of money like that in a month?"

"Not as often as I get an opportunity to lose that much making bad loans. What do you have to put up as collateral?"

"I don't have anything worth that, but trust me. The judge will rule in my favor if I raise the money. You know what I'm saying?"

Yee-aah, I know exactly what you're saying, but in my personal experience there's no such animal as a sure thing in a court of law. I'm afraid I'm going to have to pass on this deal."

"Just a minute, Mr. Boudreaux. What about one million? Loan me one million today and I'll pay you five million in a month. That's a four hundred percent gain in a month. What do you say?"

"It's still a little too risky for me. I'd consider letting you have one hundred thousand. You'll owe me one million after thirty days, with an additional one million in interest for every month after that."

"Come on, Mr. Boudreaux. You can do better than that."

"No sir, that's my final offer. Take it or leave it. It makes no difference to me."

"Alright. You've got me over a barrel. I'll do it. When can I get the cash? I need it ASAP."

"Stay close to your phone. I'll have someone contact you in a short while to explain how it works. Good day Mr. Weston."

~55~

Gordon informs Greg of the one hundred thousand dollars he was able to borrow on Sunday, saying it was the best he could do. Greg in turn informs Lauren, that same day.

"I told him it wouldn't be enough, but he wants me to call the judge in the morning and make the offer, anyway."

"You should call the judge tonight. He said he'd give you until Monday. You don't know whether that means midnight tonight, or the end of the day tomorrow. You don't want to miss the deadline, do you?"

"No, I guess not. But, I should run it by Gordon, first. He went to meet some guy about the money. He said he might be gone a couple of hours."

"I don't want you to wait on Gordon. Make the call now."

"Why, what's the rush?"

"I already told you. I don't want you to miss the deadline. And, because I'm asking you to, Greg. That's all you need to know."

"Does this have something to do with Nolan? I know you've been seeing him."

She doesn't deny or confirm it. "What if I am? I trust Nolan more than Gordon. Besides, why bet on one or the other, when I can bet on both? Go ahead, Greg. Call the judge."

Nolan is neither surprised nor disappointed to see Lauren when she shows up on his doorstep Sunday evening. Once inside, she throws her arms around his neck to pull his face to hers. He offers no resistance.

"It's been way too long, Nolan."

"You were here three days ago."

"And that's three days too many to be away from you. Pour me a drink. I have some good news to share with you, and then we can celebrate."

"A little good news is always welcome. The same is true of a celebration."

They settle onto barstools with their drinks, and Lauren begins.

"Gordon is attempting to bribe Judge Reynolds to rule in his favor. He had Greg talk to Reynolds and offer five million dollars. Gordon told Greg not to tell me, but Greg doesn't keep anything from me for very long. Reynolds agreed, so it's a done deal, except for one thing. Gordon doesn't have all the money. He wants to give Reynolds one hundred thousand now, and pay him the rest after the estate is settled."

"Until my recent experience in court, I would have thought it more difficult to buy a judge. I can't say I'm surprised that Gordon would try, though. The trouble is, I don't know who to report this to."

"Report it? Why would you do that?"

"So Gordon doesn't buy the judge and inherit Erica's estate."

"Nolan, if you did report the judge, there's no telling if it would make any difference. It's difficult to know who can be trusted. Consider this for a moment. Gordon can only come up with one hundred thousand dollars. Can you come up with more? We could top Gordon's offer."

"We?"

"Yes, we. I want you to get Erica's estate. It's what she wanted. And yes, I want my share of it. I've been honest with you about that. I have the judge's phone number, the one he told Greg to call him on. I can call him and make a deal. How much money can you put your hands on when the banks open tomorrow?"

"How much do you think it would take?"

"Unfortunately, Greg has already told the judge Gordon will pay five million, so he has that figure in mind. At the same time, he knows he has to wait to get it, and a lot of things can happen in the meantime."

"True. I'm sure Reynolds would prefer the money up front. Are you sure you want to be the one to call him? I don't want you to get in trouble."

"I can take care of myself. I won't get in any trouble."

"Yeah, I know you take care of yourself. I've seen you in action."

Nolan is quiet for a minute, wondering if he really wants to do this, and considering how best to proceed. Lauren refills their glasses as he ponders it.

"Let's set a ceiling of five million, knowing he's already accepted that from Gordon, via Greg. But, I want to start out lower. Offer him a half million cash, delivered tomorrow. If he says no, up it to a million."

"I can do that, but Nolan, I lived with you for almost a year. I know how much you keep in your bank account. Where are you going to get that kind of money, so quickly?"

"Erica named me as the beneficiary on her life insurance policy. The insurance company withheld payment until I was cleared of the murder charges."

"How much was it for?" Her eyes light up with interest. It's a reminder to exercise a degree of caution when discussing his finances with Lauren.

"There's enough to cover the payment to the judge."

"I should call him now. Greg has already called him with Gordon's offer of one hundred thousand. He hasn't accepted it, but he hasn't given a definite no, either. If he knows there's a cash offer for a lot more than the one hundred thousand, he can tell Greg he's had a change of heart."

She takes out her phone and the piece of paper with the judge's number to make the call. Then she remembers something.

"Before I make this deal with Judge Reynolds, you and I need to reach an agreement on my share, should everything go as planned. I'd like half of whatever you net after all the taxes and fees are deducted."

"Sorry, no deal."

"Nolan, don't be selfish. With half of what you're going to get you can still afford to live anywhere in the world you want, and never work another day in your life. You can travel, have your choice of women, and buy a yacht. It won't hurt you to give me the opportunity to live like that."

"It might not hurt me, but it isn't necessary. You've used me and tossed me aside one too many times. There's a buyer-beware warning stuck on your forehead. I made a tentative agreement to partner with you, but it's a limited partnership. One day at a time for as long as it works. And I never said we'd split things fifty-fifty."

"Alright, Nolan. What do you think is fair? Forty percent to me? Does that sound reasonable?"

"Five percent," Nolan counters.

"Get serious, Nolan. I'll agree to thirty-five."

"I'll up it to ten percent. That's as high as I'll go."

"Fifteen and we have a deal. That's not that much. You can do that."

"Alright," Nolan says after a beat.

They shake hands and Lauren punches in Judge Reynolds's number.

"Hello, John Smith. I would like for you to rule against Gordon Weston and let Erica Dupree's will stay as it is. I'm willing to pay you five hundred thousand dollars. I can have it delivered by whatever method you choose, after the banks open, tomorrow."

"Who are you?"

"It's best for both of us if I don't tell you. Let's just say I'm a friend of Erica Dupree who knows she wouldn't want to see Gordon Weston win."

"Attempting to bribe a judge is a criminal offense."

"Yes, I'm aware of that. I'm also aware of the arrangement with Gordon Weston. I think you know you'll never see any money beyond the one hundred thousand dollars."

The line is quiet as Reynolds considers this. She has his interest, she's certain of it, but he's still clinging to the hope of getting five million.

"Mr. Smith," Lauren prompts.

"Yes, I'm here."

"I'll up my offer to one million dollars. The same terms, delivered tomorrow."

"Since you're aware of the arrangement with the other party, I'm sure you're aware of the amount, as well."

"Gordon Weston is a seasoned con artist. He can't be taken at his word. You'd be foolish to think otherwise. Two million dollars, tomorrow. That's my final offer."

"Okay," Reynolds says. "I accept."

~56~

Nolan enters the courtroom near ten on Monday morning, and takes a seat in the back row. It looks no different than any other session he's attended. Alan Rutherford and Joseph Edgar sit impassively with their gazes trained on the papers laid out in front of them, looking as if they'd rather be anywhere but here, as Marv Feldman is questioning Dr. Rebecca Patrice. She's the third psychiatrist to be called to testify to Erica's poor mental condition. Lauren and Greg are in the row behind the plaintiff's table, where Gordon and Feldman are. Greg glances back at Nolan as he enters, then whispers to Lauren. She doesn't look at Nolan.

As usual, Judge Reynolds's expression is unreadable as he listens to the witness's testimony. For Feldman it's another day in court like all the others. He may suspect his client has bought the judge's verdict, but he can't be certain of it. Gordon has kept him out of the loop, as per Feldman's wishes.

"And how many times did you see Ms. Dupree during that period?" Feldman asks the witness.

"I saw her once a week."

"Did you prescribe any medications for her?"

"Yes, I prescribed an antipsychotic for her schizophrenia."

If Erica had taken even a small portion of the pills these phony doctors had supposedly prescribed, she would have OD'd years ago. But as with all previous witnesses for the plaintiff, Rutherford declines to cross-examine.

"I'm out of people to put on the stand," Feldman tells Gordon during the lunch recess.

"Well, you've given it your best shot. Let's leave it to the judge to decide," Gordon says confidently.

Feldman takes this to mean Gordon has gotten to Reynolds. When the trial reconvenes after lunch he tells the judge he's done.

"Mr. Rutherford, your response to the plaintiff's claim."

"Your Honor. We stand by our previous statement. The will was properly drawn, and legally signed by Erica Dupree. She was of sound mind at the time, as witnessed by myself and three other people. The plaintiff has not introduced evidence to the contrary."

"Very well. We will now adjourn, and I'll give you my decision when we reconvene at nine a.m."

~~~

Nolan didn't return to the courtroom after lunch because there was a matter to attend to at his bank—a wire transfer to a Grand Cayman Island bank account, for two million dollars. At another bank, a man who works for Jacques Boudreaux is wire transferring one hundred thousand dollars to the same bank account.

~~~

Late afternoon, Curtis Leyden comes by Nolan's house to tell him what he's found out about Tung Pham.

"He left Houston a week ago on a United Airlines flight to Tokyo. I wasn't able to pick him up from there. He's probably gone to Vietnam where he can lay low with friends or family."

"Sounds like he's on the run. That may be our last chance to find out what was in the bag, or what actually happened to Erica. I have a strong feeling Gordon is somehow involved in her death. I was counting on Tung to confirm my suspicions."

"My guess is, you'll never know. Sorry, Nolan. There's nothing more I can do on this one."

It was Nolan's wish Tung would be found, and that he would implicate Gordon in Erica's murder. It would be sweet revenge after the way Gordon lied on the witness stand during Nolan's murder trial. Not to mention, it would have had a major impact on the outcome of the suit contesting Erica's will. As it is, all his hopes are riding on the two-million-dollar bribe to Judge Reynolds. It made sense when Lauren suggested it, but now he's not so sure.

The two million is gone. There's no getting it back. It's in a Grand Cayman Island bank where it can't be touched by anyone other than Reynolds. What's to keep Reynolds from deciding in Gordon's favor? He has all the money he'll get from Nolan. If Gordon wins, he gets another four million nine hundred thousand from him.

It occurs to Nolan that Lauren realizes this, and has all along. She's playing both sides against one another. If Gordon inherits Erica's estate, she gets half. If Nolan inherits it, she doesn't get half, but she still comes out smelling like a rose. That stuff about not trusting Gordon. It's a load of crap. She's outfoxed Gordon as well as himself at every turn, and will probably continue to do so.

~~~

Greg is having the same thoughts about Lauren. When the three of them returned to his apartment after court was

303

adjourned, Gordon was euphoric. It annoyed Greg to see him like that, laughing, singing, grabbing Lauren and dancing around the room with her. Then, he whispers in her ear, and they go into the bedroom and shut the door. Greg has to turn the volume up on the TV, to drown out the sound of them screwing.

Luckily, it doesn't last long. Afterward, Lauren comes out of the bedroom in her robe, without Gordon. She sits on the couch next to Greg. He glares at her.

"Stop that, Greg. I'm taking care of business. That's all."

"Yeah, right. Tell me something. Which one do you want to see win, Nolan or Gordon?"

"It's not up to me, so it doesn't matter."

"You talked to Nolan about paying Reynolds, didn't you?"

"Why would you think that?"

"I know you. That's what you meant by, *bet on them both*. You've made a deal with Nolan, too. Haven't you?"

"I'm doing what I need to do, and that's all you need to know. Don't forget, what helps me, helps you, too. I'm going to take a shower."

While Lauren is in the shower, Gordon comes out of the bedroom. If possible, he's even happier than earlier. Greg feels like punching him, but he manages to keep his cool.

"So things look pretty good for tomorrow, don't they?" he says to Gordon.

"You bet they do. I can hardly wait to hear the judge say, 'I find in favor of the plaintiff.'"

"How long do you think it will be before you get everything?"

"A few weeks, maybe a month. And then, we're out of here. I mean, no offense, Greg. It's been good of you to put up with us for so long, but Lauren and I have decided to get married. We're thinking about buying a house on Grand Cayman Island. We've got a lot of good memories of the time we spent there."

304

Greg isn't able to hide his surprise at hearing this. "Wow, I didn't see that coming."

"Don't worry Greg. You can come visit us anytime you like. You'll love it there."

"Yeah, uh…, that sounds great. I mean, congratulations."

"Thanks, Greg. I knew you'd be happy for us. There's something else I wanted to tell you about, while it's just the two of us here. You remember Phuong's boyfriend, Tung? He was the third guy caught on the hidden cameras, the night Erica was killed."

"The police showed me the video when they questioned me, so I know who you're talking about."

"He left town suddenly, last week. When the police find out, they'll assume he's the one who killed her."

"How do you know he left town?"

"I was the one who advised him to go. He's Vietnamese. That's enough in itself to make the police suspicious. I told him it was just a matter of time before they arrested him, and then I gave him the money for airfare, so he could lay low in Vietnam for a while."

"Why are you telling me?"

"I did it for you. The DA isn't going to rest until someone is convicted of her murder. Now, they'll spend all their time chasing Tung. Don't you see? You're off the hook."

"There is no hook, Gordon. I didn't kill her. It was your idea for me to go there on that night. You did it for you, not me."

"Okay, Greg. You're right. It wasn't entirely unselfish of me, but we're on the same team here. We're family, now. Or at least we will be soon. We've got to help each other out when necessary."

~57~

Although Erica Dupree's murder is no longer front page news, there are still enough people following it to merit a story update every so often. The reporters that normally hang out around the courthouse get word Judge Reynolds is giving his decision this morning. A half dozen of them are seated in the back row, ten minutes before the show is set to begin.

Also among the folks in the gallery are Nolan, Lauren, Greg, a handful of curious onlookers, two thugs who work for Jacques Boudreaux, and Erica's brother and sister. The brother and sister are sitting in the row behind Rutherford and Edgar, and making a show of ignoring everyone else in the room.

Gordon seems unable to stop smiling. He turns his head occasionally to glance at Lauren, and give her a thumbs-up. And, he aims a giddy grin at Nolan now and again. The only time the smile seems to slacken is when Gordon catches sight of the two thugs.

"All rise, the court is now in session. The honorable Judge Irvin Reynolds presiding," the bailiff announces, as things get underway.

The judge enters, takes his place at the head of the courtroom, and waits for those gathered to settle into their seats, before beginning.

"After many hours of deliberation, I've concluded that the evidence presented by the plaintiff raises concern over the state of Erica Dupree's mental health at the time of the signing of her most recent will."

A squeal, sounding more like one from a young girl than Gordon, escapes his lips quicker than he can clamp a hand over his mouth to stop it. The judge admonishes him with a stern look before continuing.

"Furthermore, the evidence presented by the plaintiff raises concern over whether or not Ms. Dupree was capable of making rational decisions concerning her financial affairs at that time."

Gordon can barely contain himself. Nolan wants to cry. He has a vision of four hundred million dollars disappearing right before his eyes, along with the two million he wired to the Grand Cayman Island bank.

"However, according to the testimony of the psychiatrists, Ms. Dupree, has been treated for various conditions, such as schizophrenia and bipolar disorder, for the last ten years."

Everyone in the courtroom seems to sense a change in the air. It's like leaning into a strong wind that suddenly switches directions, one hundred eighty degrees, and you fall on your face.

"Mr. Rutherford, I understand you have a copy of a last will and testament signed by Ms. Dupree prior to the ten-year period in question. Is that correct?"

"Yes, Your Honor. Erica Dupree made out her original will when she was twenty-two. Thirteen years ago."

"Can I see that copy, please?" Reynolds asks.

The bailiff takes the papers from Rutherford and hands them to the judge, who quickly scans them. Not a sound can be heard as they await the judge's decision.

"This document," Reynolds says, holding the papers up for all to see, "represents the final wishes of Erica Dupree. I declare it her legitimate and final will and testament." His gavel comes down. "We're adjourned."

Gordon can't comprehend what happened. He stares at Reynolds in utter disbelief. Reynolds returns the stare with a screw-you look, then vanishes from the room. Rutherford, Edgar and Erica's siblings make a swift escape a beat after Reynolds. Nolan evades the reporters as he hurries from the courtroom and down the stairs.

"Mr. Weston," a reporter shouts, as Gordon stumbles from the courtroom. "What do you think about the judge's decision?"

"Uh…," is all Gordon can manage.

"We're still processing it," Feldman says. "No comment for now."

"Will you appeal the ruling?"

"That hasn't been decided, yet."

Feldman takes Gordon's arm and pulls him toward the elevator with the two thugs from the gallery trailing close behind. Gordon is still in a state of shock, and doesn't realize Lauren isn't with him. She bolted after Nolan as he exited the courtroom. Greg follows Lauren out a minute too late, and loses sight of her when she disappears into the stairwell.

Nolan is still trying to assimilate this latest turn of events. He's oblivious to the people and traffic around him as he makes his way to the parking garage. Lauren runs across an intersection ignoring the flashing 'Don't Walk' signal and is almost struck by a car. She catches Nolan as he's about to get into his car.

"Nolan, wait!" she shouts. "I want to talk to you."

She's sweating and panting. Her mascara is running and her hair is a mess from sprinting after him, but he still finds her every bit as beautiful as ever.

"Not now, Lauren."

"Please, Nolan. It will only take a minute."

"Alright, get in," he offers, and opens the passenger door.

She does. He closes the door before going around to the driver's side to get in himself.

"Don't be mad at me, Nolan. I had no idea this would happen."

"I'm not mad. This is my own fault. I should have known better than to try and bribe a judge. I got swept up in the whole thing—Erica's vast fortune and the lifestyle it would afford me. It was greedy of me. It's as simple as that."

"Does this mean you're giving up? You're not going to fight the decision?"

"I doubt I'll fight it. Erica leaving her estate to me was too good to be true, in the first place. Maybe she *wasn't* in her right mind when she changed her will. Who can say for sure? Besides, I have the money from her life insurance. They can't take that away from me."

"How much did you get?"

"Nice try, but I'm not saying."

She slides over a little closer. "Why not? I'm only curious. I'm happy that you've come out of this with something to show for it. That's more than I can say for Gordon or myself."

"Don't worry Lauren. You'll land on your feet. You always do. And as far as Gordon is concerned, I couldn't care less."

"Are you going back to your house, now? I'll come along with you."

"Thanks, but I'm not sure where I'm going, now. Anyway, Gordon probably needs a shoulder to cry on."

"Screw Gordon."

"Yeah, and that too. You, Gordon and Greg have a great life."

"What, like you and I are through? We've had this conversation before, Nolan. You're not getting rid of me that easily. You feel as strongly about me as I do about you. You can't forget me. It's impossible. There's no place on earth

309

you can go to get away from me. I'll always be right here." She places her hand over his heart. "I feel the same about you, Nolan."

"You're right, Lauren. We have had this conversation before. But thankfully, this is the last time we'll have it. I won't deny my feelings for you, but I have a shred of dignity and enough self-control left to resist giving in to them. You have Greg, and Gordon if you want him. The two of them should be plenty. Maybe, I'll see you around."

Lauren gets out of his car. "When you come to your senses, you know where to reach me," she says, before shutting the door and walking away.

As she steps out of the parking garage onto the sidewalk, she sees Gordon walking her way. On each side of him a thug has him by the arm coaxing him forward. Gordon stares straight ahead with a petrified expression on his face. The thugs pass within a few feet of her as they lead Gordon into the parking garage. Gordon doesn't even notice her. Marv Feldman is trailing behind the threesome. Lauren stops him.

"Who are those guys, and where are they taking Gordon?"

"I'm not sure. They got into the elevator with us and told everyone else to get out. As we rode down to the lobby, they told Gordon someone wants to talk to him, and something else about Boudreaux."

"Should we call the police?" Lauren asks.

"What would we tell them? Two guys who look like mafia goons took Gordon somewhere for a chat? That could get him in more trouble. I say we wait and see what happens."

~58~

After a week of traveling by plane, train and bus, Tung Pham arrives in Lam Dong Province in the Central Highlands of Vietnam. He'll stay with a cousin, sleep on the floor and live on a diet of mostly rice for however long it takes the police in Houston to lose interest in him. He will miss the USA. It's the country where he was born. Vietnam is a strange faraway place he's never visited before now. He's sorry he didn't tell Phuong he was leaving or where he was going, but it is best she doesn't know.

Phuong Nguyen cried herself to sleep every night for a week after Tung left. He broke her heart, but she has no choice but to try and forget about him. She has to find work, to earn money to buy the many things that will be needed for the child she carries in her belly. She never had the chance to tell Tung, because she didn't find out herself until after he left. Maybe if she had known sooner, if she had told him, maybe he wouldn't have gone. But that's a lot of ifs and too many maybes, and it just doesn't matter anymore.

~~~

Erica's murder, along with the investigation and questioning of his lover has since brought Hernando Perez and Douglas Pruitt closer to one another. Hernando hasn't found another job. Douglas helps him with his bills, though he hides it from his wife. He's even told Hernando he plans to leave his wife. Hernando doesn't really believe he ever will, but it's still nice to hear him say it.

~~~

The thugs don't stick Gordon's feet in buckets of concrete and throw him into the ship channel, as he thought they might. Instead, they drive him to Lake Charles, Louisiana, two hours east of Houston, to have a face-to-face chat with Boudreaux. It takes place in a meat locker chilled to thirty-three degrees. Boudreaux is a huge man who weighs over four hundred pounds. The cold doesn't bother him. He is sitting on a stool beside an overturned wooden barrel with a chopping block, cleaver and slab of raw meat resting on top of it, when the thugs bring Gordon in.

"I understand things didn't go as planned in court today," Boudreaux begins. "That makes me worry about not getting the money you owe me, and I hate to worry." He cleaves a large chunk of raw meat from the slab and stuffs it into his mouth.

"What happened in court was unfortunate, but this thing is a long way from over. My attorney, Marv Feldman is already working on the appeal."

"I'm glad to hear it, but the fact is, you led me to believe the money I loaned you would be enough for you to win your case. It didn't turn out that way. So either you lied to me, or that judge screwed you over. Which is it?"

"The judge reneged on our agreement. It was totally unexpected. Who would have thought a judge, of all people would do that? It's getting so you can't trust anyone these days."

"Yeah, I know the feeling. Would you like me to have someone speak to the judge, and have him change his ruling?"

"Could you? I mean, that would be great."

Boudreaux lets out a loud guffaw. The thugs laugh, too.

"I'm just joking with you. I'm not going to mess with a judge for this kind of money. That'd just be buying trouble I don't need. You go ahead and file that appeal. I'll be watching to see how things go. Don't take any trips out of town though. That sort of thing makes me worry, and like I said before, I don't like to worry."

Boudreaux shoves another chunk of meat into his mouth. Gordon watches him chew.

"We're finished talking, for now. You can go," Boudreaux tells him.

"Uh…, your men brought me here. Can one of them give me a ride back to Houston?"

"Sure. We can get you back to Houston. Jim Bob, give this man a ride to the Greyhound station, so he can get home."

~ ~ ~

Lauren is inconsolable on the drive back to the apartment after the disappointing outcome of the hearing.

"Look on the bright side," Greg says.

"Shut up, Greg. There is no bright side, you idiot."

"Now we're not tied down to Houston, and that loser Gordon. We can go somewhere else and get a fresh start."

"I'm not sure I'm through with Gordon. There's still a chance he can appeal this thing."

"I'm not sure we'll see him again. Those guys I saw him getting into the elevator with looked like they meant business. It must have something to do with the hundred grand he borrowed."

Greg and Lauren go back to the apartment and have several drinks to numb the pain of their disappointment. After a bit Greg coaxes her into bed. Gordon arrives at the

313

bus station in Houston at nine p.m. and catches a cab to the apartment. He walks in on Lauren and Greg in bed together.

"What the hell is going on, here?!" he yells at them.

"What does it look like?" Greg answers, nonchalantly.

"Your own sister? You sick bastard."

"I'm not his sister, Gordon. I didn't intend for you to find out like this, but now that you have, I might as well tell you everything. Greg and I are husband and wife."

"And you've been stringing me along, all this time?"

"Yes, the same way you've been stringing us along. A lot of big talk about what's going to happen, but somehow it never does."

Gordon begins packing his clothes into a suitcase.

"You're leaving? Just like that?" Lauren inquires.

"Let him go. We're better off without him."

"Until I walked in and saw the two of you going at it, I wasn't sure what I was going to do. Jacques Boudreaux is going to have me killed if I don't come up with a million dollars. I was going to take you with me, Lauren, but not now. This is too weird for me."

"You're not going to appeal the ruling?"

"What for? It was a long shot from the beginning."

He finishes packing and leaves.

"Do you want another drink?" Greg asks.

"Yes, and don't skimp on the vodka."

~59~

When Erica Dupree dictated her final will and testament at the age of twenty-two, it was done at the insistence of her father. At that age the girl had no concept of the value of a dollar or what it took to earn one. Or so her father thought. Without a will, if something were to happen to her, the money would have been tied up in probate for years. And afterward, a big chunk of it would be claimed by the government. Her great-grandfather would roll over in his grave if that happened.

Having no significant other or children of her own at the time, Erica bequeathed her entire estate to be divided equally among her father, mother, brother and sister. Maybe it's for the best, Nolan tells himself. The money will go to people who are already wealthy. It won't change their lives one iota. Had he inherited it, his life would have suddenly become very complicated. It would have been like winning the lottery. Friends and relatives he hadn't heard from in years would be calling day and night, attempting to reconnect with him.

The members of Erica's family meet over dinner, shortly after Judge Reynolds's decision, to discuss their inheritance. It seems only fitting that they use some portion of the money to honor Erica. Donate a plot of land to be turned into a park named after her, perhaps. Or set up a scholarship fund for gifted young girls and boys.

315

"I've been thinking about something, ever since the reading of her will. The one where she gave it all to Nolan Drake," Erica's sister, Caroline says. "I never thought he did it. I was surprised to hear he was arrested for her murder. When Alan read what he was to receive, he was in shock."

"I agree," her brother Jacob says. "In my opinion, he appeared deeply affected by her death. I think DA Hardwick jumped the gun, and as a result the real killer had plenty of time to cover his tracks and get rid of any evidence. We may never know what really happened."

"I think we should use some of her estate to find her killer," Caroline suggests. "We can put up a reward large enough a mother would turn in her own son for it."

"You'll have cranks, phonies and liars coming out of the woodwork if we do that," their father says.

"No, Dad. I think she's right," Jacob says. "Offer a huge reward. Five million dollars. Let the police sort through who's lying and who's not. It won't hurt anything to try."

~~~

The Dupree family holds a press conference to announce they're offering a five-million-dollar reward for information leading to the arrest and conviction of Erica's killer. They don't notify the police or District Attorney's Office beforehand. DA Aaron Hardwick finds out as it is happening.

"You'll want to see this," Fiona says, as she hurries into his office to turn on the TV. Jacob Dupree is standing at a podium while the news media folks ask questions. A 1-800 phone number scrolls across the bottom of the screen. "The Dupree family is offering a five-million-dollar reward for her killer," Fiona explains.

"Crap!" Hardwick exclaims. "Get me those two detectives. I want them in my office, ASAP."

The reward offer works. Two days after it is posted, Detective Gutierrez calls to report directly to Hardwick.

"We have an informant who's come forward. She says she can give us the murderer, the motive and the weapon used. She wants full immunity for her testimony."

"Who is this woman, and how does she come by the information?"

"She's Gordon Weston's former girlfriend, Lauren Malloy. She claims she overheard him talking with her brother, Greg Malloy. Weston agreed to pay Malloy to kill her."

"He's one of the men on the hidden camera video, isn't he?"

"Yes, that's right. We have him in custody. According to Ms. Malloy, he used a fireplace poker. We retrieved the poker from Ms. Dupree's home an hour ago. There appears to be blood, hair and skin fragments on the handle. The lab is going over it, now. Do you want to charge him?"

"Not yet. Hold him, but don't charge him until we get the lab results. Has he implicated Gordon Weston?"

"No. He claims he didn't do it. We have an arrest warrant out for Weston, but it appears he may have left town."

~60~

Nolan rereads Erica's posthumous note for what must be the tenth time. It saddens him, but it's the only thing of hers he has. The request to spread her ashes on the hillside near her home in Costa Rica is something he intends to honor. He hopes her family will allow him to do so. Knowing of no other way to contact them, Nolan leaves a message for Jacob Dupree at the executive offices of Dupree Oil and Gas. He returns it the next day.

"Mr. Drake, I got your message saying you wanted to speak with me. What can I do for you?"

"Thanks for returning my call. This concerns Erica."

"Yes, I presumed as much."

"Erica left a note with Alan Rutherford, with instructions to give it to me, in the event of her death. He did so after the reading of her will. In the note she makes a request of me to spread her ashes on the hillside near her home in Costa Rica. I'd like to honor her wishes. Would you ask your parents and your sister if they will allow it?"

"I see. I wasn't aware of any note, or her desire for her ashes to be spread in that manner. Would it be possible for me to have a look at the note from her?"

"Of course. I can bring it to you."

"Thank you. That would be helpful. I'd like to see it for myself, before discussing it with my family."

Nolan delivers the note to Jacob, who in turn takes it to Caroline.

"It's her handwriting," Caroline says. "I'm sure of it. I didn't realize until now how much she loved him. If Gordon hadn't contested her will, it would have all been his. It appears that's what she wanted."

"And if dad hadn't paid the judge to stop him, Gordon might have gotten it all. As it is, her money will go to a good cause. What do you think we should do about her ashes?"

~~~

The Dupree family uses two private jets to fly themselves and Nolan to Costa Rica. Jacob, Caroline, their spouses and children ride in the larger jet. Nolan rides in the smaller jet with Erica's parents. Midday they arrive at the Tamarindo Airport. They have a small memorial service at sunset, just the family and Nolan. The wind coming off the Pacific Ocean scatters the ashes across the hillside as Nolan empties them from the urn. Afterward they enjoy a meal delivered from Erica's favorite local restaurant.

Nolan appreciates meeting and spending time with her family. And he is grateful for the opportunity to relive the memories of the time spent here with Erica. At the end of the evening, after the children are in bed, Jacob calls Nolan aside to speak with him and his sister. They take a bottle of rum and paper cups to sit by the pool, overlooking the ocean and the hillside where Erica's ashes lie.

"Until I read the note from Erica, I didn't realize how close the two of you had become," Caroline tells Nolan.

"We're sorry about the way things turned out with her will," Jacob says. "If we had known sooner, maybe we could have done something. I hope it's of some consolation to you to know her money will aid several worthy causes that Erica supported over the years."

"That's not to say we expect that alone to be enough," Caroline adds. "We take our sister's wishes very seriously. We want you to have this house. I know it's what she wanted, as well."

"Uh…, I don't know what to say. Thank you. This place holds some of the best memories I have of our short time together."

"Additionally," Jacob says, "the jet you rode in on the way here is yours, now. The pilots are on the Dupree Oil and Gas payroll. It can stay that way for now. Our family will fly back in the bigger jet, tomorrow morning. You of course can stay as long as you like. Also, I've transferred fifty million dollars into a bank account for you."

"Let me guess," Nolan says. "A Grand Cayman Island bank?"

"That's right. There's some paperwork to take care of. They'll need a signature card and a password, that sort of thing. That can be done whenever you're ready. Also, we've had our attorneys draw up an agreement for you to sign. Essentially, it is a waiver of your right to contest the recent court ruling concerning Erica's will."

"Alright, I have no objection to signing the waiver," Nolan says. "This is all so unexpected, like everything else that's happened in the last couple of months."

"Nolan, can I ask you something about her last week?" Caroline says.

"Yes, of course."

"Did she express concern over the possibility Gordon might attempt to have her killed?"

"We didn't talk much about Gordon, but in the note she alluded to the chance of something happening to her."

"Do you know this Greg Malloy person the police are holding?"

"Yes, I was romantically involved with his wife, only I thought she was his sister." Caroline gives him a puzzled look. "It's a long story."

"I wonder if they'll ever find Gordon."

"Probably not," Jacob answers. "If he's smart, he'll run to some country that has no extradition treaty with the USA, and stay there."

The view and tropical climate don't hold the same allure without Erica there to share them. It's profoundly sad in the big house by himself. Nolan longs for the sound, feel and scent of a woman to ease his loneliness. Someone to share this house with. Hell, someone to share this new life of his. And not just anyone. He's had it with strangers. He wants to wake every morning beside someone who is familiar and predictable.

Two days after the Dupree family leaves, the solitude is too much to bear any longer. Nolan decides to return to Houston. He's aboard the jet with the pilots going through their preflight checklist when his phone sounds an incoming call. It's Lauren.

"Hello Lauren. I can't talk right now."

"Well, call me back when you can. When will that be?"

"I'm on a plane that's about to take off. I'll be back in Houston in five or six hours."

"Where are you?"

"It's not important. Like I say, I'll be back in Houston later today."

"Call me as soon as you get in. Something's happened. Greg is in jail, and Gordon has left town."

"Yeah, I know. I've heard all about it."

"I need you, Nolan. I don't have anyone else to turn to. Please call me."

~~~

321

In the Harris County Jail, Greg waits to hear from Lauren. Her plan is a simple one. Gordon will contact her, eventually. When he does, she'll find out where he is and notify the authorities. Once Gordon is in custody, Greg can cut a deal to testify against Gordon, in exchange for a lesser sentence. He'll swear Gordon paid him to kill her. Lauren will get the five-million-dollar-reward, and when he gets out they'll be together again. Only this time they'll be rich. It made perfect sense when Lauren explained it to him. How else are they going to put their hands on five million dollars? But with each passing day behind bars, his doubts increase.

~~~

Gordon is staying in a motel in Lyman, Wyoming. He is registered as Willis Humphry, and pays the weekly rate in advance with cash. It's a sleepy little town seven miles off the interstate, halfway between no place and nowhere. He ended up there after his sudden and unplanned departure from Houston. If he had left the country, his passport would have been scanned and there would be a record of his destination. With his connections, Jacques Boudreaux could find him.

The motel has cable TV and free Wi-Fi. Gordon is browsing the Houston Chronicle online when he comes across an article mentioning the murder of Erica Dupree. He reads it twice. A five-million-dollar reward was offered by the Dupree family. A confidential informant came forward. Greg Malloy has been arrested. Another suspect is at large.

"Crap!" Gordon says aloud. "Another suspect? Who?" Then he realizes it can only be one person, himself. "Crap and crap, again."

He uses a burner cell phone to place a call to Lauren. She doesn't recognize the number. "Hello," she answers tentatively.

"It's me."

"Gordon?"

"Yeah, what's going on there?"

"What do you mean? Where are you?"

Her response confirms his suspicions. Pretending nothing is wrong, asking where he is.

"I'm still here in Houston. I never left."

"You are? I've missed you. Can I come over?"

"Nice try, Lauren. You set me up. Why'd you do it? Don't tell me. It was for the reward, wasn't it?"

"I don't know what you're talking about, Gordon. What reward?"

"I'll get you for this, Lauren," Gordon says, before hanging up.

~61~

On that early March night when Erica Dupree is killed, the temperature dips into the forties as a brisk wind blows from the north. Lauren parks her Lexus SUV a block away, and checks the time before getting out. Ten forty. She is dressed all in black, wearing slacks, a long sleeve knit turtleneck, soft-sole shoes, hooded jacket and gloves. With her hair tied back and the hood covering her head, she walks casually down the sidewalk toward her destination. Lights are on in the houses on the block, but the drapes are drawn shut, and no one notices the darkly clad stranger passing by.

Upon reaching the house, she departs from the sidewalk, slips behind hedge bushes and over the eight-foot-tall wrought iron fence. Hidden from the traffic on the street and neighbors, by the hedgerow, she crosses through a rose garden to a courtyard beneath a second-floor balcony. She removes her jacket and pulls on a ski mask, then like a cat she scales a trellis to reach the balcony. Testing the doorknob, she finds it unlocked. It's not surprising. A second-floor door to a balcony of a house situated in a quiet neighborhood. Slowly and cautiously she opens the door, eases inside and shuts it, without so much as a click of the latch being heard.

With her back to the door she stands perfectly still, letting her eyes adjust to the darkness. It appears to be a small reading room. After a moment, she moves across it to the door. On the other side of the door is a hallway, and at the end of the hallway is a double-door leading into what must be the master bedroom suite. She moves stealthily toward it, knowing that's where her man, Nolan and the woman who wants to take him away, are sleeping. Lauren puts her ear to the bedroom door—nothing.

She silently turns the knob, and cracks the door open an inch. Still no sound. Opening the door a little more, she pokes her head in for a look. A poster bed sits against the wall opposite the door. Two lumps lie unmoving under the covers. Lauren steps inside, leaving the door ajar and creeps along the wall until reaching a dark corner where she can observe the couple without being seen. Nolan is lying on his back. Erica's head rests on his chest. She looks so content. It infuriates Lauren.

This was her plan all along, Lauren now realizes. Enticing her into the affair with Gordon wasn't done to get rid of Gordon. It was done to get Nolan away from her, so Erica could impress him with her big home, fancy car and wealth. She never intended to pay the one million for screwing Gordon. She probably didn't intend to pay the five million divorce settlement, either. It was all a ruse to keep her occupied while Erica stole Nolan.

Erica stirs. Lauren presses her back to the corner, and remains still. Suddenly, Erica's head jerks up in alarm. She looks around, and at Nolan, then she relaxes. It was only a dream. She pulls the covers back and slides out of bed, careful not to wake Nolan. Lauren watches her tiptoe into the bathroom and shut the door. The light spills out from beneath the door. It's enough that Nolan could possibly see her if he happens to wake and look in her direction.

After a moment the light is turned off, and Erica emerges wearing a robe. She goes to leave the bedroom, but pauses when she finds the door ajar. It puzzles her, that much is obvious, but she shrugs it off and continues out of the bedroom. Lauren leaves the room a few seconds later, and catches a glimpse of Erica descending the stairs to the first floor. She heads toward the kitchen, and Lauren follows. As she passes through the big room, Lauren grabs the poker from its stand beside the fireplace. Erica leaves the kitchen door open as she enters. A light goes on.

From the dining room twenty feet away, Lauren can see Erica's shadow as she moves around the kitchen. She stops in the area of the cooking island. Lauren eases closer to the open door. Erica is standing with her back to the door, looking at a message displayed on her cell phone. Until that moment, Lauren wasn't sure what she would do. She reacts without thinking, charging toward Erica while raising the poker high in the air. Gripping it with both hands, she brings it down with all her strength, striking Erica on the head, and knocking her unconscious.

The blood doesn't gush out immediately. It starts slowly trickling, and then the flow increases. Lauren's mind kicks into overdrive. The pantry closet is only ten feet away. She opens the pantry door, takes hold of Erica's hands and drags her inside. Lauren bends over to put her gloved hand to Erica's jugular vein to feel for a pulse. It's very weak, and her breathing is extremely shallow. Erica's eyes flutter open, though they don't seem to focus. Lauren grips a lock of Erica's hair, raises her head off the floor and slams it down hard. Her eyes roll back and close.

Lauren wipes up the blood from the tile floor with a kitchen towel. She throws the towel into the trash compactor and turns off the light. The house is quiet and dark. No one has heard the attack take place. Lauren returns the poker to its stand, and retraces her steps up the stairs. Before she goes, she sneaks one more look at Nolan. He's still asleep. She feels a pang of guilt over the sorrow he'll feel when he discovers her body, but it's his own damn fault. He never should have chosen Erica over her.

She leaves by the same door, locking it before pulling it shut as she does. She escapes the way she came, over the wrought iron fence, through the hedgerow, down the sidewalk and back to her SUV. She checks the time. Eleven fifteen. Greg will be at Erica's house, soon. It's not likely he'll discover her in the pantry. He plans to move through the house in the dark, grab the jewelry and get out without pausing. She'll be back at the apartment long before either Greg or Gordon return, and no one will be the wiser.

Epilogue

Six months later

There will never be another woman like Lauren, Nolan concedes. No one who can twist his heart into knots like she can. No one who can treat him like a dog, only to have him beg for more. No one who can make him feel as if life isn't worth living without her. Apparently, she has the same effect on Greg. He is willing to sacrifice his freedom, simply because Lauren asks him to. Nolan understands why he does it. He chooses to be in jail rather than being without her.

The police haven't caught Gordon, yet. Nor has Jacques Boudreaux. District Attorney Hardwick intends to try him in absentia, though the news media has already convicted him of Erica's murder. Greg cut a deal with the DA for his testimony. His own trial and sentencing won't take place until after Gordon's. Meanwhile he's out on bail. If Gordon is found guilty of Erica's murder, Lauren will be entitled to the five-million-dollar reward, even if Gordon is never apprehended and punished. Waiting for the outcome of Gordon's trial leaves Lauren restless. She decides to leave town for a while.

~~~

At an exclusive beachfront resort, Lauren enjoys a cocktail at the poolside bar, while she watches the sun slowly sink into the Pacific Ocean. She's wearing a semi-sheer minidress over a tiny black bikini. Couples lounge on the beach nearby and around the pool. It brings to mind times spent with Greg in Florida, Nolan in Jamaica, and Gordon in Grand Cayman. Those are fond memories for her. Maybe, once she gets the reward from Erica's family, she'll buy a place on a beach somewhere. She finishes the cocktail and sets the empty glass on the bar.

"May I buy you another?" a voice asks.

She turns her head to see a man she guesses to be forty-five. He's fit, a little taller than her, not bad-looking, wearing tan slacks and a tropical shirt. His reddish brown hair is peppered with gray, and he's displaying a lot of bling. Such as a diamond pinky ring, Rolex watch and gold neck chain.

"Yes, you may."

"I'm Oscar Pascal." He offers his hand, and Lauren gives it a quick squeeze.

"Lauren."

He settles himself onto the barstool beside her and signals the bartender.

"Are you here on business or pleasure, Lauren?"

"Pleasure, of course. Does anyone come here for business?"

"No one except for me, I guess. I'm the vice president of marketing for the corporation that owns this resort. Are you a guest here?"

"No. I'm staying in a house, nearby."

The bartender brings their drinks, and then vanishes immediately.

"You weren't completely honest with me, were you?" Lauren says.

"What do you mean?"

"You offered to buy me another drink, but in truth you don't pay for your drinks, do you?"

"You've got me there. That's correct. I drink for free, here. As does anyone who's with me."

"You must make a lot of friends that way."

"Yes, I do, but none as beautiful as you, Lauren."

Of course they aren't, Lauren thinks to herself, but to Oscar she says, "That's sweet of you to say so."

The sun disappears. Lauren and Oscar remain at the bar two hours longer having several more drinks and getting to know one another. There's a white band on his finger where his wedding ring belongs. He keeps glancing at his watch. He probably has to check in with his wife at some point. He's careful not to mention her at home in Los Angeles, or their three children she's looking after. If he only knew. That's the part of him Lauren finds most attractive, his vulnerability.

"I should be going," Lauren says. "It was nice meeting you, Oscar. Thanks for the drinks."

"Are you okay to drive? Some of the roads are pretty rough, here. I could get you a complimentary room for the night."

"That's good of you to offer, but I hired a car to bring me here. I told the driver I'd call him when I was ready to leave. I'll be more comfortable in the house where I'm staying."

She gets up from the barstool. Her legs are a bit rubbery. She has to stand still for a minute before taking a step.

"Here, let me help you," Oscar tells Lauren. He instructs the bartender to call the front desk and have the shuttle sent around. "There's no need for you to call for a car. I'll see that you get home safely."

Oscar is every bit as wobbly on his feet as Lauren. Clinging to one another for support they stagger from the pool area and out to the curb where the shuttle van is waiting. Lauren gives the address of the house where she is staying to the driver. As the van navigates its way along the narrow rutted roads, Lauren and Oscar make out in the back seat like a couple of teenagers. After a thirty-minute drive, they arrive at the Costa Rican hillside house once owned by Erica Dupree, where Lauren is staying.

"Come inside and stay for a while," Lauren offers. Oscar looks at the driver, and then back at Lauren. "You can have him come back for you in the morning. That is, unless you're worried about your wife finding out."

Oscar doesn't have to think about it long. He sends the shuttle back to the resort and follows Lauren into the house. The entry is on the upper level. A stairway leads down to the main living area with a wall of tall windows overlooking the infinity pool and the Pacific Ocean beyond it.

"Are you staying in this big house all by yourself?" Oscar asks.

"No, I'm here with my brothers. Come meet them."

She leads him down the stairs and outside where three men are lounging beside the pool. Their heads turn to look at the newcomer. It's unsettling for him. Something seems a little off. Three men, no women, staying in the house with their sister, just the four of them. They stand to greet Oscar and Lauren. There is no family resemblance between the brothers, nor is there between them and Lauren.

"Guys," Lauren says. "Meet Oscar. Oscar, these are my brothers, Greg, Nolan and Gordon."

Mason is hard at work on his next novel. To see what's new or ask Mason a question, visit him at:
masonmalone.com

Other books by Mason Malone

The Chamala Quest

Backbeat